CANDLELIGHT
Ecstasy Supreme

**"DOES THIS FEEL LIKE A MISTAKE, ERIN?"
LOGAN WHISPERED AGAINST HER SKIN,
PRESSING HER TO HIM.**

Feeling his power, Erin drew in a long, shaky breath as his eyes captured hers in the darkness. She struggled against her own powerful desire. What was the point of having a sharp mind if you allowed your body to overrule common sense? "It *is* a mistake, Logan. We hardly know each other, don't trust each other. There can't be anything between us, not now. Maybe not ever."

Logan released her instantly. "How I envy your professional detachment," he said in a flat, toneless voice. Then he added sarcastically, "But I'd forgotten that you're not just a woman, you're a scientist. Cold, unemotional, clinically precise. Please excuse my interruption of your orderly existence." He turned and left, closing the door quietly behind him.

CANDLELIGHT ECSTASY SUPREMES

PRIZED POSSESSION

Linda Vail

A CANDLELIGHT ECSTASY SUPREME

Published by
Dell Publishing Co., Inc.
1 Dag Hammarskjold Plaza
New York, New York 10017

ISBN: 0-440-17116-4

Printed in the United States of America

First printing—May 1985

To Our Readers:

Candlelight Ecstasy is delighted to announce the start of a brand-new series—Ecstasy Supremes! Now you can enjoy a romance series unlike all the others—longer and more exciting, filled with more passion, adventure, and intrigue—the stories you've been waiting for.

In months to come we look forward to presenting books by many of your favorite authors and the very finest work from new authors of romantic fiction as well. As always, we are striving to present the unique, absorbing love stories that you enjoy most—the very best love has to offer.

Breathtaking and unforgettable, Ecstasy Supremes will follow in the great romantic tradition you've come to expect *only* from Candlelight Ecstasy.

Your suggestions and comments are always welcome. Please let us hear from you.

Sincerely,

The Editors
Candlelight Romances
1 Dag Hammarskjold Plaza
New York, New York 10017

PROLOGUE

"Adrenaline," the silver-haired professor was saying, "is a fascinating substance. It produces an enormous variety of actions and reactions within the human body. Emotional and physical excitement; increased cardiovascular and respiratory activity; in short, adrenaline can cause your body to go berserk, often carrying your mind along for the ride. Closely related to the sex hormones . . ."

Dr. Erin Barclay blinked, and the image of her old college professor faded away. It was funny how she could still remember his lectures after all these years, perhaps because she'd had a crush on him and had hung on his every word. And, at least as far as his thoughts on adrenaline were concerned, his every word had been true.

Her skin felt flushed. Her breathing was rapid. Her heart was beating rapidly, and her mind was racing, a mixture of excitement and fear carrying her along on a wave of hyperactivity. The adrenaline coursing through her veins almost blocked out the implications of what she was doing. Almost.

Months and months of work, rendered useless in seconds with the wipe of a cloth, the flick of a switch. Hours of meticulous labor rinsed down the drain; the product of her talent, the job she'd been paid for, the property of the powerful company she worked for—all destroyed in a flash. She stood back and looked at the now silent laboratory that had been her private domain for so long, and gasped. "What have I done!"

I've done what I was told to do, she thought. Relentlessly pushing her fear into a corner of her mind, she grabbed a thick notebook and switched off the lights. She walked down a familiar corridor, past a security guard and through the front door to her car, then out the main gate to freedom. *Freedom?* She drove a short distance and pulled over to the side of the road.

She was the only one who could recreate what she had destroyed. Her notes could point another competent microbiologist in the right direction, but it took more than mere competence to achieve the end result. Dr. Erin Barclay was the required ingredient, the necessary catalyst. She'd be damned if she was going to do what she was told!

With another burst of adrenaline that made her whoop in terrified joy, she spun the car's tires on the loose gravel of the shoulder and took off in search of the nearest phone.

CHAPTER ONE

Something was wrong, horribly, dreadfully wrong. The chief administrator for Scott Research and Development stood in the center of the spotless laboratory, taking a mental inventory of the horrendously expensive and highly sophisticated equipment around him. At least the machinery looked in good order. Still, he felt an unreasoning panic rise in the pit of his stomach.

Tom Dayton was a small, balding man in his late forties. He had a sharp business mind and the rare ability to make things run smoothly. His duties, however, were administrative, not technical, and he was definitely out of his element in this wing of the scientific research complex. He did know that the work taking place in this particular lab was very, very important, not only to the Scott Corporation but to him as well. If anything went wrong, it was his tail the company would put in the wringer.

Initially set up by the Scott Corporation as a private testing facility to serve its own undersea mining interests, Scott R and D had gradually become much more. Extremely well thought of in the scientific community, the activities continually in progress ran the gamut from scholarly oceanographic research to feasibility studies of specialized ocean mining technologies. The scientists working here were an elite corp, highly paid and much respected in their diverse fields. Keeping them all happy was one of Tom Dayton's less appreciated responsibilities, because it often entailed simply keeping them out of each other's way.

But, appreciated or not, if there was trouble, he was usually the first one on the scene. As he continued his quiet survey of the lab his gaze came to rest on the face of David Turner, a technician with a particularly grating personality. If Dayton had had any say in the matter, Turner wouldn't have been hired at all, but Scott R and D had its own peculiar hierarchy. The complex was divided into three departments: administration; research; and security. They all tried to respect each other's duties as much as possible. Trying not to vent his anger and confusion, Dayton asked, "What the hell is going on here?"

From his position in the corner Turner leaned against the lab bench behind him and shrugged. "As any fool can see, Mr. Dayton, nothing at all is going on here," he replied derisively. "Absolutely nothing."

Fighting the temptation to physically throttle the younger man, Tom Dayton at last realized what was wrong. In his damnably flippant manner Turner was rubbing his nose in it. Absolutely nothing was going on.

As with most of the research at Scott, this project dealt with the mineral wealth found beneath the sea. Working full-tilt for the better part of a year, channeling knowledge from other projects that had been operating years before, the scientist in charge had also been dealing with bacteria, enzymes, and what Dayton dimly recognized as the very cutting edge of recombinant DNA technology.

Yet nothing was happening. Countertops had been cleared off, the myriad apparatus neatly put away. The large blackboards lining the walls were clean and untouched by any signs of mathematical or chemical formulae.

"Where's Barclay?"

"Gone," Turner answered with a shrug.

"Where?"

Another shrug.

Dayton ran a shaky hand over his bald pate, thinking that if this insolent jerk shrugged one more time, he would undoubtedly throttle him, anyway. With his job desperately close to being history, why not go ahead and add an assault charge to his problems? "Could you be a bit more specific?"

David Turner sighed audibly. "She's gone. Period. I haven't the slightest idea where. All I know is that when I got in this morning, someone had obviously been here long before me."

"Did you check with security?"

"Just before I called you. Our Dr. Barclay was here early all right."

"How early?" Dayton asked.

Turner shrugged, noticed with growing unease the murderous gleam in the other man's eyes, and decided to explain. Dayton was small but

13

he looked tough. "Early enough to have made this place look as if a herd of crazed cleaning people had been here. Her notes are gone, the batch tanks have been shut down, and all the bacteria cultures are either gone or destroyed."

"Any chance of going on with the project in her absence?" Tom Dayton asked hopefully, already knowing the answer.

"Are you kidding? Barclay *is* the project. She's the real hotshot around here and you know it. Without her bioengineering genius we may as well turn her lab into a greenhouse and grow orchids." Turner waved his hand expansively. "Face it. Either she's gone berserk or she made a breakthrough and decided to peddle it elsewhere."

Though he had promised his wife he would stop swearing, Tom Dayton let loose a stream of highly imaginative epithets. He suddenly felt sick to his stomach. This complex was a wholly owned subsidiary of the Scott Corporation, as were Scott Mining, Scott Shipping, and various other similar interests throughout the south and southwest. It all essentially boiled down to one man: Logan Scott. Dayton had never met him, but he had the feeling that would soon change. In view of Logan Scott's reputation as a man intolerant of failure, it was not a meeting he was looking forward to.

His only consolation was that, after he had been handed his own head, an even worse fate awaited the fool who had brought a halt to what Dayton knew to be Logan Scott's pet project. He tried to smile but his heart wasn't in it.

*   *   *

Erin Barclay wasn't thinking about being a fool or about the retribution of the Scott Corporation. She was concentrating fully on putting one foot in front of the other as fast as she could. In short, she was running, though desperately trying to make it look as if she were only hurrying.

Long legs swinging rhythmically, dark brown hair fluttering against her shoulders, she dashed toward the gate for the Muse airlines flight that would take her to Houston. Love Field in Dallas wasn't the largest air terminal she had ever been in, but it certainly felt like it at the moment. For once it actually felt good to stand in a line as she joined the rest of the passengers boarding the plane, lugging her one overloaded suitcase that just barely qualified as carry-on. A fellow passenger eyed it suspiciously as she waited for Erin to stuff the soft-sided bag into an overhead compartment.

"Business or pleasure?" the older woman inquired rather impatiently, blocked as she was by Erin's struggles.

"Excuse me?"

"Are you going to Houston for business or pleasure?"

"Oh. No, I'm sort of going for my health, actually," Erin replied. The woman gave her an odd look, then moved on down the narrow aisle when Erin stepped out of her way.

My health, Erin thought, gratefully collapsing her five-foot-eight-inch frame into her seat. *That's a good one.* The trouble was, it was also very

15

true. With a swiftness that still had her mind reeling in unaccustomed confusion, Dallas had suddenly become a very unhealthy place for her to be.

She had only moved to Texas three years ago, lured by heaven knew what. Challenge, perhaps, or just a change. *Be honest, Erin,* she thought, chiding herself. Movement was all that mattered, or at least her history bore witness to that explanation. Before Scott she had worked for BioData of Dallas. Before that it had been a company in Fort Worth, two in California, one in Denver after earning her Ph.D. at the Colorado School of Mines, and two minor positions before that. Never more than a year with one firm, sometimes barely three months. Except for Scott.

Scott Research and Development was different. At last she seemed to have found what she was looking for, whatever that was. She honestly didn't know. Just . . . something she could sink her teeth into. Scott had more than its share of office-style political infighting—which she hated— but had a lot more than its share of no-questions-asked funding, which she loved. Results were all that the big shots at the top seemed to care about, or rather *the* big shot—some man Erin had never met, who had a reputation as an absolutely ruthless businessman. Whatever, it was a convenient arrangement, because Dr. Erin Barclay was extremely good at providing results. So damn good, in fact, that she had probably gotten herself into deep trouble.

A very nice-looking man came by with a cart,

offering Erin coffee, tea, or whatever her little heart desired. "Your eyes are gray!" he exclaimed. "I've never seen anyone with gray eyes before."

She batted her thick brown lashes at him. "My eyes are black, really. It's just that I'm low on coffee."

He gave her some and moved on—reluctantly, she noted with a guilty smile of triumph. Flirting was the last thing she needed to do. She didn't want anyone remembering her on this particular flight. It wasn't as if she needed the reassurance. At thirty-six, and in what could be considered a very sedentary profession, she knew she was lucky to be so trim, though she owed more to her height and her penchant for perpetual motion than to any regular regimen of athletic behavior.

It was a quick and relatively smooth flight. When they landed, Erin wrestled her bag from the overhead compartment, wondering where the strong potential suitors were when you needed them, then disembarked, enjoying an undoubtedly false sense of security as she headed for the car rental desk. They were quick, efficient, and polite, something she had easily gotten used to in Texas. In California one could spend ten minutes watching a shop clerk stare into space before she deigned to notice you.

After assuring the personnel that she didn't mind walking out to pick up her car, Erin left the Houston Hobby terminal and made for the beige midsize Ford they had pointed out. The morning air was already steamy-hot, turning her purposeful stride into a languorous stroll.

17

She loved the heat. Born and bred in Colorado, she had had her fill of cold wind and knee-deep snow. Soon, a short drive away, she would be on the beach at Galveston, soaking up the sun and planning her next move.

Erin was so absorbed in her pleasant day-dreams, she failed to notice the two men following her until they had fallen in step on either side of her. They were oddly aristocratic in appearance, fine-boned and swarthy, with an air of command despite their casual dress of Hawaiian print shirts, khaki slacks and white sneakers. The fact that they were quite a bit shorter than Erin didn't seem to bother them at all.

The one on Erin's left side spoke. "You are going, I think, in the direction we do not wish." He had a thick, undefinable accent.

Her heart pounding with a surge of adrenaline, Erin stopped in her tracks and asked, "What?"

"Dammit, Carlos," the man to her right snapped. "You went to Harvard. Act like it!" There was no trace of an accent in the angry man's voice.

When he spoke again, his companion's accent had disappeared as well. "Sorry, Armando. I got carried away." He put his hands out, palms up, and shrugged in apology. Then he turned his black eyes on Erin. "Dr. Barclay, you will accompany us and we will discuss your future."

She couldn't run; there really wasn't anywhere to go. Her throat refused to work, so screaming was out as well. Though she looked around desperately, no one else had ventured out onto the hot asphalt of the rental parking lot. Just her luck to hit a slow moment. "I—I don't . . ." she stammered.

They obviously didn't plan on waiting for anyone to show up and interfere. "Please," the one called Carlos said, "you know as well as we do what's at stake here. Our car is this way." He took her by the arm and started to lead her toward the temporary parking zone. "You will come to no harm, I assure you."

Though there was something vaguely nonthreatening about this odd pair, Erin knew appearances could be deceiving. She fell obediently into step between them, her mind working furiously. How much did they know? More importantly, how could they have found her so quickly?

Covertly looking them over as they escorted her into the multitiered parking garage, she could detect no sign of any weapons. The whole situation caused her sense of indignation to rise. She may be in over her head but so were they. They were five feet tall at best; Erin felt as though she towered over them. Carlos and Armando were going to have to give her more of a reason to go with them than a firm hand on her arm.

Just as she was about to make a break for it, however, she found herself walking alone, taking a few steps without them before she realized what was happening. She turned around and nearly fainted.

He was, without a doubt, the largest individual Erin had ever seen. The top of his head, capped with short, curly black hair, would brush doorways when he walked through them. His chest looked to be easily the circumference of a fifty-five-gallon oil drum, tapering to a waist that was incredibly narrow for his size but still in proportion. His legs could pass for tree trunks. Wearing an expensive charcoal-gray suit, he looked like a well-dressed Sequoia.

Erin's would-be abductors had stopped because they had no choice. It was very difficult to run when your feet weren't touching the ground, but they were trying their best, anyway. The walking tree held each of them by the collar with hands the approximate size of Virginia hams.

"Hit him, Armando!" Carlos rasped. His shirtfront had ridden up on his neck, making it difficult for him to speak.

"*You* hit him! I'm busy trying to breathe," Armando said, gasping.

With an ease of movement that both intrigued and petrified Erin, the big man carried his two now-limp parcels to a blue subcompact across the way. He looked as if he were taking a pair of errant kittens back to their mother by the scruff of the neck. "Your car, gentlemen," he said in a deep, unusually soft voice as he set them down by the driver's door.

"You'll be seeing us again," one of them choked out, rubbing his throat and quickly climbing into the car. The other pushed him roughly inside and followed, starting the engine with a roar.

"Oh, good," the big man replied, seeming genuinely pleased. His craggy face broke into a

grin. "Give me a call next time. We'll do lunch."
Immense shoulders shaking with quiet laughter,
he watched them speed away, squealing the small
car's tires as they headed for the airport exit
gate.

Frozen where she stood, Erin felt her knees
threaten to buckle when her rescuer turned his
attention back to her. *Rescuer?* As far as she
knew he was simply the victor, and to the victor
go the spoils. "Um, thank you," she said, her
voice tight. "I think."

Brown eyes thoughtful, he fixed her with an
appraising gaze. "You're a very popular woman
of late, aren't you, Dr. Barclay?" he rumbled
quietly.

All thoughts of this man being a passing Good
Samaritan drained from Erin's mind, leaving
her feeling limp and dispirited. "Who are you?"

"My name is Stephanos. I've been sent to
collect you, as, I see, have at least two others.
Shall we go before a more efficient crew shows
up?"

Erin noticed he didn't look all that perturbed
by the possibility of anyone else interfering with
his task. He picked up her bag from where she
had dropped it on the concrete floor of the
garage and started walking back toward the rental
lot. He didn't take her arm. He didn't have to.
She followed, knowing full well she wouldn't
get three feet before he stopped her.

The other men would have had to force her
to go with them, but Stephanos's sheer size was
enough to insure compliance. And once again
there wasn't anywhere to run. Explaining any-

thing to the police would be decidedly tricky. "Where are you taking me?" she asked, the panic flowing through her, constricting her throat and making her mouth feel as if full of cotton.

"To see a friend of mine. He has a lot of questions too." Stephanos turned his big head to look at her. "And I think you're right. You had probably better wait until after you've answered them to thank me. You may not have all that much to be thankful for."

CHAPTER TWO

Greeted by shimmering waves of heat, a midnight-blue helicopter settled gently to earth, its rotor wash kicking up the dry Texas soil of the private landing strip. Waiting patiently until the dust settled, a single passenger got out, instinctively ducking his head as he walked under the slowly revolving blades toward the two men awaiting him.

They were dressed well enough, he supposed, but the man was well aware that he made them look slovenly. It pleased him to think that the material for his impeccably tailored suit had cost more than he paid either of these men in a month. What didn't please him was the look on their faces, a collective anxiety that told him they had failed.

"Where is she?" he demanded, glaring furiously at one bearded face and then the other.

"We didn't get her, Mr. Reynolds," the braver of the two answered.

Without a backward glance the man turned and headed toward the silver Rolls-Royce waiting behind them and got in, ordering the driver to take off as soon as he settled into the air-conditioned comfort of the spacious backseat. His two minions just barely made it to the car in time.

"What the hell do you mean you didn't get her?" he asked when his fury permitted him to speak.

"We were there, at the airport and everything, but two funny-looking little shrimps grabbed her first."

"So they have her."

"No."

The man ran a hand over his face in exasperation. "What the hell are we playing here? Twenty questions? Tell me where she is or I'll dump you out and you can walk back to the ranch."

The pair looked uneasily at each other. One of them spoke up hesitantly. "The two little guys grabbed her, and then this one great big guy grabbed them and sent 'em packing. He's got her."

Pouring himself a glass of white wine from the vehicle's built-in bar, the man sighed heavily. "I imagine that was Stephanos, Logan Scott's man. Did you even try to take the woman from him?" He looked at them and sadly shook his head. "No, I can see that you didn't." His hand tremored with the effort of holding in his anger, but he was careful not to spill any wine on his suit. "I suppose I don't pay you enough to expect any initiative on your part, let alone courage."

"He was a big guy, Mr. Reynolds, built like a brick—"

One carefully manicured hand came up to

cut the man off. "Please, spare me your analogies. Did you at least follow them to see where he took Dr. Barclay?"

"We tried, we really did." There was a growing note of desperation in the man's voice as he rushed to explain. "But that guy knew the Houston freeways like nobody I ever saw."

"Let me get this straight," Reynolds replied in a quiet, threatening voice. "Not only did you fail to get the woman, you also failed even to find out where she's been taken. Is that about right?"

"Right," they both said in near whispers. Their boss could be patronizing, intimidating, even downright strange at times, and though he didn't pay as well as they knew he could afford to, the many other benefits of working for such a powerful man kept them quite content to remain in his employ. But he was also a very dangerous man, especially at times like this. His two lieutenants would much prefer to be somewhere else—anywhere else. They tried not to show their surprise when he sighed again and continued calmly, almost placidly.

"I suppose this is really my fault. My psychiatrist tells me I surrounded myself with idiots to enlarge my own feeling of importance." He took a sip of wine, rolling it on his tongue while gazing thoughtfully at the two men seated next to him, cherishing the panic he saw in their eyes. "On the other hand, I think he's full of crap. I prefer to think that I simply failed to impress upon you the importance of your mission. I did not, after all, expect Dr. Barclay to run and therefore had little time to explain things to you."

His sudden change of mood made the pair uneasy. "Maybe I was too tough with her over the phone," one of the bearded men mumbled.

"Perhaps. Perhaps the woman is made of sterner stuff than I gave her credit for." He looked into their eyes, gauging the depth of their fear. These men were good at their work, and their work was following his orders to the letter. They hadn't performed up to their usual efficiency, but Reynolds supposed he couldn't expect them to operate efficiently without a proper briefing.

"At any rate," he continued with a benign air of infinite patience, "I shall fill you in now, so listen carefully. Dr. Erin Barclay is a brilliant microbiologist. She works with bacteria; specifically, her area of expertise is in developing new strains of organisms or altering organisms so that they work more efficiently."

"Wait a minute. Are you saying she's involved in germ warfare or something?" the spokesman for the pair inquired in horror.

"She's bright enough to do that kind of work, I'm sure, but she doesn't. Her interests, and her talents, are in industrial bioengineering, or at least her somewhat frantic career has been largely in that direction."

Both men gave a sigh of relief. At least they didn't have to worry about getting infected or locking horns with the government. The big guy at the airport would be bad enough. "Why's she so important?"

The Rolls pulled up in front of the largest of a sprawling complex of buildings, the Reynolds ranch, actually more of a combined security headquarters and retreat than a working ranch, though cattle were run to keep up appearances. Reynolds gazed fondly at the Tudor-style house before continuing his briefing.

"Essentially *she* isn't. However, the process she has developed *is* important, and since she's the only one who knows exactly what that process entails, I need both it and her."

The three men got out of the car and went inside, walking down a long hallway to a den with paneling of dark walnut. Reynolds leaned against the mantel of an unlit stone fireplace while his two slightly bewildered employees took seats in wing chairs in front of him.

Picking up from the mantel an object that looked like a black, misshapen baseball, Reynolds threw it to the man nearest him. "That, gentlemen, is a manganese nodule. They are found on the very bottom of the ocean, so thick in some places that the seabed is literally paved with them."

"It's lighter than it looks," remarked the man holding the sphere. He threw it to his companion, who dropped it. The lump of metal hit the floor with a thud.

Their employer closed his eyes and sighed. "Manganese is a light metal. Typically the nodules also contain iron and, to a lesser extent, zinc, copper, nickel, and other trace minerals." He opened his eyes and looked at the two men, smiling reflectively. "The Barclay woman is important to the Scott Corporation—and to me—because my sources tell me she has developed a bacteria, or an enzyme, to be more precise, that can economically separate these metals from the dross that surrounds them."

"So?"

"So the process is worth millions."

"Um, correct me if I'm wrong, Mr. Reynolds, but if the process is as good as you say, and these things as easy to find," the other man said, nervously recovering the nodule from the floor, "wouldn't that drive the price of the metals down, not up?"

"Ah!" Reynolds exclaimed, pleasantly surprised. "Poorly handled, that would be precisely true, but I doubt Logan Scott would handle it that way. On the other hand, I doubt he sees—or will take advantage of—the real opportunity here."

The two men looked at each other and shrugged. "What's that?" one asked.

"There are a lot of people who would like to see things stay just the way they are, as far as the current market of certain metals is concerned. I am one of those people." Reynolds smiled enigmatically. "Or at least I am for the time being. I won't burden you with the full extent of my plans. Suffice it to say that I consider it *very* important indeed for you two gentlemen to deliver Dr. Barclay to me as soon as possible."

That was a cue, and the two men took it gladly. It was a rare occasion when their boss was in such a forgiving, expansive mood, and they didn't plan on waiting around for that mood to change again. They got up to leave. "We'll get her. Now that we know who has her, it shouldn't be that hard."

"Gentlemen." The bantering, informative tone was gone from Reynolds's voice. His face was as hard and cold as the stone of the fireplace behind him. "First, it seems my contact at Scott has not been faithful to me. Despite my cautions to the contrary, he has obviously decided to sell his information to more than one buyer. That accounts for your diminutive competition at the airport."

"Our what?"

"The two shrimps," Reynolds bit out.

"Oh."

He took a deep breath to calm himself, then continued in a quiet voice, "Please visit him and give him my regards."

The two bearded men smiled at each other. This was more like the Reynolds they knew, and a situation they were more comfortable with. "Our pleasure, Mr. Reynolds."

"Secondly, I advise you both not to underestimate Logan Scott. I will not tolerate another failure. Consider it, if you will, to be a matter of life and death."

How the big man named Stephanos had managed to fold his bulk behind the wheel of her rented car, Erin would never understand, but he had done so with grace and humor. He was also one of the most accomplished drivers she had ever had the pleasure to witness, whipping the reluctant car through the maze of asphalt that was Houston with calm assurance. She was definitely in good hands, but into whose hands was she being delivered? Stephanos wasn't talking. It didn't matter. Erin was shaking so badly, she couldn't speak.

Stephanos had taken special care to make sure her suitcase was safely stowed in the trunk of the car, and Erin doubted his concern was for her belongings. He obviously knew her notebook was inside, among her hurriedly packed clothes. Or perhaps he just had orders to collect her and anything she was carrying. Erin tried not to think about what other orders he may have, about the threats that had caused her to run in the first place. This unusual man had shown no signs of doing her harm, but she was infinitely aware of his ability to do so should he deem it necessary. Was Stephanos taking her to the man who had called, the man she had so foolishly decided to run from?

Her stomach tightened into a knot, and she thought she might be physically ill. She forced herself to stare numbly out the window at the passing scenery, swallowing her fear. *My notes are only a small part of the whole package,* she thought, trying to calm her panicked mind. *I'm the key, the most important link in the chain. Nothing serious can happen to me—at least not right away.*

Having been to Houston only a few times before, Erin quickly lost all sense of direction. The signs on the highway whizzed by in a confusing mass, the midmorning traffic as bad as Dallas at high noon. She had the vague feeling of going south, a feeling that was confirmed by the landscape as urban sprawl flattened out to fields and, eventually, the bayous and salt marshes that signaled the nearness of the ocean.

Perhaps she would get to Galveston yet, she thought, almost managing to convince herself that none of this was happening. Her nervous shakes finally subsided as a sort of overall stiffness took over.

At last Stephanos pulled the car up in front of a very high-brow-looking marina, switched off the engine, then led her through a security gate and down a planked walkway between rows of moored boats. Or were they ships? Erin settled for calling them yachts. They were all quite large, quite well cared for, and definitely the kind of seagoing vessel one didn't inquire about as to cost. If you had to ask, you couldn't afford one.

The yacht they boarded—via a stainless steel ramp—was the biggest of the lot, with a pristine white hull that made it look even larger. It had teak decks and brass fittings that gleamed in the strong, clean sunlight pouring down on the seaside marina. The noisy squawks of sea gulls competed with the sounds of ocean business nearby. If she hadn't been so scared, Erin would have gasped in delight.

As it was, she merely stole glances around her as she followed Stephanos down a companionway, bumping into him when he stopped abruptly in front of a polished mahogany door. It was like walking into a concrete bridge abutment.

"Excuse me," she said.

"For what?" Stephanos inquired with a smile

before rapping sharply on the door in front of them.

"Never mind," Erin muttered.

"Come in," a deep male voice requested from the other side of the door.

They went in. This was all so hard to believe, and even harder to accept. Erin was fed up with being threatened and chased and led around like a pet on a leash. Pulling herself up to her full height, she entered the well-appointed cabin with the most regal bearing she could muster. She was a gifted and respected scientist, a pioneer in the field of industrial DNA research. Whoever these people were, they had no right to treat her this way, and she intended to tell them so in no uncertain terms.

Once through the doorway, however, some of her defiance drained away. She found herself looking into a pair of dark eyes, a deep cobalt blue, the most threatening, hypnotizing, masculine eyes she had ever encountered in her life.

Sitting behind a massive oak desk, surrounded by paperwork, the man who possessed those eyes was as magnetically dynamic as Stephanos was large. Not that he was a small man, himself, by any means, or at least as much of him as Erin could see above the top of the desk.

He was dark, his longish, thick black hair scattered with traces of silver gray throughout. A lock of it had fallen over his furrowed black brows, and he pushed it back negligently as he pinned Erin in her place with those magnificent eyes. If this was the captain, his face fit the title, pleasantly weathered and masculine and totally

32

arresting. His nose was strong, his jaw firm and determined.

At the moment, that jaw was set with impatient annoyance. "Who's this?" he asked. His voice had an odd melodic quality to it, deep and somehow reassuring. Had he not dismissed her so offhandedly, Erin might have even felt reassured herself.

"Dr. Erin Barclay," Stephanos replied. He had closed the door and was standing beside it, a peaceful look on his face which Erin knew to be incredibly deceptive.

"You're sure?" the man behind the desk asked. "I somehow had in mind—"

"Gray herringbone tweed and thirty extra pounds?" Stephanos remarked, breaking into a grin. "Me too. Everything else fits, though. At any rate she was the only woman being kidnapped at the airport, at least as far as I could see."

"Which is quite far indeed," the man murmured. "Thank you, old friend."

"My pleasure."

"Did she have anything with her?"

Stephanos negligently lifted Erin's suitcase into view with one finger. "Her purse and this. I didn't look inside either one."

"Modesty?" the other man inquired, a friendly banter in his tone that made Erin feel somehow excluded. It was obvious that these two men were good friends, and she was nothing more to them than another irritant in a day's work.

He shrugged. "Discreet, that's me. Besides, she didn't look the type to pull a gun."

33

Those cold, cobalt eyes looked Erin up and down. "I suppose not."

Confused, angry, and definitely tired of being discussed as if she weren't there, Erin announced, "I *am* Erin Barclay." She subconsciously smoothed the skirt of her tan A-line suit and stared at the man behind the desk. "Now, who are you?" she finished, her gray eyes boring into him.

His dark brows arched. He stood up, meeting Erin's glare with equal heat. Erin was glad of the inches that put her above average female height, for though not in the giant redwood category as was Stephanos, this was a big man. He was over six feet with a tautly muscled frame Erin was acutely aware of even through his gray slacks and black knit shirt. "Not at all what we expected, eh, Stephanos?" he commented dryly.

"A far cry, I'd say," Stephanos agreed.

The smile disappeared as he leaned on the desk with arms that looked like bronze pillars. His face was rugged and deeply tanned as well, handsome not in a classical, but in a purely elemental, way, though his mouth bordered on the classical form for masculine sensuality. He spoke, however, not with sensuality but with a flaming anger that made Erin tremble with its sudden ferocity. "Who am I? I, Dr. Barclay," he bit out through shining white teeth, "am your judge and your jury. My name is Logan Scott."

Erin tried to hide the shock she felt as her confused mind absorbed the knowledge of where she was—and in whose presence. This was her employer, the ruthless man whose business successes were legend. By the age of thirty-eight

Logan Scott had created an empire; he was an emperor, and she was in his domain.

"Did you say Logan Scott?" she asked in quiet disbelief.

He continued to stare coldly at her. "Why so surprised, Dr. Barclay? You have something of mine, and rest assured that I am going to get it back. One way or another."

Despite the potent threat in his voice, Erin felt tension drain from her in waves. "Oh, God," she said with a sigh, collapsing into a leather-covered chair in front of the desk. "What a relief." Eyes fluttering closed, she gulped in air, feeling on the verge of passing out.

One of Logan's eyebrows shot up in surprise as he watched her. She was really quite a beautiful woman. High cheekbones, face perhaps a bit too thin, but that could be just stress. Her lips were full and soft-looking, making him feel a sudden desire to know what they would be like to kiss.

That slim body of hers is intriguing as well, he thought. He would be willing to bet that there was more to her than her conservative suit divulged. Maybe a lot more. Nice long legs too.

With a start he pulled himself out of his perusal of Erin's attributes, unexpectedly angry with himself. "What do you mean, *relief*?"

Erin slowly opened her eyes, realizing that her anger had been covering up sheer terror. She had been so frightened, she hadn't been breathing properly since those two men had grabbed her at the airport. "I need a drink," she said with a gasp.

Stephanos looked at Logan, received a nod, and poured a healthy shot of brandy into a snifter he procured from a well-stocked bar off to one side. Erin accepted the drink gratefully and tossed the fiery liquor down in one gulp, feeling color flow back to her face.

Watching these proceedings irritably, Logan Scott returned to his seat behind the desk, leaned back in his chair, and glared at the woman seated before him. For a few seconds he seemed transfixed by the depths of her gray eyes.

"You're either one hell of a cool customer or just plain stupid," he said at last. "Don't you realize the trouble you're in?"

The brandy hit Erin hard, and she stared numbly at him for a moment, regaining her composure. "I—I know how this must look—"

"At the moment it looks like you're some kind of a nut!" he interrupted heatedly.

"I'm a scientist," Erin objected.

"You, Miss Erin Barclay, are a thief! You have brought a very important project to a screeching halt, absconded with company secrets, and were probably on your way to sell those secrets when we stopped you. And you say you're relieved?" He tapped his forehead with one long finger. "Sounds pretty crazy to me, lady."

Erin's eyes widened. "But I wasn't!" she cried. "I mean, I did shut down the lab, and I am in possession of classified material, but I wasn't going to sell it!"

"Then what were you doing?" Logan asked

sarcastically. "Taking some bacteria out for a stroll?"

Cursing under her breath, Erin fought to remember that he had a perfect right to be asking her these questions. But did he have to be so nasty about it? "All right. I developed the enzyme, and the patent agreement I signed when I went to work for Scott Research makes it yours. Technically I suppose I did steal it. But you must let me explain—"

Logan cut her off, his eyes gleaming with sudden interest. "Wait a minute. Did you just say you've already developed the enzyme?"

"Yes, but—"

Logan banged his fist on the desk top in triumph. "Damn! I wasn't aware you had gotten that far. I thought you had just stolen some kind of intermediate step, something to sweeten the deal on another of your job-hopping sprees." His deep voice was controlled, but there was no mistaking his excitement. "It works?"

"I am *not* a job-hopper! I've just had trouble finding a company I liked, that's all." It disturbed her to realize that he undoubtedly had a file on her and had probably read it thoroughly. Since most of what she knew about the reclusive Logan Scott was rumor or gossip, she felt at a distinct disadvantage.

"Does it work?" Logan demanded again.

Now he had gone too far. She could understand being accused of not having much loyalty to the companies she had worked for in the past, could even see how this looked to be theft on her part. But now this rash, opinionated man was impugning her abilities! "Of course it works!" Erin shot back indignantly. "I tried a test batch on those deep-sea nodules at the lab. The process rate was ninety-six percent for most of the main metals." Her brow furrowed in thought. "Slightly lower on nickel for some reason. With a bit more work—"

Logan's excitement faded somewhat as he looked at Erin, something cold and forbidding in his eyes. "And you stole it."

Fists clenched at her sides, she stood up and glowered at him. "I'm sick and tired of your accusations! Are you going to listen to me or not?"

"Oh, by all means," he returned acidly. "Stephanos and I are just breathless with anticipation."

Fury flowing hot in her veins, Erin spoke through clenched teeth. "I had been working by myself for some time. I tend to do that when I get close to a breakthrough." She looked directly into Logan's deep blue eyes and added curtly, "Unlike some people, I don't go around looking for someone to blame when things go wrong."

Stephanos chuckled, a deep rumble of mirth that ceased immediately when Logan gave him a perturbed glance. A poorly concealed smirk remained on his craggy face.

"Get on with it," Logan said.

"When the culture I was working with was ready, I tried a test, and as I said, it worked well. Shortly thereafter I got the call, at home."

"Call? What call?"

"A man's voice—no one I recognized—telling

38

me to destroy my work at the lab, then bring all my notes to an address in Fort Worth."

"So naturally, smelling money, you—"

"No! Dammit, just listen," Erin said, seething. "He told me to meet him or else."

Logan leaned toward her, frowning. "Or else, what?"

Her face paled as she remembered the gruff voice, the vile threats made in conversational tones. "I-I'd rather not repeat . . ." She trailed off and sat down, feeling dizzy. "I got the impression that eventually he'd force me to do what he told me," Erin finished quietly. Thinking about the call again, she wondered where she had gotten the courage to defy those orders.

"And yet you didn't contact plant security, did you?" Logan pointed out sharply.

"Don't you see? I told you I was working alone, and the project is hardly public knowledge. Whoever he was, he had inside information. I didn't know who I could trust."

"Why didn't you go to the police?"

Now that, Erin thought, is a very good question. By deciding to take matters into her own hands like this, she could have easily ended up in the hands of her caller instead of sitting here in Logan Scott's plush shipboard office. The very thought started her trembling again, but she quickly pushed the fear down. Somehow she had to make Logan believe her, and he was obviously a man with little sympathy for frailty of any kind.

Her decision to run could be traced to the fact she was self-reliant to the point of absurdity.

And though she knew it would be hard for him to believe, she also had developed a sense of loyalty to Scott Research. "We already had one information leak, and I didn't see any sense in discussing a sensitive project with the police. Especially since there wasn't much they could do, anyway. It was only a threatening phone call."

"*We* had a leak? My, such team spirit." Logan lifted one dark eyebrow, looking at Erin speculatively. If the story she was telling him was true, she had probably saved his bacon. Still, something didn't feel right. "I'm having a hard time understanding what you thought you were doing. Where were you running *to*?"

"I don't know. I'm a microbiologist, not James Bond. Just away, that's all."

"No, James Bond you're not," Logan remarked, a trace of real humor in his voice, which made Erin look up. She noticed that the humor didn't reach his eyes. "For future reference, if you're trying to disappear, you don't make airline or car rental reservations in your own name."

"Oh." Lord, she felt mortified. It had all happened so fast this morning that the reality of it still hadn't sunk in. "I didn't even think about that."

She looked at Logan hesitantly. He may as well have the whole truth. His opinion of her obviously wasn't that high, anyway. "I started out doing exactly as I was told, shutting down the lab, packing up my notes. Then, when I should have been at the address I'd been given, I picked up the phone, made reservations, and ran. *I* developed this process," Erin continued, her voice growing stronger. "I know it's Scott—your property—but it's mine, too, and I wasn't about to give it all up over one threatening phone call."

Not a talkative man, Stephanos finally spoke up. "Still, it took guts to run like that, Erin," he rumbled softly.

Logan looked at the big man in surprise. "Erin?" he asked him sardonically.

Stephanos shrugged. "I believe her. I kind of like her style too."

She looked up at Stephanos with a wide smile. "Thanks."

"You are entirely welcome."

"How about you, Mr. Scott? Do you believe me?" Erin asked.

He sighed heavily, then stared at her for a full minute. There was certainly more to Erin Barclay than met the eye, and unfortunately, not all of it had to do with her deceptively slim body. "Where are your notes?"

Erin got up and grabbed her bag, sat back down with it on her lap, then opened it and withdrew her notebook. She handed it to him triumphantly. "There."

Logan took the thick package, nodding his head slowly. "Yes, I believe you. Nobody's that good an actress. But," he added, pinning Erin to her seat with a penetrating stare, "I still don't trust you. I'm not as easily swayed by a pretty face as is Stephanos." He stood up decisively, a somewhat wistful smile on his tanned face. "And I won't have to trust you far, anyway.

41

You're going to be under my protective custody till we get this thing settled."

"What?"

Logan ignored her. "Stephanos, arrange to have Dr. Barclay's—I mean, Erin's—car returned to the rental agency. She won't be needing it. Then get me the files on anyone who might have even *conceivably* had access to that lab." He jerked his thumb in Erin's direction. "She can probably prove helpful there. After lunch we'll get her settled in here, and then you and I are paying a visit to a certain address in Fort Worth."

"You can't hold me here against my will!" Erin cried in outrage. He was talking as if she were nothing more than a piece of furniture, to be moved around at his discretion.

"Think of it as a vacation," Logan said. "Sun, sea, good food. Besides, you don't have a choice. You are a commodity now, and a very valuable one."

So this was the Logan Scott she had heard so much about. A ruthless man, totally without scruples. Her stomach felt tied in a knot. "You don't own me, Logan Scott."

He turned and sat on the edge of the desk, leaning close to emphasize his words. "Oh, yes, I do, lady. I'm not about to let you, the process you've developed, or any further information about it fall into someone else's hands. There is a tremendous potential for exploitation involved here, and it has to be controlled."

"By you, I suppose?" she bit out.

Logan smiled with maddening self-assurance. "I can't think of a better choice."

CHAPTER THREE

Logan and Stephanos were on their way to the research complex in Dallas, having touched down at Addison Airport moments earlier. Logan had piloted the company's private jet, but the big man was the more accomplished driver of the two, so he was behind the wheel of the modified Jeep truck the Scott Corporation kept at the small local airport.

"Why don't you trust her?"

"I don't know," Logan replied. "Maybe it's her work history. Most research scientists go with one company and stay till they drop."

"Could be like she said. She had trouble finding one she wanted to stay with."

"Or it could be she had trouble finding one with secrets worth stealing." He thought for a moment, then admitted, "Of course, the discovery itself was hers. And it was a pretty loyal move on her part not to go to the police. If it *was* a loyal move."

"I thought you said you believed her," Stephanos stated, a touch of reproach in his voice.

The two men had fought in Vietnam together. Since then they had done battle with politicians, other corporations, and the demanding world of ocean business as well. More partners than anything, they had stood shoulder to shoulder in more deadly encounters—both physical and financial—than either cared to count. They had no secrets.

"Oh, I believe her story, as far as it goes. I just wonder what would have happened if we hadn't caught—or rather, rescued her."

"That's the point, isn't it?" Stephanos said. "Whatever she may or may not have been planning in the back of her mind, there are just too many people after her now to make what she wants of any consequence. Even if she's honest, any kidnappers won't be. And, as we both know, what can't be bought for money can be acquired by force."

"Yes. There does seem to be at least two factions working here, and more will probably turn up. There's the guy who called her, and something tells me that the two guys who grabbed her at the airport are another group," Logan replied.

"The munchkins? I think you're probably right. Someone who makes threats like that over the phone and gets left twiddling his thumbs would probably send more muscle than those two."

Logan shook his head irritably. "Too many unknown forces working in this for my taste, old friend."

"Maybe we can narrow them down some here," Stephanos said happily as they pulled up to the security gate of Scott Research and Development.

A security crew cleared them through the

44

gate and again at the main desk. Logan hoped they were always so efficient but knew it was probably for his benefit. Erin had pretty much been able to do what she wanted, and he took full responsibility for that. He detested the idea of treating people as if they were working in some kind of prison camp.

Logan had changed his casual attire of earlier for a classic gray pinstripe business suit with pale pink shirt and regimental tie. An imposing man, even in jeans, his appearance alone in what he called his corporate clothes was enough to undermine the confidence of most executives.

Tom Dayton hardly needed any more intimidation. His face ashen, he ushered them into his office, his carefully rehearsed apology disappearing from his memory immediately. The congenial smile on Logan's face only made his dread grow by the second. Scott, by reputation, did not tolerate failure—in himself or anyone else. He gobbled up competition like a shark among squid. It was a well-known fact that he was on a first name, back-slapping basis with movers and shakers in powerful political circles. Dayton fully expected to be summarily chewed up and spit out.

"I'm sorry, Mr. Scott," was all he could manage to say.

"Relax, Tom," Logan said, shaking the older man's hand firmly. "It's good to meet you in person at last."

Dayton blinked, then concealed a sigh of relief. "Yes. I mean, it's good to meet you, too, Mr. Scott." Confusion written all over his face, he waved a hand at the chairs in front of his desk. If he didn't sit down, he would fall down.

"Logan. And this is Stephanos." They all sat down, and Logan continued. "Let me start by saying that I don't want your resignation."

Dayton's eyebrows arched. It had never entered his mind to offer his resignation. Perhaps that was what one was expected to do in this situation, but he hadn't planned on leaving this job unless he was kicking and screaming. Still, he found himself saying, "I don't know why not. I really messed up."

"My notoriety in the news media notwithstanding, I've never fired anybody yet for circumstances beyond their control," Logan replied, chuckling at the bewilderment on the administrator's face. "Dr. Barclay had a free hand, and we've yet to see if that was a mistake or not. If it was, the responsibility is all mine. For the moment the situation is under control." Logan settled himself more comfortably in his chair. "Right now what I want is to get to the bottom of all this."

"There's not an awful lot I can tell you. As you well know, we're quite compartmentalized here. Except in emergencies, or to smooth things out, we all keep to our own departments and don't cross over much. My main responsibility is to make sure the funding goes where it's supposed to, where it needs to, and where you say it should."

Logan saw Dayton's tension easing and smiled. "And you're good at it, Tom. I set this place up the way it is because I've found everyone works better if they're allowed to do what they're good at. You watch the bucks, the scientists watch the experiments, and security watches everybody."

"Obviously not quite everybody," Dayton remarked dryly.

Stephanos chuckled. "Good point."

"A head or two may roll there," Logan agreed. "But one of the advantages of a strictly compartmentalized structure is that the compartments are independent of each other. In a ship, if one section floods, it can be shut off from the others before the whole ship sinks. Here at Scott R and D, if a problem develops somewhere, it can be pinpointed more easily; a limited number of people are involved at any one time."

"I see. And which of *our* compartments has flooded, Logan?" Tom Dayton asked. Reassured that his job wasn't in jeopardy, he was rapidly returning to his usual efficiency. In the back of his mind he realized that however ruthless Logan Scott might be, he was also very adept at managing people.

"Well, we're certainly taking on some water in security, but the leak itself is in research. We've had an information spill, and they're the only ones with access to that information. Specifically, we now have reason to suspect one individual."

"Dr. Barclay?"

Logan shook his head. "At this point it appears that Erin is just a pawn. We want to see a technician named David Turner."

Dayton's face, which had finally returned to its naturally ruddy hue, suddenly paled again. A stream of expletives managed to slip through the tight lines of his mouth. "Excuse me," he finished.

"How long were you in the Navy, Mr. Dayton?" Stephanos asked.

"Ten years. How did you know?"

"Just a hunch."

"What's the problem?" Logan interjected.

"I was just informed before you arrived that David Turner is two hours late in getting back from lunch, without explanation. We're pretty loose around here as research facilities go but not *that* loose."

Tempete. That was the name of Logan's yacht. It figured. Tempete meant "storm" in French—the feminine form naturally—and Logan was very much a stormy kind of man. The name fit the boat as well, because, for all its luxurious appointments, there was a quiet strength about it, a solidity that spoke of its oceangoing design. Erin had had some time to look it over thoroughly.

After some intense interrogation over lunch, Logan and Stephanos had left on what Logan called a "fact-finding tour." He had cautioned Erin to remain on board but otherwise told her to make herself at home. Neither Logan nor Stephanos mentioned it, but Erin got the impression that there were people on the dock who could and would stop her from leaving the yacht. They *had* quietly informed her that the guard at the marina's entrance was there to keep unauthorized personnel out—and was under orders to keep her in. The only other way would be to swim, a prospect that didn't exactly thrill her. She wasn't that good a swimmer, and the waters of the intracoastal waterway outside the safe harbor of the marina looked decidedly inhospitable.

Left to her own devices, Erin had finished her self-guided tour and then stretched out on a comfortable chaise on the deck of the *Tempete,* listening to the sounds around her with eyes closed, clothed in a tangerine-colored, French-cut one-piece swimsuit. She had given up on the idea of escaping the clutches of Logan Scott, for the moment at least.

Heaven knew they weren't such bad clutches. Lying in the hot sun with a cold drink in her hand, the gulls overhead and the waves lapping against the hull for company, it wasn't too hard for Erin to convince herself that she was on vacation. To her great surprise Stephanos had fixed their lunch earlier and proved himself to be a marvelous cook. And, however long her stay might be, the stateroom that was to be hers for the duration was comfortable and cozy, with a not-too-soft bed and an adjoining bathroom with shower. At least she would be well fed, well rested, and tanned. In fact, everything was perfect.

Except that she couldn't leave.

Turning over on her belly, Erin sighed and resigned herself to her fate. Logan Scott was, after all, a pirate of industry, not a pirate of the high seas. She was safe enough. Or was she? Truthfully, she was more worried about the direction her own thoughts had taken since she

49

had met Logan than anything he or anyone else might be planning.

Erin had always been fascinated with ships and the sea. She had even tried her hand at sailing, piloting the small craft of a friend in the waters around Catalina, and had done quite well. Maybe one day she would buy her own, but she would fly in the face of convention and give her boat a masculine name. Yes, she thought drowsily, a strong masculine name.

Erin could call her boat the *Logan*. She imagined bragging about its attributes, but instead of "she's a fine craft," she would say, "He's a fine craft." A trim ship, *Logan*. Clean, hard lines. A bit of wear and tear, but it just makes him more attractive, gives him character. Strong. Lean. Capable. The sexiest . . .

A low, appreciative whistle sounded behind her, followed by a deep, melodic voice. "So this is what you've been doing all afternoon while I was out trying to unravel the mess you've gotten yourself into. Had I known you were here, dressed—or should I say undressed—like that, I would have pushed the old corporate jet even faster to get back." Logan's gaze traveled over every inch of her lovely form, surprised at the hunger she aroused within him. "You don't look like any Ph.D. I've ever met," he remarked.

Erin had flipped over to face him, knowing her suit to be more revealing from behind than from the front. He was standing with his back to the setting sun, so she couldn't see his face clearly, but she could feel his eyes following the long line of her legs, pausing with interest on the lush, tanned skin of her slightly parted thighs, then moving up past her barely rounded stomach to the soft cleavage of her breasts.

His gaze at last came to rest on her face. "I knew it," he murmured softly. A woman like this had no business wearing conservative clothes to hide her figure.

If her thoughts of a moment ago hadn't caused her to blush in his unexpected presence, his leisurely perusal of her body would have. She met his gaze as boldly as she could under the circumstances, her gray eyes cloudy with tension. "You knew what?"

"That you . . . never mind." Logan leaned casually against the railing behind him. "I'm glad to see you're adapting to your environment."

Erin grabbed her terry-cloth robe from the deck and shrugged into it, tying it around her waist. She lowered her sunglasses over her eyes from their perch on top of her head. "My captivity, you mean," she said brusquely.

Grinning broadly, he continued to look at her as if her skin were still uncovered to his view. In truth it was a sight he would not soon forget. "Feel better now that you have your armor on?"

Maybe she *did* have more to worry about than her own thoughts. "Just adapting to my environment." Erin made a point of pulling her robe tighter around her.

Clearing his throat laboriously, Stephanos stepped out on deck. "I have a date tonight, but I prepared a meal for you." His craggy face was animated by a wide grin. "Just a cozy dinner for two."

"Oh, joy," Erin said.

The big man guffawed, then took off for the marina gate.

Logan shook his head, looking as though he couldn't decide whether to be amused or disgusted. "I thought scientists were supposed to be mousy and quiet. *You* have quite a mouth on you, lady."

Smug, arrogant jerk. "Like I said, I'm just—"

"Yeah, I know," Logan interrupted. "Just adapting to your environment. And that's what I mean. I should think you'd be grateful."

Most of her sour attitude could be attributed to being held there like some sort of criminal, but there was also the way Logan made her feel, the way he looked at her as if he would like to swallow her in one gulp. All her nerve endings felt like they itched, and it made her irritable beyond reason.

"Why should I be grateful?"

"People usually are when they've been rescued from kidnappers."

"Oh. I didn't know I *had* been rescued. I thought I'd just been transferred."

Throwing his hands in the air in exasperation, Logan went below deck and into his office, muttering to himself all the way. Erin followed, enjoying the cool, relatively dark atmosphere of the cabin. She removed her sunglasses and watched his brusque movements as he took off his coat and tie, then mixed himself a drink at the bar.

"How long do you intend to keep me here?" she asked.

"Until I decide it's safe for you to leave," Logan replied tersely. He looked at the annoyed expression on her face and sighed, sitting down behind his desk. "Look, lady, I don't want you here any more than you want to be here. Is there anything else?"

So he didn't want her here. You couldn't prove it to her, not from the way he had been looking at her earlier. "I at least have a right to know what's going on. Did you find out anything this afternoon?"

"Not a hell of a lot." Logan watched as she went to the bar and poured herself some more orange juice, then sat down in front of the desk. "It looks like David Turner is the one who leaked the information about the project."

"Did you talk to him?"

"No, that's why I suspect him. He's disappeared."

Erin frowned. "How about the address in Fort Worth?"

"It is a supermarket. I doubt your caller would have let you do any shopping, though. You probably would have been grabbed as soon as you got out of your car."

Erin shifted in her chair. The leather felt cold against the back of her legs after her time in the sun. "So, until you figure out what's going on, I have to stay here," she said glumly.

Something snapped inside him, and Logan was suddenly furious with her. "You obviously don't realize it," he said sarcastically, "but you are in great danger, and that means that the project is in danger. Many years and a lot of money have gone into this, and I'll let nothing stand in the way now that it's so close to bearing fruit." His strong jaw set with a fierce determination, he continued in a less violent tone, "Anyway, I would think you'd be happy to stay here. Your experience at the airport this morning should have taught you a lesson."

Logan obviously had a mercurial temper. She was glad he seemed able to hold it in check. When he was angry, his will became a tangible force flowing around her, dizzying in its ferocity. She had no desire to become the object of his wrath. "What lesson is that?"

"You need protection. The pair who tried to pick you up may or may not have been sent by your caller. It would be foolish to assume that Turner leaked the information to only one person. It's possible you have quite a number of people after you by now, and some of them could have less of an interest in stealing the secret than in making sure it—and you—disappear."

Erin's healthy complexion paled at the thought. She had been comforting herself with the knowledge that as long as she was the only one who could reconstruct the enzyme, she would be relatively safe. "I don't understand. Why—"

"Let's just say, not everyone will be as overjoyed by your discovery as I am," Logan interrupted in exasperation. "There are investors in metals who like the current situation of high demand and low supply. There are also land-based producers of the metals found in the nodules, most of them smaller countries who wouldn't exactly relish the competition."

54

Erin nodded slowly. "I never stopped to think about all the ramifications of the project. I was simply excited to be involved in the creation of a process that could end our foreign dependence on some metals."

"I understand. I'm excited about it too. Just keep in mind that handling the distribution of the enzyme is just as complicated as the steps you went through to create it. Blackmail is even a possibility."

"Blackmail!"

Logan's expression turned thoughtful. "As much money as there is to be made from the process itself, possibly even more—or at least easier—money could be made by *not* using it. For a portion of the profits from investors and producers, the person controlling the enzyme could agree not to put it into production. See?"

"Yes." Erin saw, all right. She saw that in the wrong hands the product of her hard work could be turned into nothing more than a political tool or a bargaining chip between unscrupulous corporations. An uneasy suspicion nagged at her as she looked into Logan's eyes. Which hands were his, right or wrong? "Tempting possibility, isn't it?" she probed.

Logan looked up at her sharply. "One could say that, yes."

They stared at each other for a moment, the tension between them so thick, Erin imagined she could see it, like a mist floating in the air. What kind of man *was* Logan Scott? Now that she had been alerted to the possibility, she realized that her process was indeed wide open for exploitation, either for the good of the country or the personal profits of one individual. As its creator she felt a great responsibility to make sure the enzyme was put to its fullest and best use, even if that should mean keeping it away from its rightful owner.

Maybe it would be the wisest thing all around for her to remain under Logan's protective custody. He could watch over her, and she could keep an eye on him—and on his plans. Getting to know this enigma of a man could hardly be called an unpleasant task. Erin was most definitely attracted to him, and no matter what he said about not wanting her there, she could tell by the look in his eyes that Logan was interested in more than her secrets, more than her professional abilities. Not all the tension between them was caused by their lack of trust in one another.

"I'm going to shower and change for dinner," Logan announced in an abrupt change of subject. "Do you want to use the bathroom first?"

"Yes, I'd like a shower, too, if that's all right," Erin answered, more than a little taken aback. One moment he was at her throat, the next he was treating her like a small child. But she had hardly expected him to be so polite.

"As long as you don't use all the hot water." He dismissed Erin with a wave of his hand and turned his attention to some paperwork on his desk.

The bathroom was compact, spotless, and modern, as was everything else she had seen aboard the *Tempete*. It was quite obvious that the yacht was Logan's home, as well as his office and a preferred means of travel. Was it any wonder that the man was something of a mystery? If anyone bothered him, he could simply start up the yacht's powerful engines and leave.

It was an unusual way to live but one Erin could identify with. She was a nomad herself, never bothering to put down very deep roots in any one spot. Her nesting instincts weren't strong at all: not surprising for a person who worked as long and hard as she often did. Home was a place to sleep; living was done elsewhere.

After a quick shower she spent some time in her cabin fiddling with her hair. The conservative, shoulder-length cut was becoming, if rather functional. Two clips and it could be pulled to the back of her head and out of her way. Loose, the thick, dark-brown tendrils curled inward toward her throat to frame the high-cheekboned lines of her face.

She jumped when the shower started up next door. There was something disturbingly intimate about sharing a bathroom with Logan Scott. Indeed, Erin decided, this whole situation was like sharing a man's apartment.

This was Logan's home, and she would be required to stay until he decided to let her leave or until she decided she had to leave. Since he worked here as well, they would be seeing a lot of each other. It would be wise not to get too carried away with thoughts of the kind she had earlier.

Remembering the predatory gleam in his eyes when he had surprised her on deck, it would probably be wise not to do any sunbathing at all when Logan was near. Even if she didn't mean to, Logan was far too much man to tease. With the effect they so obviously had on each other, things could easily get out of hand.

Erin's wandering thoughts were interrupted by a knock on her door, and she opened it hesitantly. The limited attire she had brought with her held little in the way of anything formal, save the suit she had worn on the plane. Clad in sandals, jeans, and a pale blue halter top, she was comfortable but would feel at a disadvantage if Logan wore the likes of the suit in which he had looked so devastating earlier.

She was in for a pleasant surprise. "I'm glad to see you don't dress for dinner around here," Erin remarked upon seeing him. He had on black canvas deck shoes, jeans, and a white cotton shirt, short-sleeved and unbuttoned at the neck. He was *still* devastating.

"I get enough of that everywhere else." He preceded her down the companionway. "Let's eat. Everything's set out up here."

They had dinner on deck in the pleasant evening air, enjoying Stephanos's talent with seafood. Logan apparently surrounded himself with quiet, capable people, and he obviously cherished his privacy. Erin felt as if she were intruding.

Even bathed in the soft light of the moon and the cheery deck lamps, the silence between them felt awkward to her. She took a bite of the delicious cold crab salad and sighed. "If one has to be a captive, this is the way to go."

He looked at her irritably. "Are you going to keep doing that?"

58

"What?" Didn't he like conversation over dinner, or was it just her he didn't like?

"Making me feel like a jailer."

Though tempted to make another of the flip remarks she had been handing him all day, she could hear the disgust in his voice and thought better of antagonizing him further. "I'm sorry. I'm being unfair. You really don't want me here, do you?" She looked into his eyes and felt the power there. To her great surprise—and pleasure—he gave her a genuine smile.

"Actually I'm beginning to wonder about that," Logan replied. He looked her over, then winked slyly. "I think you adorn the decks quite nicely."

Erin felt a warm flush course through her as she remembered his eyes devouring her in her swimsuit. "You could easily have much less troublesome ornaments than me, I'm sure."

"Hmm. But not one of them a Ph.D." He had been grinning at her frustration, but now he continued more seriously. "Perhaps I should have said that I dislike playing the role of warden as much as you do that of prisoner. I don't like restricting anyone's freedom, neither physical nor creative. Unless, as in this case, it's absolutely necessary."

They were enjoying a vintage white wine with dinner, its finish fruity and cool. Erin sipped hers thoughtfully. "I should have guessed as much from working for you. Some of the other research facilities I've been associated with are very restrictive. Guards everywhere, vehicle searches when you arrive and when you leave.

Even magnetically coded cards for *all* the doors, including the rest rooms."

"I know. I was advised to set up the same kind of system when I started my research section. In view of recent developments," Logan added wryly, "perhaps I should have listened."

Erin looked horrified. "No! Don't let what I did spoil the freedom you give the people at Scott R and D. For what it's worth, that freedom is the reason I developed a sense of loyalty to your corporation," she said earnestly. "Loyalty isn't easy to come by, especially from me. Anything that helps it grow has to be a step in the right direction."

"All right," Logan said. His laughter was as pleasing to Erin's ear as any sound she ever heard. "I wasn't intending to change a thing. If you hadn't had the freedom to take off like you did, your process might have fallen into the wrong hands. As it is, everything's working out fine. Let's keep it that way, okay?"

She smiled. "Okay. I don't see how you can say everything's working out, though. I've been threatened and have to remain a captive—"

"Hey!" Logan exclaimed in outrage.

"Sorry. How about incognito?"

"Much better."

"I have to remain incognito, and meanwhile, to hear you tell it, evil forces are gathering all around me. Not to mention that I'm here at your sufferance. How can you describe this situation as working fine?"

Logan sighed and shook his head, then refilled their wineglasses. "First, it's not just the way I tell it, it's the truth. There really are nasty people in the world, Erin, and some of them are going to be after you. You know your business, and you're good at it. I'm just as good at mine."

Yes, Erin thought, Logan was like the people he hired. Quietly efficient. Top-flight talent was all he would accept, and she imagined that he would accept nothing less from himself. "Okay. The big bad wolf is at my door. What's next?"

Pursing his lips at her glib turn of phrase, Logan continued. "Second, everything's working well at the moment because I've got you, and the big bad wolf doesn't. And I'm going to keep you. As a matter of fact," he added, lifting his glass to hers, "I'm kind of getting to like having you around. I agree with Stephanos. I like your style. Besides, how could a woman with legs like yours be imposing on me by staying on my yacht?"

Eyes wide, Erin exclaimed, "You're outrageous!"

"I thought you'd never notice," he replied innocently.

The wine warming her, the soft, humid air of the deepening night surrounding and soothing her senses, Erin had to agree. There were worse ways to spend time. She worked hard and hadn't had a vacation in years. What could be better than to be here, near the sea, eating well and drinking fine wine in the tantalizing presence of *the* most interesting bachelor in ten states?

Getting up from the table, Erin went to the railing and looked out at the water, past the harbor, and to the ocean beyond. She reminded herself that all of the wolves weren't necessarily elsewhere. There was a change in Logan this evening, a change in the way he thought of her, spoke to her. This was a man used to getting his own way; she might be playing with fire. What would she do if Logan sailed out onto the open sea with her still aboard? Would she go? Would he give her any choice?

Logan followed her to the edge of the deck, standing right behind her. Her body seemed to emanate heat, a heat he was being drawn into with each breath of her intoxicating scent. Why was it so hard to keep his perspective around her? "How did you happen to choose microbiology as a career?" he asked softly.

His voice, so close behind her, startled Erin. She tried not to jump. "You disapprove?" Erin turned to look at his face and almost wished she hadn't. His eyes caught and held hers in their hypnotic depths.

"How could I? Your talents stand to net my company a tidy profit. I meant, it seems a rather staid profession for someone as restless as you are," Logan explained.

"Am I?"

"Restless? I'd say so. You were with—what— six companies before coming to work for me?"

Erin studied the angular planes of his face, the hard line of his jaw. "Seven, but who's counting." She turned back to look out at the water, wondering if he were really interested or just making conversation. "I was one of those kids everyone despises in school. High grade-

62

point averages without much effort, used up all my electives on chemistry and math courses. In college I just naturally flowed in the direction of the most challenge. There was so much unbroken ground in microbiology. I was intrigued by the promise of DNA research, of the discoveries waiting to be made."

"Fame and fortune?"

Turning back to him and leaning against the railing, Erin grinned. "You sound shocked."

"I am, I suppose. I have this image of the quintessential scientist. Selfless devotion to a cause, total dedication to the betterment of mankind through chemistry. The idea of earning money and recognition doesn't fit my stereotype." Logan chuckled and joined her at the yacht's railing, folding his arms across his broad chest as he leaned his back against it to look up at the night sky. "I guess that's a pretty naive view of the scientific community."

"Not naive, just outdated. These days, the entire structure of the system turns out very competitive scientists. You have to get the grants to do the research, and you have to get noticed to get the grants. And that's just at the hard research level, medical breakthroughs and such. Once you become involved in the commercial side of things, the competition gets even stiffer."

"How so?"

At first Erin thought that Logan was simply trying to pigeonhole her, get a handle on just who this person was who had suddenly become so important to his company. And though she still had the suspicion that she was being subtly interrogated, she could almost feel his curiosity and interest. For some unexplainable reason this genuine interest in her was thrilling. "Almost everything we eat, drink, or put on or in us has been altered or improved in some way by a hardworking scientist like me. The wine we had with dinner is one of the oldest examples of bioengineering."

Logan looked as though he had swallowed something dreadful. "Trust a scientist to spoil my carefully nurtured illusions about the magic of the vintner's art."

Erin laughed. "It *is* magic, in a way. At first our ancestors made their beer and what have you by allowing wild yeasts to perform the fermentation. Gradually they found that certain strains of yeast produced a better brew, and they cultivated those strains. They even improved some strains by selectively using only the best species. That's a simple form of genetic engineering."

"I think I'd rather keep my illusions, thank you."

"Maybe so, but remember," Erin pointed out, "my kind of magic is very profitable. One of the most lucrative projects I ever worked on was creating a better, faster enzyme for the production of corn sweetener, and that's used in everything from soda pop to barbecue sauce. 'Better living through chemistry' isn't just a phrase, it's a reality."

"We laymen prefer to believe that everything springs from the ground. It's startling to think that some guy in a lab coat was responsible for your breakfast," Logan stated with a sigh.

"Yeasts, molds, enzymes, bacteria, they're all natural processes. We fiddle with them to make them perform better or more economically. That economy is, ideally, passed on to the consumer."

"Optimist."

Erin shrugged. "I guess you could say that. Even though I'm an industrial bioengineer, paid by industry, I still like to think of myself as a do-gooder," Erin finished reflectively.

They continued to watch the stars in thoughtful silence for a moment. When Erin stole a glance at him, however, Logan seemed far more interested in gazing at her.

"It's the competition, isn't it?" he asked.

"What is?"

"The real reason you do what you do. Getting there first, being the one responsible for a totally new way of doing things. You're in it for the glory, aren't you?"

Erin saw now why this man had been able to build an empire before he even turned forty. He could pick out the reason behind a person's actions and motivation, even if they weren't entirely sure of it themselves.

She nodded, a small and speculative smile on her face. "Yes. The fame and fortune bit's okay, but the personal satisfaction is the best part. It's why I chose industrial research over medical. Mine is a profession where I can control everything, from start to finish. I like it a lot."

"We're not really so different after all, you and I." The moonlight reflecting in Logan's eyes gave his gaze an intense, penetrating quality as he looked at her. "We're control freaks. We like to be in command of every situation. That way we can take the glory as our own."

Erin laughed nervously. Logan was indeed an intuitive man, and he was getting a bit too close to her psyche for comfort. She was well aware that she liked to be in control. It was her need for control and self-reliance that had put her in this awkward situation in the first place, a situation that had perversely ended with her being under *his* control.

She didn't want him to know just how much it bothered her to be here, to have so little say about what was happening. She especially didn't want him on guard, watching for any attempt on her part to wrest back the control she desperately needed. Using the process she had created was one thing, abusing it another. If Logan Scott's plans for her and her discovery took a wrong turn, he would be in for the fight of his life.

"*You* picked an odd environment for a control freak. I mean, shipping and ocean mining? The ocean has to be the least controllable thing imaginable," Erin said, as much to change the subject as to get him to talk about himself. Telling him her life story wasn't getting her any closer to finding out what made Logan Scott tick.

A gleam came to his eyes. "Ah, but that's the whole point! Nothing on earth can challenge like the sea. To gain even a small amount of mastery over such an untamed force is real glory."

Erin strolled back to the table and finished her wine, her mouth suddenly dry. He was such a dominant male! Should it become necessary to take flight from him, could she manage it without clashing with his indomitable will? "You sound like an Old World sailing man, a character out of a Joseph Conrad novel." She looked at him, extremely aware of his rakish good looks, his strength and masculinity. The touches of gray in his hair made him at once distinguished and devilish. "Or a pirate," she added.

Logan threw back his head and laughed uproariously, nearly succeeding in pitching himself overboard. He returned to his seat, still chuckling. "And you are the fair maiden I've kidnapped and claimed as my property."

"I don't think I care for that analogy," Erin replied dryly. She didn't like it at all. It was too close to the truth. Hadn't he called her a valuable property earlier, one that was his to control?

"Don't worry, Erin. Rapine and pillage aren't my style at all." His eyes roved over her slim form, lingering with great interest on the swell of her breasts beneath her halter top. "I often resort to subterfuge and intrigue, but I very rarely indulge myself in force."

"Subtle, that's you," she shot back, crossing her arms pointedly over her breasts. An image kept trying to form in her mind, but she fought it desperately. If he could make her tingle like this with a look, what would it be like if he touched her?

"Subtle? Never. Sneaky, perhaps, but not subtle. Life's too short. If I want something, I go after it."

"I thought you said rapine wasn't your style."

He returned his gaze to her face after a slow perusal of her jean-clad thighs. He grinned with great amusement. "I thought we were discussing business attributes. If you want to get personal—"

"I think not, Mr. Scott," Erin answered quickly. "My stay here with you will be trying enough without that."

"Trying, or *tiring?*" Logan arched his brows roguishly.

With an impatient exhalation, Erin got up and looked him in the eye. "Thanks for the hospitality, Logan," she said sardonically. "It's been a long day for me, and I'm going to bed now." Her heart racing from his casual innuendos, she turned on her heel and strode across the deck.

"Join you in a little while?" Logan called out hopefully.

"Only in your dreams, Mr. Scott," she tossed back blithely over her shoulder. "Only in your dreams."

Logan watched the graceful movement of her backside as she disappeared below deck, then sighed and finished his wine. She was probably right. He would be seeing her in his dreams. Even now the vision of Erin in her swimsuit returned to taunt him, a luscious nymph lying in the sun, her flawless skin glossy with a thin sheen of perspiration. "God," he muttered under his breath, "having her here *is* going to be trying."

68

CHAPTER FOUR

At first the gentle, rolling motion of the *Tempete* was disquieting to Erin, then somehow soothing. Finally she had fallen into a deep sleep, the sea air clearing her mind and relaxing her nerves.

Early in the morning she awoke with a jolt to a clanking and thumping overhead. Thinking Logan might be preparing to head out to sea, she hurriedly pulled on jeans and a pale blue T-shirt, then dashed down the companionway and up the stairs to the deck.

Blinking back the bright sunlight, Erin looked around in confusion, trying to locate the source of all the noise. Still in her bare feet, she went through the cool morning air toward the rear of the boat, where she found Logan and Stephanos working out with a set of weights. A thick rubber pad covered the deck and protected it from the exercise equipment.

"Good morning," Stephanos said solicitously. Both men wore only shorts and sleeveless sweat shirts, darkened with perspiration. Stephanos was adding weights to a long, heavy metal bar. The bar was suspended on two poles attached to a bench, and on the bench Logan lay on his back, breathing deeply.

"Sleep well?" Logan inquired.

"Yes, thank you." She watched as Stephanos fitted a retaining collar on each end of the bar, then stood at the head of the bench. She glanced at her wristwatch. Six o'clock. "Good God! Do you two always start the day like this?"

"Every other day," Logan replied blandly. "Care to join us?"

"Are you kidding? I have trouble lifting a coffee cup in the morning, let alone . . . Just how much weight is that, anyway?" Erin asked, looking askance at the weight-laden bar Logan was preparing to lower to his chest.

"Two twenty-five. We're just about done, and then I'll make breakfast," Stephanos promised.

With a final explosive exhalation Logan hoisted the bar from the poles—Stephanos steadying it with one massive hand—and started pressing it up and down. When he reached ten repetitions, Stephanos assisted him in setting the bar back in place. Erin felt dizzy just watching, but Logan seemed only mildly out of breath.

"I think I'm going to throw up," she remarked, sitting down on a nearby chair.

Both men laughed. Logan sat up on the bench and wrapped a towel around his neck, wiping his glistening face with one end. "Not a morning person?"

"As a matter of fact, I am. But you two are nuts!"

Logan took a deep breath, blew it out in a whoosh, and got to his feet. "No argument there.

70

You have to be a little nuts to do something just because it feels so good when you stop," he said with a grin. "Stephanos enjoys pumping iron, but I hate it."

"Then why do it?" Erin asked, bewildered.

Logan shrugged. "Habit. We started in the service, and I can't seem to stop."

Erin remembered something she had read about Logan, about his being a hardened combat veteran and how the threatening attitude he protrayed at board meetings had real substance. Logan Scott was not a paper tiger, a fact that became even more apparent when he stripped off his shirt before going below deck.

"I'm going to grab a quick shower." He turned back and looked at her, humor in his eyes as he caught her staring at his powerful, lean lines. "Care to join me?"

Erin blinked, then turned bright red. "Dream on, Mr. Scott."

He shrugged again, then disappeared.

"What would you like for breakfast?" Stephanos asked, a broad grin the only indication that he had noticed the interchange between her and Logan.

"Fresh fruit too much to ask?"

"Coming right up, as soon as I clear the deck and take a shower myself."

"Can I help?"

"I can manage."

Erin thought that nothing the big man did would amaze her anymore, but she was wrong. With one hand he picked up the heavy bar, weights and all. In the other he grabbed the bench and carried both to a storage locker just behind the wheel house, looking for all the world like a traveler carrying suitcases. The amazing thing was, he didn't look overdeveloped, either. He was simply massive. Everything twice normal size but in proportion, like looking at a physically fit specimen through a magnifying glass.

Logan and Stephanos were definitely an odd pair. For all his bulk and obvious power, Stephanos was even-tempered; jovial, in fact. Logan, on the other hand, was capable of sharp anger, impatience, and a temper that was quick to boil over but just as quick to cool. There appeared to be a deep camaraderie between them, more than friendship and yet not quite a fifty-fifty partnership. It wasn't that Stephanos was so much a follower as it was that Logan was such a leader. Logan didn't bend you to his will; you flowed along with it, feeling all the while that it was your idea in the first place.

Charisma, force of personality, there were words for the kind of influence Logan Scott projected. All the words failed to represent the facts. Until you were in his presence, you couldn't begin to imagine how in control he really was. His force of will was stronger than all of Stephanos's muscles combined. Logan was alluring, hypnotizing, and to Erin he was also quite frightening—in an impossibly attractive way.

She didn't trust Logan Scott, couldn't trust him, and yet was drawn to him with such strong, elemental force, she could scarcely keep her mind on the business of learning more about him. As a scientist, objectivity was a quality she had painstakingly developed, but it all flew out the window when he was near. "Erin," she muttered to herself, "you could be in big trouble."

From a higher vantage point on the fantail of an ancient ore freighter about a quarter of a mile away, two bearded men were observing the activities aboard the *Tempete* through high-powered binoculars.

"I'm glad Mr. Reynolds told us to watch for a while before making a play for the woman. That guy Stephanos worries me."

"Tell me about it. Look at that! There must be three hundred pounds of weights in that stack he just picked up, and he's carrying 'em like they were dinner plates!"

"Yeah. Then there's the guard, and Logan Scott isn't exactly Tinker Bell. One thing's for sure. We're going to have to wait until Dr. Barclay's alone before we make a move on that yacht."

"I'm all for that. But Reynolds won't wait forever, you know."

"I know. Still, it won't do him any good if we move too soon and get splattered all over the wharf, now will it?"

"Won't do *us* an awful lot of good, either."

"Stephanos, where did you learn to cook like this?" Erin asked as she bit into her third croissant. He had made the buttery pastry himself and had managed, with some kind of delicious liqueur, to turn a simple fruit compote into a heavenly delight.

"The army."

"Don't listen to him," Logan said. "He's a cordon-bleu chef. Could be in a five-star restaurant somewhere instead of chasing all over the world for the Scott Corporation."

"Why aren't you?" Erin could swear the big man was blushing, but with his dark complexion, it was hard to tell.

"I was, actually, until Logan came and saved me," he replied in the unusually soft voice Erin still wasn't used to.

"I don't understand."

"I love to cook. But I hate to take orders. I was working under this chef, Henri something, and I swear, he was the reincarnation of Napoleon. Ran that kitchen like a little general." Stephanos was shaking his head sadly at the thought. "I'd served with Logan in 'Nam, but we sort of lost track of each other. Then one day he walks into the kitchen, says he has a business proposition for me, and starts to drag me out the door."

Erin grinned at his choice of words and at the number of them. Perhaps she'd been wrong about Stephanos being a quiet man. Perhaps he simply needed to trust you before he spoke much. She hoped so. One way of finding out more about Logan was through Stephanos, and Erin was hungry for information. "And that's how you got involved with the Scott Corporation?" she said.

"Not exactly," Logan replied. "I was talking

to him as we headed for the back door, and he wasn't at all enthusiastic."

Stephanos waved his comment aside and turned back to Erin. "He was muttering something about mining gravel and how we were going to make a killing on sand." He lifted one finger and circled it near his ear. "I thought he'd gone crazy. Delayed stress or something. Then the little general catches us and starts screaming at me to get back to work."

"And?" Erin prompted.

"Henri au jus," Stephanos sputtered, stricken by a fit of laughter.

"What?"

"I dumped a big vat of chicken stock on him," Logan said, as if it were the most natural thing in the world.

"I *knew* he was crazy then," Stephanos finally managed to say, "but I also didn't have a job anymore. So I went along with it. Best move I ever made. Somehow Logan had gotten his hands on an old dredger, and we fixed it up, swung a deal on an area near the mouth of the Mississippi, and darned if we didn't make a killing on sand and gravel!"

So, Erin thought, that was the start of the Scott Corporation. Unlikely but somehow fitting. "I wasn't aware that's where sand and gravel came from."

Logan nodded and swallowed some coffee. "Especially around the coastal areas. In the Midwest they have sand and gravel pits, but down here the soil is mostly what's called gumbo, sort of like adobe. Sand and other aggregates have

75

to be dredged off the sea bottom, and the best place is near the mouth of a big river where Mother Nature has already done most of the work for you."

Erin remembered a colleague of hers at Scott who was working on new methods of separating and grading sand. She'd thought it odd at the time, but now she understood. "It must still be a large part of your business."

"The backbone, you might say," Stephanos answered. "It's what financed the other expansions, into shipping and other forms of ocean mining."

"And research and development," Logan added pointedly. "Such as your own illustrious project." He fixed Erin with one of his penetrating looks. "How long will it take to reproduce the enzyme?"

Erin should have been expecting the question, but she wasn't. She had been absorbed in trying to figure out her two protectors—especially Logan Scott. "I . . . I don't know. Wouldn't it be better to wait a while?"

"Why?" Logan asked sharply.

"B-because we still don't know all the facts," Erin stammered, blessing her stars for a sudden flash of insight.

"What facts?" Logan's eyes were full of doubt.

"We need more facts about who threatened me, where David is, and who else he may have told."

Black brows arched, Logan spoke sarcastically. "Oh, it's *David* now, is it? You two pretty chummy, are you?"

"What is that supposed to mean?"

"Just what it sounded like."

"It sounded," Erin said, leaning back in her chair and regarding Logan with a glacial expression, "like jealousy."

Stephanos cleared his throat. "I think I'll just go below and tidy up the galley." He got up and quietly disappeared.

Logan was shaking his head in disbelief. "Jealousy! What cause would I have to be jealous? You're only an employee, Erin, and a troublesome one at that."

"Exactly my point, Mr. Scott. You have no reason to regard me as anything other than an employee." Erin looked at him with slightly narrowed eyes. "And you never will," she added, frost in her voice.

"Is that a challenge?" The melodic quality was back in his tone, but anger still rode on an undercurrent.

"I would never issue you a challenge, Logan. You enjoy them too much, and I'm not here for your enjoyment."

Their eyes remained locked for a moment, then Erin threw her napkin onto the table and stood up, angrily retreating to the railing behind the awning-covered dining area. She looked out at the water, the waves on the marina's sheltered bay choppier than yesterday but still too small to affect the *Tempete* more than slightly.

Erin was tearing the rest of her croissant into little bits and throwing them overboard when Logan at last got his temper under control enough to join her.

"Don't do that," he said chidingly.

"Don't do this, don't do that," Erin mocked. "Is that all you know how to do, order people around?" She turned and looked at him defiantly.

Logan took a deep breath, then let it out slowly. "Besides the fact that it's illegal to throw anything into the water of this marina, you'll also draw sea gulls."

"So?"

"So, she who feeds the gulls, swabs the decks."

Erin smiled wryly in spite of her foul mood. "An old saying of the sea?"

"Guano in a ship's hold is profitable; on deck it's just a nuisance."

"That's right," she said, shielding her eyes from the sun so as to see his face more clearly. "Guano is another Scott Corporation endeavor. Collected for the nitrates it contains." She grinned at him. "I'd forgotten I was in the presence of an expert on sea gull poop."

Logan leaned both forearms on the railing and laughed, his broad shoulders shaking. "Boy oh boy. You're really something. I like you, Erin Barclay. I don't know why, but I do."

Feeling a tingle run through her at his words, Erin tried to remember that she was furious with him. "I thought you said I was just a troublesome employee."

"You're that, all right." He straightened and faced her fully. "Look, this whole situation has me ready to chew nails. I'm not at my best when I don't have something solid to fight against, and so far I feel like I'm chasing shadows."

"So do I." One of those shadows was Logan

himself, but she didn't want him to know that. "Like I said earlier, we need more facts."

"You're awfully free with the plurals. *We* aren't going to do anything. Stephanos and I will get to the bottom of this one way or another—and soon. I'm anxious to get on with my plans. You are going to stay here, where you're safe."

"By then I won't be of any use to anyone," Erin countered. She had no intention of reproducing the enzyme until she knew more about the enigmatic Scott and his company. Simply coming out and telling him that, however, would only make him mad. She wanted him pliable, not angry.

Logan stiffened perceptibly. "And why is that?" he asked in a cold, threatening voice.

"Because I'll be ready for a padded room, that's why! What you said last night, about us not being so different—it's true."

"What's that got to do with—"

"Control, remember?" Erin interrupted. "I'm not kidding, Logan. I was the one who was threatened, not you. Sure, you stand to lose money, but I was *physically* threatened. If you don't involve me in this, the uncertainty of it all will weigh on my mind until I split apart at the seams."

She was trying to convince him because she needed to know what was going on. She couldn't make a decision about what to do with her discovery if he kept her in the dark. Oddly enough, however, what she was telling him *was* true. Sitting around, waiting for something to happen . . . she really *would* go crazy.

79

"Think how you would feel," Erin continued, her voice holding a note of desperation that was very real now. "What if you couldn't go out and take matters into your own hands, meet them head-on? What if all you could do was sit and wait?"

Logan ran a hand over his chin, as if checking the condition of his shave. He looked hard at her, considering her words. "I don't know. It could be dangerous."

"More dangerous than leaving me here? If I'm with you, at least you'll know for sure that I'm okay. Right?"

He pursed his lips, perturbed. She had managed to put her finger on the problem, all right. Her safety was definitely a consideration, but at the moment, he wanted her close at hand for an entirely different reason. Logan didn't really trust Erin out of his sight.

Too many questions remained unanswered. The instability in her past still bothered him. Erin Barclay could just as easily be a very clever mastermind as she might be a bewildered pawn. He could keep an eye on her, learn more about her in the process, and carefully watch her reaction when and if they found Turner. "I'll think about it."

Erin pressed her advantage. "When do we start?"

Logan smiled and shook his head. "Pushy, aren't you?" He looked over her shoulder and broke into a broad grin. "I told you I'll think about it. Meanwhile you have some work to do.

80

Every hand on a boat has to do his or her fair share."

He pointed behind her. "A mop's not that heavy."

Erin turned, and saw at least ten sea gulls lined up on the bow railing, looking at her expectantly. She ran forward and chased them off, accompanied by Logan's cheerful laughter. Then she looked down at the deck where the birds had been. "Oh . . . Oh, guano!" she cried in disgust.

"Yep," Logan agreed. "Take the word of an expert. That's what it is, all right."

The trio spent the rest of the morning cleaning up around the *Tempete*. Never much of a housekeeper, Erin was the only one who didn't seem to enjoy the work. The two men went about their tasks almost as if they would rather do nothing else. Sailors, Erin decided, were a demented lot.

Logan and Stephanos finished their chores first and were taking a break in the shade of the afterdeck awning when Erin joined them. They were all similarly attired in cleaning garb—jeans and T-shirts—and for the first time since her arrival, Erin was starting to feel at home on the *Tempete*.

"I would think," she said as she flopped in a deck chair beside them, "that a man of your means would hire people to do this sort of thing."

"I do, usually. From the ship chandler down the wharf a ways," Logan replied. He smiled at her and held out a tall glass of iced tea.

She accepted it gladly, drank it down, then

held it out for a refill. "I knew you had an ulterior motive for keeping me here. You needed a scullery maid."

"I just thought that the fewer people who knew you were here, the better," Logan explained. "So, for the duration we three will have to keep the *Tempete* in the state of cleanliness to which she's accustomed. And that she deserves," he added proudly.

Now that he'd put it into words, Erin did feel a certain sense of accomplishment at having put the *Tempete*'s decks in order. Scrubbing the kitchen floor in her town house just wasn't the same. The yacht seemed a living thing somehow. Lord, she'd even started thinking of it as a she! "Just what kind of ship is this, anyway?"

"Boat," Logan corrected. "The *Queen Elizabeth* is a ship. The *Tempete* is an eighty-foot cabin cruiser, luxury-class, but she's weathered typhoons and hurricanes as well as any oceangoing tugboat. She's the love of my life." Logan sipped at his cold drink, a wistful smile on his face.

The love of his life. Odd that Erin hadn't thought to wonder why a man like Logan Scott didn't have women fawning all over him. Maybe the unexpected problems she had gotten him involved in had simply curtailed his love life. For some reason it pleased Erin to think that she might be causing him frustrations in his amorous pursuits. It was his own fault for keeping her here, and it wasn't as if he weren't frustrating enough himself.

Logan cocked his head and looked at her,

frowning at her curious expression. He'd been watching her all morning as she worked, enjoying the way she moved, the way the sunlight played in her windblown mane of dark brown hair. He felt captivated by her mysterious gray eyes, sparkling with inner purpose, flashing defiance whenever she caught him looking at her.

"There's nothing quite like the feeling of being surrounded by sea and sky with a solid teak deck and throbbing engines beneath you," Logan said.

Was it just Erin's overactive imagination or had he made that sound sensual, almost lustful? "I think I'd like that," she murmured.

Lord, Logan thought. *What a beautiful woman you are, Erin Barclay.* "I'm sure you would." What *he'd* like is to forget his doubts about her, chuck his responsibilities, and carry her off to some deserted island. But he couldn't, and he knew it, so there was no use in fantasizing any further.

For an instant Erin had seen something in his eyes, a hungry look that made her pulse quicken and her nerves tingle. Then the look was gone, replaced by the now-familiar shield of cold cobalt blue. How could she be so attracted to him and yet so afraid of him? She couldn't allow herself to forget that he was totally in control—for the moment at least. She had to walk an emotional tightrope, keeping her distance from him, yet getting him to trust her enough to keep her informed of his plans for her and her process.

Thankfully, Stephanos announced that he would be serving lunch shortly. Erin took the opportunity to freshen up a bit first and went below to her room. After changing into his usual shipboard attire of gray slacks, black knit shirt, and deck shoes, Logan decided to help Stephanos prepare the meal, something he didn't often do, but he had a lot on his mind and needed to talk to his friend.

"What's up?" the big man asked when Logan strolled into the spotless, modern cooking area.

"Need some help?" Logan inquired.

"Ha! The last time I let you into my galley, you burned my soufflé. Stand right there and you can stay," Stephanos replied amiably.

Logan did as instructed, obviously deep in thought. He watched as Stephanos chopped some chives with flashing movements of a sharp knife. "What do you think of our guest?" he asked at last.

"Hey, anybody who raves about my cooking has a permanent place in my heart. But I don't suppose that's what you mean."

"Do you trust her?"

"As far as I can throw her."

"You could throw her," Logan remarked dryly, "to Chicago if you put your mind to it."

"I trust her as much as I can with the knowledge we have of her. What are you getting at?"

"She wants to take more of an active role in this whole affair. I'm thinking of keeping her with us when we start shaking the trees to see who falls out."

"Makes sense. If you're so worried about her, what better way to watch her than have her by

84

your side?" Stephanos smirked. "Not a bad assignment, that."

"No. Having her around is hardly a distasteful business duty." Logan leaned back against the counter behind him and folded his arms on his chest. "What I really want is to get on with this."

Stephanos finished his chopping and turned, looking at Logan with raised eyebrows. "This?" he asked, his tone leaving no doubt that he meant his friend's obvious attraction to Erin.

"Not *that*. Business," Logan answered impatiently. "I want to get set up to produce the enzyme and begin a carefully secured and supervised experiment on a larger scale, just to prove its worth."

"At least that would keep her busy."

Logan shook his head. "In order to do that and still protect the project and Erin, I'd practically have to have armed guards standing over her day and night. I don't think she'd go for that. Just holding her here seems to set her on edge."

"So I've noticed," Stephanos said with a deep chuckle.

"Besides, I'm not sure I trust her enough to allow her to have possession of the enzyme again. Knowing how to produce it and having the actual article in hand are two different things, temptation-wise."

A bell went off, and Stephanos gingerly pulled three big baked potatoes out of the oven. He dabbed butter and sour cream into each one, then sprinkled the chives on top. Setting them aside, he checked the temperature of a pot of oil on the stove and started deep-frying some batter-covered shrimp.

"Do you really think Erin is capable of taking the enzyme and selling it to someone else?"

Logan sighed heavily. "I just don't know. I think it's a possibility she and Turner may be in cahoots. It's possible she was threatened because she was double-dealing somebody." Logan's mind returned to what Erin had told him last night and again this morning. She was as much a take-charge person in her world as he was in his. "It's even possible that she has her own idealistic ideas about how the process should be used and wants to be in control."

"I think I like the sound of that last possibility the best," Stephanos remarked. The shrimp were done, and he completed his tempura with rice and steamed vegetables.

"So do I. We can work with that, reeducate her, so to speak. But I'm not going to tell her *anything* until I know more about what's going on," Logan finished.

"Want my advice?" Stephanos asked, putting the full plates on a tray.

"When have I not?"

"Get to know her." He winked. "We've already determined that that's nice work if you can get it. Let her get involved with the search for Turner and the threatening phone caller. Meanwhile start getting things ready to experiment with the enzyme. And for heaven's sake," Stephanos added, hoisting the tray and inhaling the delightful aroma with a blissful expression, "stop worrying so much!"

CHAPTER FIVE

Right in the middle of their late-afternoon lunch, storm clouds started rolling in off the Gulf, and as Stephanos was serving coffee, the sky opened up. Driven by a fierce wind, the rain came down in an almost horizontal sheet, sending the trio scurrying from under the deck awning to the cozy confines of Logan's office. They dried off and had their coffee, listening to the howling wind and roar of rain on the decks overhead.

"All that cleaning for nothing. We could have let the rain wash the dirt away," Erin complained.

"The salt spray will foul all the fittings I polished," Logan agreed.

"And all my windows," Stephanos said, moaning.

They looked at each other and laughed, struck at the same moment by the absurdity of their complaints.

"I had an aunt who covered all her furniture with these gross plastic covers," Stephanos remarked in his deep, soft voice. "She had some really nice pieces, but you couldn't see them. Wouldn't even let anyone sit on them."

"A ship in harbor is safe," Logan announced. "But that is not what ships were built for."

"Nice sentiment," Erin said.

"I read it on a bathroom wall somewhere."

"You must hang out in high-class rest rooms."

Logan shot her a perturbed glance. "It was on a little plaque, signed Anonymous."

"Oh."

Stephanos got up from his seat near the desk and went to a radio receiver on the far wall. He put on a set of headphones, turned a few dials, and listened intently.

Erin watched him curiously, but Logan just sighed and leaned back in his chair. "At any rate, I have a newfound appreciation for the people I hire to clean up around here. It's a thankless task."

"One I suppose we'll be repeating tomorrow," Erin observed.

"I suppose."

"Maybe not." Stephanos removed the headphones and switched off the radio. "The thunderstorm watch in effect for this morning has been changed to a small craft advisory. Heavy rain and high winds expected on and off for the next forty-eight hours. The worst should pass through tonight sometime, though."

"Serious?" Erin asked with a frown.

"Not for the *Tempete*," Logan assured her. "Could bounce a few small pleasure boats around and slow up some of the ship traffic out there"— he motioned vaguely in the direction of the intracoastal waterway—"but this is a protected anchorage. Short of a hurricane, we'll be fine."

"No hurricane," Stephanos joined in. "Just some heavy weather." He grinned and rubbed his big hands together. "No cleaning for a while, either."

Thus reassured, Erin's mind turned to other matters. "What *will* we do with our time?"

Logan observed her intently for a moment. Looking at her now, with her damp blouse still conforming to the gentle swell of her breasts and her hair in fetching disarray, he certainly had some thoughts on what *he'd* like to do. *Discipline, Logan,* he told himself. *Business before pleasure.*

"We make some plans," he said at last, "about what we're going to do with this mess. I don't like it, but there isn't much I can do with the project until we clear up the waters you've managed to muddy."

Erin breathed an inner sigh of relief. She even let his comment slip by—an obvious attempt to put the blame on her shoulders—in favor of picking up on the content of his words.

"We?" she asked. "Does that mean you've decided to stop treating me like some prized possession locked in a closet and let me help?"

"It does," Logan replied, ignoring her accusing tone.

"Then let's go!"

His eyebrows shot up. "Go where?"

"Chase the baddies!" Erin answered, feeling a rush of excitement. How nice it would be to switch roles, become the hunter instead of the hunted.

Stephanos's laugh boomed through the stateroom. "I, for one, am going to the grocery store. When the going gets tough, the tough go shopping."

"I'll come too." Erin started to get up.

"Forget it," Logan said sternly.

"Excuse me?"

"Sit down. You're not going anywhere."

She obeyed his sharp command without thinking, and watched Stephanos leave. He closed the door firmly behind him, quietly reinforcing Logan's order. "I thought you said—"

"I said I'd decided to let you help unravel this situation," he interrupted forcefully. "I emphatically did not say you were free to go anywhere you please."

Erin was confused. She thought everything was going so well. Cleaning the ship this morning, then over lunch she was sure she had felt the beginning of a camaraderie, a more solid working relationship with Logan. Now he was back to bullying her. She matched his unyielding tone with anger.

"So I'm still under house arrest," she said sarcastically, knowing now how much he hated being thought of as a jailer and wanting him to realize how mad she was.

His expression turned stony and cold. "I don't care what you want to call it. Your safety is vital to the project, and the project comes before your petty concerns about being under my control!"

Logan realized that he was shouting at her and also saw an unusual, terrified look in her eyes. He continued, trying to remain calm. "You said it yourself, Erin. You are a prized possession. I haven't locked you in a closet yet, but believe me, I will if you give me reason to believe you're interfering with me in any way. Got that?" he finished with quiet menace.

"Got it." Erin's voice was barely above a whisper. Where was the man she had laughed with this morning, the man whose eyes on her last night had made her wish for his touch? This was a fiercely competitive man, a man willing to suspend right and wrong to get what he wanted. A man capable of anything.

She had to concentrate on something else. She was definitely under Logan's control, a fact he seemed intent on reminding her of at every turn. A captive she was, but hers was a relatively velvet captivity, and at the moment, Logan was extending to her a small, but significant, amount of trust. If she wanted to retain that trust and build on it, she would have to be careful not to irritate him.

Logan was staring at her. He didn't know what he had expected, but quiet acquiescence didn't suit Erin. He had the suspicion that a dangerous force was building within her and was now very glad he had decided to keep her on a shorter string.

"Now," he continued, "I'd like you to go over the whole thing again, from the breakthrough till Stephanos picked you up."

"I told it all to you yesterday," Erin said with a sigh. Had it really been so short a time? "Before you left for Dallas."

"I want to hear it again. Take your time."

Erin repeated it all, her excitement about the project, the long hours as she drew near the breakthrough, the phone call, her decision to run. At last, with evening closing in, Logan appeared satisfied.

"In your opinion, then," he said, "David Turner is most likely the key to this?"

Despite her willingness to help and her need to stay on Logan's good side, Erin was getting irritable. "I told you. He's really the only other person who had access to such information. I was working alone at the end, but he was still my authorized assistant. And he *has* disappeared," she finished impatiently.

"Then I think our first priority is to find him, don't you?" Logan asked.

"Where do we look?"

Logan leaned back in his chair and tapped his lower lip with steepled fingers. "I thought you might be able to shed some light on where we could find good old David," he replied.

"Me?" Erin exclaimed. "I'm not James Bond, remember?"

"You don't have to be a detective to figure out where a friend might be."

"He is *not* a friend! He's my assistant, that's all. I didn't even like the man," Erin objected.

"Why not?" Logan inquired with sudden interest.

"He was . . . I don't know. I just didn't like him."

"Did he interfere with your work?"

"In what way?" Erin wrinkled her brow in confusion.

"Did he make passes at you?"

Erin jumped up from her chair in outrage. "Is this the way you get your kicks? Probing into other people's love lives?" she cried.

"So you *were* involved with him," Logan concluded.

"Listen to *me*." Erin was seething now. "I wasn't involved with him, not that it's the least business of yours. He was overly ambitious but didn't like to work, nor was he very good at his job. And he had an obnoxiously high opinion of himself." She folded her arms over her breasts and fixed Logan with a cold glare. "Rather a lot like your opinion of yourself!"

Logan glared back for a moment, then a smile tugged at the corners of his mouth. He'd gotten carried away with his questioning, and he knew it. He had suspected that Erin knew more about David Turner than she was telling, and he had intended to force some kind of an admission out of her. The thought of Erin being romantically involved with Turner had made his blood boil.

He held up his hands in a pacifying gesture. "All right, all right! Truce, okay?" Logan asked, offering her another cup of coffee.

Erin watched him mistrustfully as he refilled her coffee cup, then she sat back down and glowered at him. "Try to remember, Logan," Erin said, her voice still tight with anger, "that I am a scientist, and a respected one at that. I do not have to put up with your browbeating. I'm willing to help in any way I can, because by doing so I am protecting not only myself but

93

my professional and scientific interests as well. As I told you before: I am not here for your personal amusement."

"You're right, of course," Logan replied crisply. "I apologize."

Erin's eyes widened. The last thing she expected from Logan Scott was an apology. He must want the enzyme very badly indeed. In her eyes it only made him more suspect.

"Do you have any idea at all where David Turner might be found?" he asked calmly. The distant chill was back in his eyes.

"You checked his apartment, of course?"

"Naturally."

"Well," she said, resting her chin in her hand, "we did go out for a drink on occasion." Erin fought a blush, knowing what he must be thinking. His expression didn't change, though she did see an odd light flare in his eyes.

"I think he must have gone there quite often, because the bartender and all the regular customers seemed to know him. I only agreed to go along once or twice, after a particularly grueling day." Now why, Erin asked herself, did she say that? She didn't owe him any explanations. "I don't like bars," she added, then shut her mouth, realizing that she was only making things worse by explaining further.

Logan was aware of her predicament, but he only smiled slightly. "I see. And what was the name of this bar?"

"The . . . um, The Chase Place, I believe." Her face reddened slightly.

"You're kidding," Logan remarked, starting

to laugh. "And did they chase you?" he asked with a wide grin.

"Yes!" she answered defiantly. "As a matter of fact, they did! The place draws a younger crowd, and all kinds of good-looking hunks just pleaded with me to dance with them. Is that what you wanted to hear?" Erin leaned forward in her chair and looked him right in the eye.

Logan wasn't about to give her the satisfaction of telling her it was the *last* thing he wanted to hear. He continued to smile—rather stiffly—and said, "I'm glad you like it. We'll just hop over there tomorrow evening and see what we can see."

A knock sounded on the cabin door. His eyes still locked with Erin's, Logan answered and Stephanos entered. "May I speak with you a moment?" he said, glancing from Logan to Erin, then back again. "Alone."

"Excuse me," Logan said to Erin. He got up and went out into the companionway, closing the door behind him. "Something wrong?" he asked, though he could tell from his friend's expression that something was.

"You remember what I said earlier, about not worrying so much? Well, you can start worrying again."

Logan frowned. "Company?"

Stephanos nodded, then turned and went up on deck. Logan followed. They went hurriedly through the pouring rain to the darkened wheelhouse, where Stephanos handed him an odd-looking device shaped like an overgrown rifle sight. "A quarter of a mile off our starboard bow at three o'clock."

Logan peered into the growing darkness. "Ore freighter?"

"On the fantail."

Rain fell with a hiss into the water of the marina, and an occasional violent puff of wind whipped it against the windows of the wheelhouse. Except for an occasional fiery streak of lightning, the clouds and rain made it very dark outside. Through a bit of scientific magic the night scope Logan held to his eye attenuated his vision through the murky evening gloom, magnifying the lights on the marina and the wharf beyond. He could see almost as clearly as if it had been broad daylight.

"They look very uncomfortable, don't they?" Logan said when he had located the two men on the freighter.

"That's what I thought," Stephanos agreed. "Anyone with sense would be under cover on a night like this. Even someone on deck watch."

Logan observed for a moment longer, then put the night scope back in its place near the *Tempete*'s helm. "They could catch pneumonia like that. I think we ought to go over and tell them."

The big man at his side grinned. "That's what I like about you, Logan. You're so considerate of others."

The door behind them burst open, and both men fell flat on the deck. "Whew! Wet out there!" Erin exclaimed.

"Oh for . . ." They both sighed heavily.

"What are you doing on the floor?" she asked, just barely able to see them in the light from the open door behind her.

They got up, and Logan reached her in one long stride. He slammed the door shut, then grabbed her by the arms. "Don't *ever* do that again," he yelled. "Ever!"

Logan's hands bit into the flesh of her upper arms like steel clamps. He shook her once, then let her go, running a hand over his face in exasperation.

"Easy, Logan," Stephanos said quietly. "She didn't know."

"Know what? What's going on?" Erin asked in bewildered confusion.

"You could have gotten yourself . . ." Logan shouted, then trailed off. "Just knock next time, okay?" he finished in an anguished tone.

"I'm sorry," Erin replied, rubbing her sore arms. "I didn't know you had secrets of such importance to keep from me. I'll just go below like a good girl!" she finished sarcastically, turning to leave.

"Stay put," Logan said vehemently. "And as long as we're on the subject, from now on, when I tell you to do something, you do it. No questions, just follow my instructions to the letter. Understand?"

"No, I don't understand, you overbearing—"

"Erin," Stephanos interrupted, "We're under someone's surveillance. It's a spooky night. When you came crashing through that door, we thought, well, you were still in the office. Please don't sneak around like that again. Please?"

Erin looked at him, then back at Logan, a lump of fear forming in her stomach. These were big men, strong men. They were veterans of a particularly nasty part of American history, survivors. The thought of something dangerous enough to frighten them made her sick with fear.

Logan took her by the hand, suddenly gentle, and led her to the broad expanse of windows in front of the helm. "Stand right here." He handed her the night scope, pointed it in the direction of the freighter anchored down the wharf from them, and said, "Take a look."

Erin looked, at first too surprised by how clearly she could see to make out detail. Then she saw two shapes huddled in the shadows on the deck of the ship. "They're watching us?" She shrank back from the window.

"I doubt that they can see us at the moment. Recognize them?" Logan asked.

"All I see are two black shapes. How can you be so sure they're even looking over here?"

"Every now and then one of them will move closer to the railing of the freighter with a pair of binoculars," Stephanos said. "I spotted them on my way back from the store."

Erin shuddered. "How long have they been there?" Had they been watching all day? Yesterday? Had they been watching her sunbathe? "What do they want?" she whispered.

"I don't think they've been there long. I think it's a pretty safe guess as to what they're after," Logan replied.

"Me." It wasn't a question. Erin knew the

answer. She could feel it. The situation she was in suddenly took on the very ugly face of reality. "What are we going to do?"

Logan chuckled, startling Erin and breaking the tension. "Can you cook?" he asked.

"What are you going to do, invite them over for dinner?"

"Only neighborly thing to do.' I figured you wouldn't want just to stay put in your room—"

"You figured right!" Erin interrupted.

"And Stephanos could use a break from the galley," he continued, unperturbed. "So you fix us a hearty meal while we go visiting."

He made it sound so commonplace, his voice nonchalant. Erin knew better. Logan didn't want her along because he anticipated danger. "Shouldn't we just call the police?"

"And tell them what?" Logan replied impatiently. "The only way it would make any sense would be to tell them the whole story, and we've already decided that's not such a good idea just yet." He looked at her, and even in the darkness of the wheelhouse Erin could tell he was gauging her reaction suspiciously. "Haven't we?"

"The fewer involved, the better," she answered quietly.

"Right. So you just go on to the galley and stay off the deck while we're gone."

"I'll show her where everything is," Stephanos said, leading the way through the door.

Erin followed, then Logan. The rain had eased to a few scattered drops but seemed only to be catching its breath for another downpour. Before she went below, Erin stopped in her tracks

99

and turned around. Logan was right behind her. "You're not going to . . ."

"To what?"

"They're only watching us. We don't even know who they are or what they want."

An ethereal moonlit fog was rolling in off the water, casting an erie glow on Logan's face. His expression was very hard and distant. "You let me worry about that. Now get below."

Erin looked up into his eyes. "Be careful," she said softly, then went to join Stephanos.

It had been nearly an hour since Logan and Stephanos had left Erin in the *Tempete*'s well-equipped galley. At first she couldn't seem to concentrate, then had gotten so involved in preparing the meal that she hadn't been aware of time passing. Now, dinner ready to serve, she was worried.

Ordinary noises seemed magnified to her. The persistent sound of rain and wind overhead, the barely audible gurgle of water on the boat's hull around her, even the *Tempete*'s normal creaks and groans that Erin had come to find familiar and comforting took on evil proportions. What if something had happened to them? What would she do? *Damn!* she thought. *I don't even know where I am!* On the Gulf, near the intracoastal waterway, but where?

Erin was just about to make a run for the guard at the marina entrance when she heard footsteps in the companionway. Quiet footsteps. Like someone sneaking toward her. She pressed her ear against the wall and thought she could hear hushed voices, two of them, unclear and unfamiliar.

In a fit of panic she grabbed one of Stephanos's devilishly sharp knives from the wooden holder bolted to the counter behind her. She reached out a shaking hand and snapped off the light, waiting in the semidarkness for a silhouetted form to appear at the galley's open door. And appear the form did, furtively at first, then standing directly in the doorway, nearly blocking out the light from the companionway behind. She could hear labored breathing, a rasping sound in the silence. A hand reached out, and the galley flooded with light, momentarily blinding her.

"Erin?"

"Damn you!" she screamed at Logan. "Don't *ever* do that to me again!"

She started to come at him, and Logan stepped back, his eyes flicking from her angry red face to the butcher knife she held in her hand. "Do you intend to use that on me, or were you just chopping onions in the dark?" he said quietly, his face tense.

Erin looked at the knife, pointed threateningly in Logan's direction, scarcely able to believe it was her hand holding it. Did he really trust her so little as to think she would deliberately hurt him?

Stephanos hurtled into view at the far end of the companionway, then stopped short. "What the— What's going on here?"

"Ask Erin," Logan replied stiffly.

"You two scared me!" Erin cried. "That's what's

101

going on here!" She backed up a few steps and put the knife down on the counter. "And you screamed at *me* for sneaking around? Why didn't you make more of a racket or call my name or something?" Crossing her arms angrily, Erin glared at each of them in turn.

Logan let out a tense breath. "Sorry. Whoever was on that freighter didn't hang around long enough for us to catch them. We thought maybe they'd seen us leave and had come over here to get you." He was still breathing deeply. "I ran all the way. With all the silence and a dark galley, you scared *me* pretty good, too, you know."

"Good!" Erin shot back, giving him a withering glance.

Stephanos started to chuckle. "Whoa! That look she's giving you is sharper than the knife."

Logan broke into a lopsided grin. "Yeah. I think I would have been better off getting stabbed." He raised an eyebrow. "Dinner ready?"

"All except the arsenic topping," Erin replied with a tight-lipped smile.

"Mmm," Stephanos hummed. "My favorite. I'll just go change and help get it on the table." He headed for his room.

Erin chuckled reluctantly. She noticed for the first time that Logan was dripping wet from his foray into the rainy night, his black wool turtleneck and jeans soaked through. "You'd better change too. You'll catch your death," she said in a syrupy sweet voice.

"Why do I get the feeling that you'd dance at my funeral?" He stepped over to her, his grin fading. "I really am sorry. I was very worried about you."

Erin shrugged nervously. "Like you said, we're even." He smelled not unpleasantly of damp wool and wet skin, a decidedly male scent that quickened her senses. Bits and pieces of a distant memory played at the back of her mind. A wool army blanket, a sudden rainstorm, and a picnic with an all but forgotten boyfriend. They had waited out the shower in the backseat of his car, cuddled together under the blanket, and on that day, the teenaged Erin first felt the intoxicating thrill of her own awakening sexuality. Hesitant, unsure, feathery touches were given and received, her startled cries of joy as frightening as they were exciting. She shivered at the powerful memory and then felt Logan's hands tenderly grasp her arms.

"Hey. Are you all right?" he asked softly.

She looked up at him. "I-I'm still a bit shaky, that's all," she murmured. A momentary weakness in her legs made her lean forward slightly, and she was in Logan's arms, crushed against his broad chest, his breath hot on her cheek. Their lips brushed softly in the merest whisper of a kiss, then they both drew away, looking into each other's eyes with mutual surprise at what had happened.

Stephanos strolled into the galley with a spritely step, whistling a tune from a Disney movie. "Hi ho!" he sang, then he saw the embracing pair before him. "Uh-oh!" He turned on one heel and quickly returned the way he came.

Logan released Erin, still caught in the maelstrom of her eyes. "I'd better go change," he said, his voice gruff and hoarse.

When he was gone, Erin leaned back against the counter and closed her eyes, fighting back the arousal coursing hotly through her veins. It would be much easier on her mind if Logan had forced the moment, but they had both been taken by surprise, Erin as much a dazed participant as he had been. She now knew for sure that the attraction she felt for Logan was very mutual. How was it possible for two people who mistrusted each other so much to be so physically drawn to one another?

She mustn't allow it to happen again. It felt too good, too disturbingly right to be held in Logan's arms. He already had more control over her life than she felt she could tolerate for long; must she now fight against her own instincts as well?

"Knock, knock," a deep, sheepish voice announced from just beyond the doorway.

Erin smiled and beckoned to Stephanos. "Come in. *You* can have your food before I add the poison."

He raised his thick black brows, started to say something, then obviously thought better of it. "Whatever you say." Sniffing the air elaborately while looking around the galley, Stephanos asked, "Find everything okay?"

"If by that you mean, did I manage to cook a meal without destroying the place, the answer is yes. Whether you'll like it or not is another story. I'm hardly in your class."

The big man smiled benignly. "I'll eat anybody's cooking. Except Logan's." He glanced over his shoulder with the air of a conspirator, then whispered, "He's really a nice guy when you get to know him, and he has a mind like a well-oiled steel trap. But the man makes a tuna casserole that would gag a cat."

Logan entered the small room to the sound of laughter, and the bewildered look he gave them started them off again. They finally quieted down enough to serve dinner, relatively simple fare of hot roast beef sandwiches and salad. Logan watched the pair suspiciously throughout the meal.

Finishing with a sigh, Stephanos nodded in appreciation. "Fantastic, Erin. A truly memorable gravy."

"Oh, anyone can make gravy," she demurred, immensely pleased by the compliment.

Stephanos looked pointedly at Logan. "Not everyone."

Erin started chuckling again. "Gravy too?"

"With raisins," Stephanos said solemnly.

"Hey!" Logan cried. "Is that what this is all about? My cooking?" He looked disgusted. "I don't have to take this abuse. I happen to make a very good tuna casserole."

As predicted, the worst of the storm passed through on its way inland late that night. Rain hammered the decks, waking Erin with a start. In her berth the roll of the *Tempete* was more pronounced than Erin had experienced before, and for a moment she thought she might be ill, but the feeling quickly passed. She was proud of the steady stomach she was developing. Logan would undoubtedly have little patience with a seasick woman.

The thought of his lips against hers jumped into Erin's mind then, and she snuggled back under her covers, feeling luxuriously warm and dry. Perhaps she was being overly paranoid about Logan. "He's a nice guy when you get to know him," she murmured to herself, echoing Stephanos's comment of earlier.

That was a problem. Logan was a hard man to get close to. His motives were not clear, nor were his actions easy to figure out. He could be light, funny, tender, even, and then hard as nails the next moment. Stephanos was much easier to fathom, because Erin felt there was no such depth or secrecy to him. And he was Logan's friend. Was a man really known by the company he kept?

She imagined Logan capable of anything, sensed his competitive resolve, felt the underlying current of violence in his nature. Stephanos appeared to be one of the world's truly nice people, in spite of the fact he was also a survivor and eminently capable in his own right. Could such a man befriend an unscrupulous character?

Erin decided Stephanos's obvious respect and even devotion to Logan couldn't be used as a ruler to measure Logan as an individual. It was a matter of point of view, of involvement. And somehow she had to keep trying to see things from Logan's point of view, because an important scientific discovery and, quite possibly, her professional reputation were at stake. *She* had her fair share of commitment and resolve as well.

Quite another matter was the terrifying, exciting, beguiling feelings Logan had awakened in her in the galley earlier that evening. It may have taken her by surprise, but she had *wanted* him to touch her, to kiss her. She couldn't deny that: from almost the moment she'd first met him she had wondered what it would be like to have that magnificent body of his pressed against her.

Uncomfortable with her own inner revelations, Erin got out of bed and went to look out the porthole at the wind-driven rain outside. The lights from the dock and rows of boats moored at the marina were filtered through a haze, making them seem more distant than they were. She felt cut-off and alone. *I am alone,* she thought. *On one side is a man I'm unsure of, and these reckless, sensuous feelings I have for him, while on the other there are people lurking in the night, maybe even watching me right now, people who are out to kidnap me, buy or sell me and my knowledge, or worse.*

For the first time since she received the threatening phone call, Erin broke down under the pressure of the insane situation she'd gotten involved in. She wept softly, bitter at the unfairness of it all. Why was she cursed with this restlessness, this inability to stay in one place and make a normal life for herself?

She'd had other jobs, boring perhaps, but ones where the most danger and intrigue was some culprit filching sweet rolls from the cafeteria. She'd known some nice men, equally boring, and yet she hadn't had to contend with such powerful feelings, such fearful fascination about what she might find just beneath the surface of their characters. Why couldn't she have settled into one of those boring jobs with an average man? Why was she so consumed with finding something more, so compelled to search for some undefinable quality she seemed to feel her life was lacking?

A barely audible knock sounded on the door to the bathroom she shared with Logan. Erin didn't answer and suppressed a sob when the door opened and Logan stepped in.

"Erin? Is something wrong?" he asked softly.

"Wrong?" She sniffed, her voice roughened by tears. "Now, what could possibly be wrong? I've been pushed and shoved, both in person and over the phone. I've been ogled at through binoculars, held under guard, yelled at, and scared to death." Tears ran anew down her face, her throat so tight, she could barely speak. "All in a day's work for me, Captain Scott, sir." Erin turned from the window to face him, the soft fabric of her nightgown swirling around her ankles. She gave him a sarcastic salute.

"I see," Logan said when she finished. He pushed his hands deeper into the pockets of his dark velour robe. "If all you're doing is feeling sorry for yourself, I think I'll go back to bed. Self-pity isn't my forte."

Glad to have someone to take her rage out on, Erin angrily pushed tears from her eyes with the backs of her hands. "And what is your forte, Logan?"

He took his hand from the doorknob and faced her once again, his face illuminated by the pale light from the porthole. "All the usual things. Kidnapping, holding beautiful women captive. Blackmail and murder. All the things you seem to think me capable of."

"You're right," Erin countered. "I do."

"I know you do. What I can't figure out is why."

His eyes were not clearly visible in the darkness of her room, but she could tell from his tone that he was getting angry. "You're so damned enigmatic, that's why."

"For instance?"

"What are your plans for the enzyme?" She didn't think it would do much good to ask, but she had to start somewhere.

"Quite simple," he answered. "Once we clear up this mess, I want to produce, test, and then market it."

"Market it how?" Erin was surprised he had spoken so directly. Maybe she was getting close after all.

"That's my affair," he replied bluntly.

She sighed irritably. "Mine is not to reason why, is that it? Just produce and keep my mouth shut."

Logan came closer. His gaze, when it met hers, was not cold, but it wasn't warm, either. "That's exactly the point, Erin. You've already produced the enzyme. This isn't a normal situation, and you know it," he argued. "Your commitment to Scott R and D was for the enzyme project. Had it failed, your responsibilities would have been fulfilled. But it didn't fail. It was interrupted, by you, at the crucial, final phase."

"But—"

Logan cut her off. "It doesn't matter *why* it was interrupted or what forced you to take the action you did. That's academic at this point, except to get those forces resolved so we can move ahead." He put his hands on her shoulders. "What matters is that your responsibilities to the project remain. You made a commitment, and you're going to live up to that commitment."

The skin of his hands was warm and exciting. It was an oddly paternal, employer-to-employee gesture, but the feelings it caused to explode through Erin were far from reassuring. She felt as if every inch of her was begging for his strong, masculine attention.

"You mean, I'll live up to it or else, right?" she said, her throat dry.

Logan felt her body tremble beneath his touch. A feeling of power coursed through him, dangerous in its direction, as well as disregard for the situation between them. He had her under his control well enough—for now. Erin was an exciting, deliciously independent woman; whatever control he had over her was tenuous at best. As for his control over himself, that was weakening by the moment.

"Why do you insist on making this so hard on yourself?" he asked, his voice barely above a whisper. "And on me?"

Erin looked at him, at the hard planes of his face, her chin tilted at a defiant angle. "I have loyalties and responsibilities of a much higher order than simple commitment to your company, Logan. At the moment our goals are one and the same, and I really have no choice except to cooperate, but that doesn't mean I have to cheerfully submit to your will."

"And what do you call what happened earlier, Erin?" Logan taunted softly, removing a hand from her shoulder and running his fingertip along the sensitive skin of her full lips. "Was that submission, or cooperation?"

"Damn you!" she whispered hoarsely. She pushed against his chest, but she may as well have been trying to fend off a brick wall. "What happened earlier was a—a mistake in judgment. That's all."

Logan pulled her against him, locking his hands at the base of her spine. He reveled in the feel of her body as she struggled to free herself. "No," he said, his lips close to her ear. How soft and fragrant her hair was! "It was too soon, perhaps, and probably not wise, but kissing you could never be called a mistake."

His lips trailed from her ear to her mouth, then swallowed the startled gasp that rose from her throat when his tongue probed softly in search of hers. Erin's resistance to him wasn't strong in the first place, and she relaxed in his arms, her concern about the consequences of her actions slipping away. Their tongues twisted and danced in ecstatic exploration, tasting and discovering. Erin couldn't seem to catch her

111

breath, lost as she was in the intoxicating feeling of Logan's hungry assault.

She was hungry, too, hungry for the feel of his hands as they moved along the sensitive ridge of her spine. A deep, urgent, and yet languorous longing filled her when his lips left hers, his teeth nipping gently at her neck and throat as he kissed his way to her shoulder.

"Does this feel like a mistake, Erin?" he whispered against her skin. "Or this?" Logan cupped her breast in one hand while with the other pressed her hips to his. Feeling his power, his arousal, Erin drew in a long, shaky breath as his eyes captured hers in the darkness.

She struggled against her own powerful desire, her heart hammering under his intimate touch. This was insane! What was the point of having a sharp mind if you didn't use it, allowed your body to rule over common sense? "It *is* a mistake, Logan," she said, scarcely able to breathe. "I'm very attracted to you. It would be senseless to deny that. But can't you see how equally senseless this is?" Her voice grew stronger. She didn't know if she was convincing him, but she was managing to convince herself. "We hardly know each other; we don't even trust each other. There can't be anything between us, not now. Maybe not ever."

Logan released her instantly, his arms dropping to his sides. "You're right, of course," he said in a flat, toneless voice. "How I envy your dedication and professional detachment." A cold anger flared in his eyes, and he added sarcastically, "But then, I'd forgotten for a moment that you're

112

not just a woman, you're a scientist. Cold, unemotional, analyzing every aspect of life with clinical precision. Please excuse my interruption of your orderly existence." He turned and left, closing the door quietly behind him.

CHAPTER SIX

The weather was bleak again the next morning, and Erin thought that fitting. Her mood was as gray as the day. She certainly wasn't alone. At breakfast Logan was silent and sullen, looking as if he hadn't slept well after he'd left her last night. Erin remained equally closemouthed, pleased with the bags under his eyes. His parting comment had hurt, causing her to lose sleep as well.

Though thrilling, Logan's touch had also been curiously comforting, an offer of close human contact at a time when Erin was alone and unsure. Thinking back on last night, she even felt that Logan actually *had* been trying to comfort her—in a decidedly sensuous way. She was glad he couldn't see into her mind, or he would have known how close she had been to accepting his offer. Only her fear of falling even further under his possessive control had allowed her to reject his tempting advances. Now he thought her cold and unemotional.

That was a laugh! At the moment Erin was a mixed-up bundle of heated thoughts and dangerous emotion. It was playing with fire trying to get closer to Logan, because the closer she got, the stronger her awareness of the attraction between them. Sooner or later someone was going to get burned.

Stephanos was his usual cheerful self until he saw the two of them studiously ignoring each other, then gradually caught their foul disposition when both refused to make conversation. Obviously disgusted, he left right after cleaning up the breakfast dishes, ostensibly on business for the Scott Corporation. Erin decided he just wanted to get away from the black cloud she and Logan were creating over the *Tempete*.

She didn't blame him. She would have given anything to leave, herself. Logan seemed determined today to impress upon her the nature of his position and how much the situation she had caused interfered with his usually efficient running of the Scott Corporation.

He spent most of the day working in his office, plowing through mounds of paperwork and having heated phone and radio conversations with representatives of his widely spread business interests. He obviously wanted her aware of the fact that he had let things slide while watching over her. She didn't envy the people doing business with him today; actually, she was rather glad he wasn't talking to her. His angry voice could be heard from anywhere on board.

A constant drizzle kept her off the deck. Her cozy cabin felt claustrophobic all of a sudden, and so Erin found herself watching television in the saloon. The saloon was like a plush living room, except that all the furniture was bolted down. She vindictively decided that even the sofa would run away from Logan if he didn't weld it to the wall.

By five o'clock Erin had consumed an entire pot of coffee and three ham sandwiches out of sheer boredom. She also had an irrational urge to go out and buy the improved version of every product she'd seen advertised on television. A naturally active person who was busy every minute she wasn't sleeping, Erin was suffering from severe cabin fever. If this kept up, she knew she would be in a straitjacket by the end of the week.

She had about decided to go strangle Logan with his own phone cord—just for the sheer pleasure of having something to do—when he strolled into the room.

"Are you ready to go?"

Erin eyed him suspiciously. He looked washed, shaved, and despicably handsome in black dress boots, black slacks, and a gray summer-weight Harris tweed sport coat. His tanned face and throat contrasted nicely with the white of his shirt, which he wore open at the neck.

"Go where?" she asked, torn between the desire to go *anywhere* and the queasy feeling that she'd forgotten something.

Logan sighed impatiently. "To Dallas. The Chase Place. Remember?"

Now Erin was torn by another decision. Should she jump for joy at the thought of an exciting evening, quietly stalk off and get ready, or punch him in the eye for not reminding her sooner? "I forgot."

116

"Well, get a move-on! I want to get there before it gets too crowded, so we can pick an unobtrusive corner," he said, sitting down in a leather wing chair to wait for her. "That way we can observe the comings and goings of the clientele, some of which I hope you can point out as friends of Turner's." Logan crossed his arms and looked at her pointedly. "If your memory improves by then, that is."

Though socking him in the eye was definitely Erin's first choice, she stalked off to her room. Since she had showered earlier and certainly hadn't done anything to get dirty since, she splashed cold water on her face, applied a bit of makeup, then took stock of her wardrobe. Somehow she had to convince Logan to let her pick up more of her clothes from her house while they were in Dallas, or at least take her shopping tomorrow.

Finally she paired an ecru blouse with her beige A-line skirt, added a thin gold chain around her neck, and put on a pair of white enameled earrings shaped like seashells. She looked quietly elegant, yet casual.

Logan's eyebrows rose when she walked back into the saloon, a covetous gleam in his eyes. Then his frigid demeanor descended again and he said, "Very nice."

"Thank you," she replied just as coolly.

Logan glanced at his watch. "And quick too."

"You said to hurry. Besides, my wardrobe is quite limited. It doesn't take much time to choose between a business suit, three blouses, two pairs of jeans, and a handful of casual tops," Erin

117

said in a dry, accusing tone. "I hadn't planned on being held . . . incognito."

He met her eyes with a stony stare. "What *had* you planned on doing?" he asked intently.

"Go shopping, what else?" Erin knew that wasn't what he meant. He still labored under the suspicion that she had been planning to sell her notebook and disappear. Well, she thought, let him! She was secretly pleased that he thought her capable of such intrigue, and in a way it felt good to know she had him as worried as he had her. "Or I might have eventually slipped back to my place."

Logan stood up, a wry smile on his face. "You would. Ever stop to think that they probably have your home under a watchful eye?"

"My degrees are in biochemistry, not espionage," Erin returned defensively. How could she possibly be attracted to this man?

He looked as if he didn't entirely believe her, but he said, "Meaning that I do have that knowledge, I suppose."

"You have the paranoid personality for it."

Logan chuckled. "My, you're in rare form this evening. Save some of that animosity for the opposition, okay? You may need it." He smiled enigmatically and added, "Let's get going."

"Lead on, Sherlock."

It was no longer raining, but a low, gray cloud cover lingered on. Even though Logan stayed close at her side, an absolutely divine feeling of freedom met Erin as they left the yacht and went through the security gate to his car. His eyes were unreadable as he held the door of the burgundy-colored Lincoln for her, but she instinctively felt that his interest wasn't confined to keeping her from making a break for it. He most certainly watched her legs closely enough to detect even the slightest sign that she was trying to run away.

His watchful gaze reminded her of something she'd rather forget. "What about our mysterious observers?"

"Let 'em look," Logan replied simply.

"Won't they—"

"Follow us? If they're fast enough. The more the merrier, I always say." He pulled out of the parking lot and onto a narrow strip of road, rapidly picking up speed.

"You mean, you want them to know where we're going?" This was confusing. What scheme was he working on now?

Logan grinned. "I don't think they're *that* fast, but it won't bother me much if they are. I'm tired of this waiting game. Getting them to make a move when I know where they are is better than when I least expect it." He glanced in his rearview mirror. Nobody was following. "I guess we took them by surprise."

"You sound disppointed," Erin said, feeling a shiver run through her.

"I am. How can we get a handle on them if they remain in the shadows? We either have to catch them or draw them out. As it is, they have an advantage, and I don't like that at all."

Erin settled back to enjoy the ride, which she discovered she was doing in spite of the fact that she felt like bait on a hook. The change of

119

scenery lightened her spirits and recharged her optimism.

Logan looked happier, too, and probably for the same reason. Erin was glad. A happier Logan was a more talkative Logan, and besides needing the company, she still had much to learn before this snag in his plans was resolved. Once he had straightened this situation out, Logan would begin to make demands of her, demands not as easily put aside as their mutually recognized attraction for each other.

Not that that was an easy task in itself. Her sexual awareness of him smoldered beneath the surface, waiting to jump out like a tightly coiled spring. It wouldn't take many more close calls like the one in her room last night for her to totally destroy his image of her as cold and unemotional! The problem was, Erin had to fight not only his obvious desire *and* her own, but also another dangerously seductive need growing within her as well—to prove to him just how wrong he was about her. In *every* way.

"Just where are we, anyway?" Erin asked, swiveling her head this way and that.

"Why?"

Erin shrugged, trying to sound nonchalant. "Just curious."

He turned and looked at her, not buying her innocent demeanor for a second. "Freeport would be the nearest town large enough to get lost in, if that's what you mean. Not thinking of leaving me, are you?"

"Not at the moment."

"Good. If I didn't get you, our friends back

120

there would." He jerked his thumb over his shoulder.

Erin looked and saw a car behind theirs, quite some distance back. "How do you know they're . . ." she began, then the road curved gradually so she could see the vehicle more clearly. It was a blue subcompact. "That's the car from the airport!" She snapped her head around and faced front again, a surge of adrenaline making her fingertips tingle.

"That's interesting," Logan remarked calmly. "The two on the freighter last night looked quite tall. Stephanos referred to the pair from the airport as munchkins."

"To him anybody's a munchkin. They were shorter than I am, though."

"Then you really do have two different groups vying for your attentions." Logan increased the speed of the big Lincoln, and the car behind them sped up too. He slowed down, and so did they.

"Isn't it possible they're working together?" Erin asked hopefully. Having just one group after her seemed less terrifying somehow than having a whole slew of people to worry about.

"How would I know?" Logan answered, irritated by the obvious caution of the men on their tail. "I can't tell where *anybody's* loyalties are in this mess!"

Erin knew that included her as well but saw the exasperation on his face and thought better of objecting. He wouldn't listen, anyway. "What are we going to do?"

"We're headed for a small airport up the road,"

121

Logan replied. "When we get there, I want you to go inside and stay there until I come for you. Understand?"

"I . . . yes." This wasn't what Erin had in mind when she'd wished for an exciting evening. Her concern for her own safety was all but washed away by a sudden panic for Logan's.

A cleared stretch of land with several out-buildings and scattered aircraft came into view around the next curve. Logan slowed down and pulled onto a small side road, then parked the car in front of a neat, white building with red trim and lots of windows. A sign proclaimed it to be the Airport Diner. He waited until he was sure the blue car was on the side road and headed in their direction.

"Go inside now," he prompted.

Erin put a tentative hand on his thigh. "Logan . . ."

"I wish I knew if that was concern for me or them I see in those pretty gray eyes."

"Neither," she said, jerking her hand back as if scorched. "I was going to ask for a dime for the rest room." She got out of the car and went into the diner. Inside, she turned and watched nervously through a window.

Carlos and Armando pulled into the dusty gravel lot, their eyes glued to the Lincoln. When Logan appeared from behind a parked car and started toward them, they cursed loudly and imaginatively in two languages at once.

"Now what?"

"Let's get out of here before the big one shows up and steps on the car or something!"

Churning up dirt and gravel, Armando swung wildly around Logan and sped away, leaving him in a choking cloud.

"Damn!" Logan exclaimed, coughing and dusting himself off. Angry that he wasn't able to confront them, he turned back toward the diner, wiping his eyes with a handkerchief.

Erin was fairly well traveled and considered herself a veteran plane passenger, but riding in the cockpit of the Scott Corporation's private jet was a bit more than she'd bargained for. A full forward view was vastly different from an occasional glance out the window of a 747, giving her a much better idea of how fast they were going. In a jumbo jet there wasn't really much sensation of flying at all. It felt more like being jostled around in a living room easy chair than being thousands of feet in the air. She was *very* aware of all that open space below them at the moment, and she couldn't decide if she liked it or not.

Logan had been so cool after the incident in front of the Airport Diner, she almost accused him of pouting. Then she had watched in fascination as he went through a mind-boggling number of preflight checks, confusing conversations with the control tower, and, finally, the complex task of getting them airborne. At last he relaxed, glanced over at her, and laughed.

"That was really embarrassing."

Erin smiled. "The other people in the diner seemed to get a big kick out of it." In truth, though she knew there were people after her and was aware of being watched, being followed on a deserted road had terrified her. Logan's embarrassing episode had broken the grip on her fear, made it all seem less threatening. She put her hand on his thigh again, and this time she didn't pull away when he gave her a questioning glance.

"It was a brave thing to do. Thank you." Erin looked at him seriously, enjoying the warmth she found in his eyes.

"It was nothing." Something caught his attention on the control panel, and he made an adjustment. "Really nothing," he added in a mutter. "I didn't even get a very good look at them, let alone have the chance to chat. Damn!"

Erin jumped and looked around wildly. "What?"

Logan looked startled by her reaction, then grinned. "Don't worry. This thing practically flies itself. I'm just so mad. I hope we find something to grab on to at this watering hole of Turner's."

Letting out a long sigh of relief, Erin settled back in her seat. "Lord, don't scare me like that!"

"Take it easy." Logan put his hand on hers and patted it reassuringly. "First time in a small aircraft?"

Erin nodded. Once again she knew he was trying to comfort her, but his touch sent a completely different message to her brain. She was glad he kept taking his gaze from her to scan the horizon and barrage of instruments in front of them. It was all too easy to get lost in the depth of his eyes.

"You're in good hands. I have over five hundred hours in this particular craft and over five times that in the air."

"I thought you were in the army, not the air force."

"I was," Logan answered. "Aside from the business end of it, flying is just a hobby of mine. But I was in the Special Forces, and I did have a chance to do some qualifying flights here and there."

Logan didn't seem all that comfortable talking about his experiences overseas, so Erin aimed her curiosity in other directions. "With a hobby like flying how did you get involved with ocean mining?" she wondered aloud.

He removed his hand from hers. "I suppose you're just being curious again?" Some of the gruff edge had returned to his voice.

"Not entirely," Erin replied honestly, returning her hand to her lap. "I think I have a legitimate right to know something about my employer, especially when at the moment he is also my . . . my . . ."

"Jailer?" Logan supplied.

"Protector," Erin ground out through clenched teeth.

Logan shook his head. "Sorry. Must be that paranoid personality of mine you keep talking about." He sighed. "As a protector I haven't been that great. All I have so far for my trouble is a mouthful of dust."

"Are you going to answer my question or just

125

indulge in self-pity?" she asked with a playful grin.

Giving her a sidelong glance, Logan began his story. "The Scott Corporation was founded by my father. He was a navy man, a diver, and when he retired, he started a small salvage business. He had a lot of plans, but he died before he could act on most of them. He made me promise to carry on, and I did." He laughed and added, "I often wonder if he would have been proud of me. He was a greasy-overalls kind of guy, running things from the inside out. I manage the company with a phone, not a wrench, and I think he always had serious doubts about anyone in a three-piece suit."

"The newspapers and magazines never mentioned the origins of the company in any of the articles I've read."

"Naturally not. They're only interested in the sordid details. Logan Scott under investigation for price fixing," he said in sarcastic mimicry of a newspaper headline. "Scott Corporation's meteoric rise attributed to possible link with organized crime. Logan Scott, the Attila the Hun of the business world, brutalizes and nearly drowns reporter during investigative interview."

"And?"

"And what?" Logan muttered irritably.

"Price fixing? Organized crime?"

He laughed derisively. "No comment."

"Because you'd incriminate yourself?" Erin asked.

"No, dammit!" Logan exclaimed, his voice loud in the small cockpit of the jet. "Because allegations like that don't *deserve* comment. They'd be slander if they weren't couched in such ambiguous terms. 'Under investigation,' for instance. I was, along with ninety percent of the American shipping industry. The Scott Corporation was singled out because we were more up-front about how well we were doing," he explained angrily. "And we were doing well because of shrewd decisions and wise investments, *not* because of 'possible' links with organized crime. I should have sued over that one, but I'm considered a public figure and would have to prove actual malice. It wasn't worth the time and money. Any retraction I would have won would have appeared in the homemaking section of Sunday's paper."

Logan was silent for a moment, and Erin could see him gradually gain control over his temper. She hesitated, not wanting to irritate him further. But he seemed in an expansive mood, and she wanted to hear his side of things.

"How about that poor reporter?"

Logan surprised her by chuckling. It was a bit sarcastic, but it was definitely humor. "*That* one I'm always glad to answer. And I did, but my version never saw print. This guy managed to weasel past the guard at the marina and came charging into my stateroom at one in the morning." He waved a hand at Erin's lap. "Tighten that seat belt now. We'll be making our approch in a few minutes."

She did so, then looked at him expectantly. She remembered reading this particular story, and her interest was piqued. "His behavior was unprofessional, maybe even criminal. But did you have to beat him up and try to drown him?"

Even through his concentration, Logan was obviously greatly amused. He did look at her a bit hesitantly before he spoke, however. "I was . . . um . . . with a friend at the time. Anyway, this guy says something like, 'This underworld figure has got *some* figure,' and pans the camera up and down her rather scantily clad frame."

"Oh, *that* kind of friend," Erin observed wryly.

Logan ignored her. "I went berserk. I grabbed the camera, took it topside, and chucked it overboard. Then the reporter punched me. I had a hell of a shiner that would have supported my side of things, so naturally they used an old file photo for the newspaper story. I didn't even touch the guy, except to throw *him* overboard too." His face lit up in a wide grin. "How was I supposed to know he couldn't swim?"

Erin tried not to laugh but couldn't help it. Here was one of the top executives in the country, someone who should be constantly concerned about his public image, and yet he did things like dump chicken soup on people and toss reporters off his yacht. "No wonder the press takes every opportunity to rake you over the coals. You ask for it." She looked at him suspiciously. "As a matter of fact, in spite of your howls of outrage, I think you kind of like the notoriety."

The corners of Logan's mouth lifted in the hint of a smile. "Sssh! I'm trying to concentrate."

Perturbed, Erin watched and listened as Logan prepared to land, his efficient, yet congenial, conversations with the tower forestalling further questioning. She shifted her gaze forward, then immediately closed her eyes. The sight of the runway below getting larger by the second was more than she could take.

Seth Reynolds was about to have an apoplectic fit. It wasn't so bad that his men had almost gotten caught last night, or even that they had once again lost track of the Barclay woman this evening. They were men of action, and it was in that area that they were at their best. Asking them to lie low and watch went against their nature, and he knew it.

What *was* bad and had him so mad he could barely see straight was that he now had no idea where Scott and Dr. Barclay were. Nothing angered him more than not knowing what was going on. He had made a few phone calls and had found out that the Scott Corporation jet was now at Addison Airport. A flight plan had also been filed for a return trip that night. But that meant nothing and he knew it. He often filed flight plans as a ruse himself, pretending to go in one direction while actually heading in another.

Pouring himself a glass of wine, Reynolds stopped his restless pacing and returned to his desk. Moonlight poured through the window at his left, and he heard the far-off lowing of cattle somewhere on the ranch. He picked up the phone and dialed angrily.

"Airport Diner," a thin, nasal voice replied.

129

"May I speak with Brian or Robert Johnson please?"

"Who?"

He sighed heavily. "Two tall men with beards. Are they there?"

"Yeah."

"Well? May I speak with one of them?" Reynolds almost shouted. Then he realized that if he angered this person, he might have the phone slammed down on him, and he'd have to go through all this again. "Please?" he added in a cultured, coaxing tone.

There was silence over the phone lines for what seemed to him an interminable length of time, during which he heard snatches of shouted conversations, a dish breaking, and the sounds of people eating and talking. A gruff voice came on at last.

"Who's there?"

Reynolds drained the last of his wine in a gulp and hurled the glass at the fireplace. It shattered with a satisfying crash. "Who the hell do you think it is?" he replied in a quiet, deadly voice. "Santa Claus?"

"Sorry, Mr. Reynolds. I've got this cold, and I can't hear very well."

"Yes, I know, you got it from standing around in the rain for the last two days." This wasn't getting him anywhere. It was immensely satisfying to have someone to yell at, but it wasn't helping him find Dr. Barclay. "Have you asked around to see if anyone at that airport knows where Scott was going?"

"The waitress—she knows Scott because he

flies out of here regularly—said he had some kind of problem in the parking lot with two guys in a blue car, then grabbed the lady he was with and left. That's all."

Reynolds cursed softly under his breath. In a move he would have never made in front of anyone, he shrugged out of his jacket and rolled up his shirt-sleeves while he spoke.

"We know that Scott has been moving machinery out of the lab in Addison, but we don't know where it's going. His man Stephanos is in Dallas right now, presumably overseeing that operation. He's one slippery character."

"Yeah. And big too," the man added stuffily. He blew his nose with a noisy snort.

"I suppose they could be up here looking for our friend, Mr. Turner. If that's the case, I wish them the best of luck." He chuckled, but the sound was cold. "You said that two men in a blue car gave Scott a hard time?" Reynolds asked.

"We think it was those two guys from the airport the other day. They were somewhere near the marina when Scott and the broad took off. We saw them follow, but we didn't make the connection right away."

"Maybe I should be hiring them and not you," Reynolds muttered under his breath. "Do you have any thoughts on this matter?"

A scuffling could be heard over the phone, then the other of the Johnson brothers came on the line. "Dr. Barclay and Scott aren't at the lab?"

"No. That's about the only thing I'm sure of, however."

"Do we still have anyone at her house?"

"No. I abandoned that when Stephanos took her to Scott's yacht."

"It's just a wild guess, Mr. Reynolds, but I'll bet that's where they're headed." He chuckled, then coughed. His cough wasn't as bad as his brother's. "That Dr. Barclay is a good-looking woman. Couldn't blame Scott for wanting to get her alone in surroundings she'd be more at home in, if you catch my drift."

"I don't know whether Scott would get involved with her or not. He's known to have an eye for the ladies, yet he wouldn't jeopardize his business over some passing fancy." Reynolds thought for a moment, then a smile spread across his face. "However, I do know how inconvenient it must be for Dr. Barclay on board that yacht, with only the one suitcase." He tucked the phone under his chin and rubbed his hands together in anticipation. "Listen to me. There is a charter service at that airport, and I want you two to get up here as fast as you can. My instincts tell me that tonight's the night to make our move. I'll have a car waiting for you at the airport. Get to Barclay's house as soon as you can. Understand?"

Ever through his dense growth of beard, a malevolent smile could easily be seen on the man's face. That freak Stephanos was out of the way, and no matter what Reynolds said, Logan Scott probably had romance on his mind. Picking up the Barclay woman would be easy as pie. Who knows? Even might be some fun in all of this after all! "We'll be there with bells on, Mr.

132

Reynolds." He got so excited, he started coughing, then blew his nose sloppily.

"God, you two are disgusting," Reynolds remarked. "Buy yourselves some medicine or something. And I remind you at this point that we want Dr. Barclay cooperative. If she has your fingerprints all over her when you bring her to me, I'll have you both shot."

Efficient air conditioning in Dallas was a way of life, but in August it was practically a religion. The taxi Logan and Erin took from the airport, the restaurant where they had a spicy, but delicious, dinner of Texas-style Mexican food, and the cozy little club called The Chase Place all had their cooling plants on high. In fact, if not for the jalepeño peppers warming her insides, the interior of the white-collar bar would have been too cold for Erin. As it was, she was perfectly comfortable.

Logan may have been just as comfortable, but he wasn't happy. Almost everyone he struck up a casual conversation with either knew or knew of David Turner, but Logan wasn't interested in Turner's popularity. He wanted to find the missing lab assistant, and they all told him the same thing. They hadn't seen him lately.

The club was filled to capacity when the band started playing at nine. Logan looked around at the crowd with dismay. "Between us we've talked to just about everyone here," he said, having to speak into Erin's ear to be heard above the music. "Did you do any better than I did?"

Erin smiled mischievously. "All I got were

133

two indecent suggestions and one proposal of marriage."

Logan glared at her. "And how did you reply?"

"I told him I was too young to get married."

Maybe it was frustration, or maybe it was the suspicious looks he'd been getting all evening. But for one reason or another Logan felt as irritable as hell. Hearing about the passes Erin had had to fend off didn't help. He couldn't get over the feeling that if he had any sense, he'd be spending his time talking with Erin instead of on this wild-goose chase.

Where had this possessive streak come from, anyway? He had no claims on Erin, other than those dictated by his business and the enzyme. As she had pointed out to him there could be nothing between them. And he knew she was right. They didn't trust each other, didn't know each other, didn't even have that much in common except for the enzyme and a similar psychological need to be in control.

He looked at her, taking in her teasing smile and bewitching eyes, and felt a surge of desire flow through him. Her face no longer had the drawn, tense look of their first meeting. He had seen and felt enough of her lovely body to no longer be deceived by her slim appearance, and those glimpses left him hungry for more. He wanted her and was experienced enough to know she wanted him as well—even if she was so obviously fighting her desires.

Was mutual desire enough common ground to start building the trust they both needed? Perhaps not, but Logan didn't know how much longer the voice of reason could fight off the passion he felt for her. Already he had come very close to claiming her as his own. He felt very sure that there would be another time, and then they would see if their doubts were as strong as their desire.

The band ended one raucous song and started playing a soft, slow country tune. He saw Erin sway slightly to the music and decided he couldn't wait another moment to hold her in his arms. "Would you like to dance?"

"Yes, I would," Erin answered, not stopping to think about what she was doing. Only after they were on the small, crowded dance floor did she realize how unwise it was to accept his invitation. Logan's hips pressed to hers, her breasts gliding against his broad chest as they danced to the slow music; she was so intensely aware of him, it took her breath away.

She was amazed at his graceful movements and couldn't help wondering what it would be like to make love with him. He was so big, so strong. Would he be rough? Gentle? Probably a mixture of both. She wanted him, practically burned for him. His hand was running slowly up and down her spine in rhythm to the music while the other held hers tightly near his chest as if he thought she would pull away. She rested her head on his shoulder as they danced, intoxicated by the feel of his body pressed to hers.

When the band stopped playing, she lifted her head to look at him and could see in his eyes the same curiosity that had just filled her thoughts. Had he been wondering what it would be like to take her, fill her, feel her surround him?

He kissed her, a kiss that was interrupted all too soon by the band as they launched into another loud song. Erin held on to him for support as they made their way back to the table. In their absence someone had taken their places, but it didn't seem to matter to either of them. She grabbed her purse and went with Logan out of the club, the heat and humidity hitting them immediately, still a force to be reckoned with even at this time of night.

In the parking lot across from the club they saw a taxi waiting for a fare and made their way toward it through the dark. Erin stopped suddenly and turned to him, rousing from the spell she had fallen under on the dance floor.

"I—I don't want you to take this wrong, Logan, but would you take me home?"

Logan looked at her curiously, breathing in her fragrance as they stood in the dark. "What did you have in mind?"

Erin didn't want him to think she was giving in to him. In truth she was almost ready to, but the whole idea still frightened her so much, she couldn't think clearly. "I need to get some more of my clothes," she explained, unable to look him in the eye.

He thought for a moment. It might be dangerous, but then again, he hadn't accomplished anything tonight talking to Turner's friends. "Your house is probably being watched, but that might work to our advantage. If we can push them a little, maybe even get them to push us a little, that'll be one heck of a lot more action than we've seen so far." Logan took her hand in his. Her skin felt cool and exciting in the heat. "But let's be honest with each other, Erin. Back there, on the dance floor, we both had something on our minds that has nothing to do with our doubts about each other or this enzyme business. Don't you agree?"

What use would her denial be now? He had felt her respond to his touch, and she knew the desire she saw in his eyes must be mirrored in her own. "Yes," she answered quietly.

"Then let's stop playing games. We'll go to your house, pick up your things, and see if the opposition throws us a curve." He took her by the arms and pulled her against him. "But that may not be all that happens."

"I thought we had agreed—"

"I didn't agree to anything," Logan interrupted in a husky voice. "I told you. No more games. I don't get what I want out of life by force, but neither do I sit around and wait for things to come to me. I may not wait for you to make up your mind about what kind of man I am, Erin. I may just show you."

The cab was waiting for someone who had called from the club, and though they hadn't made the call, neither Erin nor Logan told the driver that. They got in, and Erin gave him her address, and soon they were on their way to her town house. Though Erin knew it wasn't far, she was so deep in thought, it seemed like mere moments had passed when the cab pulled up in front of the red brick structure.

She thought back to what Logan had said—not that he would take her against her will. He had simply told her that he wasn't going to sit back and wait for her to come to him. That implied that the next time he wouldn't stop just because her voice told him to; her body would have to say no as well. And her body betrayed her every time he touched her. Logan would be with her in her weakest moments, and she had been around him long enough to know he was a man who could take advantage of almost any situation.

When she started to get out of the cab, Logan pulled her back. "Wait."

"That'll be three-fifty," the driver drawled. He had an immense, fluffy Afro and an easy smile.

Logan handed him a twenty-dollar bill. "Once more around the block, and you can keep the change."

The man shrugged and started off. "Whatever."

"Slowly," Logan added. "Like you're looking for an address or something."

The driver complied with Logan's orders, obviously thinking his passengers were behaving suspiciously but not saying a word. A tip was a tip. When he had completed his circuit of the fashionable block of homes, he once again pulled up at the curb and waited.

"Okay," Logan said. "Thanks."

"Sure thing." He glanced at the couple in his rearview mirror and couldn't help but notice that the woman looked like a scared rabbit. He smiled, not thinking much of this guy's chances tonight. "You want me to wait?"

Logan opened the door and got out, holding it for Erin as she climbed out of the backseat. He leaned over and returned the driver's smile. "That won't be necessary."

"That's what I like," the driver said quietly with a conspiratorial wink. "Optimism." He waved and drove off.

Once through the front door, Erin turned on the lights. Then she moaned. "Oh, no!"·

"Must have been some party," Logan remarked, looking around at the wreckage and disarray. Tables were overturned, stuffing from sofas and chairs lay scattered here and there throughout the living room, and the contents of drawers had been strewn everywhere. Light fixtures and lamp shades had even been removed or pulled from the wall.

"It isn't funny!" Erin cried, nearly tripping on the carpet where it had been slashed and pulled back from the baseboards.

"No," Logan agreed seriously, "it's not. Stay behind me and let's go see what the rest of the place looks like."

The rest of the rooms had been similarly redecorated, the kitchen being the worst. Food lay all over, spoiling and beginning to smell. Logan cautiously led the way upstairs to Erin's bedroom, picking his way through the clutter.

When she saw what had been done to her room, Erin sat down on the torn-up bed and started to cry. Clothes had been ripped to shreds, the lacy contents of her dresser trampled underfoot. She felt totally violated, and an intense anger started to burn within her, blocking out all other emotions.

Logan sat beside her, putting his arm around her shoulder and holding her, saying nothing until her outraged tears had passed. Then he took her face in his hands and kissed her tenderly on the forehead.

"I'm sorry, Erin. I'll put all this right, I promise. There'll be a cleaning crew in here first thing tomorrow morning, and you can have a shopping spree on the Scott Corporation. How about that?"

Logan knew it was small compensation. In addition, he silently vowed to get those responsible. But that and giving her a shoulder to lean on was the best he could do under the circumstances. A nonthreatening shoulder. She was too vulnerable now, and seduction would have to wait.

Erin brushed impatiently at her tears, looking at Logan's gentle, compassionate expression. And she thought the only kind of comfort he knew how to offer was sexual. "Can I go to Neiman-Marcus?" she asked, trying to smile.

With a responding smile that warmed her to her toes, Logan nodded. "Anywhere you want."

There was a strength to Erin he hadn't been aware of before, an inner core of toughness. It occurred to him then that she would make either a powerful ally or a forbidding enemy. One thing was for sure. Wherever her loyalties might lie, she couldn't have planned this, not even to draw suspicion from herself.

Erin got up and went to the adjoining bathroom. "You'd think they could have at least left me a tissue," she complained as she rummaged around noisily.

Logan chuckled sympathetically, then went to the bathroom doorway and handed her his handkerchief. "If you're okay, I think we should get the hell out of here," he said.

"I'm all right. It's not the destruction that bothers me as much as it is the terrible unfairness, the disregard for my feelings these . . . these . . ."

"Animals?" Logan supplied.

"Good choice." Erin took another look around and sighed. "I agree. Let's get out of here."

They went downstairs, and Erin started looking for the phone to call a cab. She remembered then what might have happened had they not walked in to find this mess. Logan had sent the cab away, and he had said that picking up her things might not be all that happened here tonight. As unwise as the whole idea was, it appealed to her in an insane, seductive way. To have Logan hold her, caress her, make love to her. Here, in what had been her beautiful home; in her own room, her own bed.

Would that really have happened? Erin had to admit that it probably would. She still doubted Logan, didn't trust him or his plans for her. But her doubts were small defense against the powerful desire they had for one another. Perhaps she should be thankful that something had interfered with such a chain of events, but she wasn't. At least not the part of her that burned for Logan's touch. How she hated the animals who had robbed her of such a fantasy! How Logan must hate those who had robbed him of his conquest!

The sound of Logan's voice dragged Erin from her dangerous thoughts. He was standing near the front window, peering through a slit in the curtains, muttering curses under his breath. "Oh, brother," he said. "All of a sudden it's Grand Central Station out there."

Erin joined him at the front of the house, looking out from the other side of the window. In the light of a full moon she could easily see two men sitting inside a parked car across the quiet street. As she watched, another car came into view as it slowly turned the corner a block down from her town house. There were two shapes in it as well.

"This is their second trip around the block," Logan told her. "The other pair just pulled up and parked, bold as you please."

"Like they'd been here before, huh?" Erin whispered angrily.

"Why are you whispering?" Logan whispered.

"Seemed like the thing to do."

"Well, don't," he replied in a normal voice. "It makes me nervous."

He was nervous? She cleared her throat. "Do you suppose they're all together?"

"We'll find out in a moment."

They continued to watch as the second car drew nearer. Its driver seemed to hesitate for a moment, as if confused by the presence of the parked car. Logan noticed that both vehicles were nearly identical in make, model, and color, indicating that they were probably rentals from the same location. But if the men inside knew each other, they certainly weren't friendly. The moving car suddenly took off down the street and accelerated out of sight.

"What was that all about?" Erin wondered aloud.

"I'm not sure, but I have a pretty good idea." He crossed over to her in front of the window, bent low so he wouldn't throw a shadow. "The back door's in the kitchen, right?" Erin nodded, and he continued. "Any other outside doors?"

"No. Just front and back. The back leads out to a covered patio and fenced yard. Behind that is the alley."

Logan smiled at her efficiency. "Okay. Stay put and keep your eye on the two out front. If they move, give a yell." He moved away from her and headed for the kitchen.

"Shouldn't we call the police?"

"No! They'd get here too late, anyway," Logan answered vehemently. He heard her sharp intake of breath and added, "Don't worry. We'll be just fine." He smiled, pointed at the window as an indication that she should be watching and not talking, then disappeared.

Erin didn't hear the door open, but somehow she knew she was now alone in the house. The two men outside were just watching, and that was all. Occasionally she saw the red glow of a lighted cigarette in the darkened car.

As she continued to watch she felt the hair on the back of her neck stand on end. Still another vehicle—this time a rather noisy pickup truck—

pulled into view on her street. It, too, slowed down at the sight of the parked car, then continued on at a normal pace. But it pulled over and stopped up the block. Its lights went out, and the sound of the engine stopped. Once again all was quiet.

No one got out of the truck. The two men stayed where they were. Erin couldn't hear a sound except that of her own pulse, loud in her ears. Finally she couldn't stand it any longer and decided to find Logan, to tell him about the new development.

The back door was locked. Now, why had he done that? He wouldn't be able to get back in. She unlocked it and swung it open, peering into the darkness. Beyond the patio, the full moon illuminated the small yard, but no one was there. Under the patio cover near the back door it was too dark to see anything. She called in a whisper, "Logan?" Then she remembered that whispering made him nervous. "Logan?" she repeated, loudly this time.

Then she heard the sound of the front door being forced open, slamming against a wall with a loud bang. She turned in the direction of the noise and started to scream, but a hand grabbed her from behind, covering her mouth and pulling her into the smothering blackness of the patio.

Twisting and turning, she flailed out blindly with both arms, managing only to graze something that felt covered in hair before whoever held her wrapped an arm around her and pinned her arms to her sides. She could hear breathing in the shadows on both sides of her, oddly labored and stuffy-sounding. Then she felt a hand on her thigh, and her teeth dug into the hand over her mouth.

"Dammit!" a gruff voice yelled. "Would you quit fooling around? She's biting me!" he yelled again, then let Erin go.

A coarse hand still grasped her thigh, and the grip tightened, moving upward. In the dark Erin prayed for true aim and brought her knee up quickly, feeling it collide with something soft, a choked cry from very near her face telling her she'd found her mark.

"Logan!" she screamed. She made a dash for the kitchen door but bumped into the man doubled up in front of her. Unable to see, she backed straight into the arms of the other one. He grabbed her by the arm from behind, pulling her against his chest. Then Erin heard a deadly-sounding click, and the stray light from the kitchen window reflected off something shiny he held in front of her face. Without warning, her knees gave out, her whole body threatening to go limp.

"Shut up!" He pulled her toward the edge of the yard. Though Erin tried to turn and get a look at him, he was dragging her too fast, and she couldn't manage it. "Move!" At the gate to the alley he stopped and turned back to his companion, still somewhere on the pitch-black patio behind them. "Just pick 'em up off the floor and let's go!" he bit out derisively.

"Oh, oof. I . . . can't . . . breathe," the other

one gasped. He stumbled into the moonlight, still doubled over.

"Serves you right, stud."

From the street out front, frenzied yelling could be heard, and then the sound of screeching tires and a roaring engine fading away down the block. The man holding Erin by the arm turned nervously, following the sound. The knife he held in his free hand looked wicked and cold in the moonlight as he brought it out in front of him.

"What the—"

He never finished his sentence. Erin heard his startled gasp and saw a hand whip through the gate, grabbing him by the wrist and twisting until the knife fell to the ground. Then, like a puppet that was suddenly jerked offstage by the puppeteer who held its strings, he flew backward through the gate. Her arm jerked free of the man's grasp, and Erin stumbled forward a few steps into the yard. From behind the wooden fence she heard a hoarse cry, followed by a loud thud.

Logan stepped warily through the gate. "Are you all right, Erin?" he asked, his voice steely and quiet.

Before she could answer, a dark form hurtled past her, heading for the gate where Logan stood. It was the man she had kneed, still doubled over, but that didn't stop him from shoving Erin from behind as he went by. She sprawled into Logan's arms, spoiling his grab for the other man. He let him escape and held on to her to keep her from falling.

"They'll get away!" Erin cried, dizzy from the fear pumping through her veins.

Logan held up a set of keys. His teeth shone white in the moonlight when he smiled. "They won't get far."

But the sudden sound of a car screeching to a halt behind the fence wiped the smile off his face. Releasing Erin, he kicked the gate open just in time to see the two men awkwardly helping each other into the backseat of a silver Rolls-Royce that had pulled into the alley. Since it was blocked from the front by the other car, it backed up quickly down the alley to the street and sped off, lights out and license plates unreadable. One of the men still hung halfway out the back door.

Erin nearly jumped out of her skin when a voice behind her said, "Lost yours, too, I see."

She spun around, and there was Stephanos, grinning ruefully, the outside mirror of a car clutched in his immense fist.

Logan nodded. "Yes, dammit. And all I could really tell about them was that they were hairy. Big, fluffy beards. Get a good look at your two?"

"It was the pair from the airport. And how two guys that small could move so fast is beyond me. I was sitting in the truck, trying to figure out what was going on, and all of a sudden they dashed over and broke in the front door."

"That was *you* in the truck?" Erin exclaimed. "Why didn't you signal me or something! I went looking for Logan because I thought some more bad guys had showed up."

147

"After I told you to stay put—" Logan pointed out, coming over to her and fixing her with a reprimanding stare.

"Anyway," Stephanos interrupted, impatient to get on with his story, "I chased them around what's left of Erin's living room, then out into the yard, under bushes and up trees, you name it. Finally they made it to their car and took off." He held up the car mirror. "This is all I have to remember them by," the big man stated wistfully.

Logan chuckled, but his attention was fixed on Erin. He could tell that the excitement was wearing thin for her and was watching her closely to see how she was reacting to all this. "You sure you're all right?" he asked.

"I'm fine," she replied, but her voice sounded weak to her. She cleared her throat. "Just tired all of a sudden."

"Come on," Logan coaxed. "Let's go home."

She started to remind him that this *was* her home but found that she didn't really feel that way. Home, for the moment, at least, was with him, in his possessive, but secure, custody. She walked beside him, her arm around his waist, following Stephanos with his gleaming chrome trophy, and felt strangely a part of them, of their world. She was a survivor too. Now that she had faced the enemy head-on she didn't think they would scare her quite as much anymore.

"You know something, Logan Scott?" she said.

"What?"

"You may be a hotshot business man, but you've got a lot to learn about showing a lady a good time."

CHAPTER SEVEN

The jungle was hot and steamy. Thick foliage reached out to grab at her ankles, tearing at her, trying to hold her down. Her heart pounded in her chest as she ran, and every breath rasped in her lungs, loud in her ears. Louder still were the sounds close at her heels, a crashing in the dense green growth behind her, the taunting shouts of her pursuers. She could hear the ring of their machetes growing closer as they hacked their way through the jungle after her, could feel their eyes following her twisting, turning path. Voices talked to her. *You can't escape. You have to rest. Wait for us, and we won't hurt you.*

A clearing appeared in front of her, and Erin dashed into it, suddenly free and unfettered, escape within her grasp. But as she neared the other side, a terrifying feeling gripped her. She had fallen into a trap! Stopping in her tracks, she scanned the edge of the jungle in front of her, and there he was. Logan, handsome and smiling at her, reassuring her. He held out his hand, and she reached for it, realizing a sudden silence all around her. The men chasing her were gone, the jungle still.

She looked at Logan, at his helping hand, and tried to grasp it, but he pulled it away. He held it out again, palm up, his face calm and questioning. Then she realized that he wasn't offering his help, he wanted something. The men that had been chasing her wanted something too. Panic gripped her then. She didn't have what he wanted, and he was turning his back on her, leaving her alone in the jungle, and the sound of the machetes started again. . . .

Erin jerked awake and sat bolt upright in bed, drenched in a cold sweat, looking wildly around her stateroom. It was cool and quiet, the safe, familiar noises of the *Tempete* comforting and real. Slowly the nightmare released its grip on her mind, her taut muscles relaxing as she breathed deeply in the darkness.

It was just a dream, a silly dream. Logan had saved her, risked injury himself to protect her. And he wanted her, desired her. His eyes hadn't left her for more than a few minutes at a time, even on the flight back. She could almost feel his possessive influence surrounding her even now.

Erin restlessly got out of bed and put on her robe, then quietly went up on deck. A new day would soon begin, but right now it was dark and still, an hour or more before dawn. The air was heavy with the humid smell of the sea. In the distance she could see the running lights of transport ships making their way along the channel, plodding behemoths of never-sleeping ocean commerce. She leaned against the railing and sighed.

It had just been a nightmare, but Erin knew dreams often had meanings, messages from the unconscious to the conscious that shouldn't always be ignored. In this case she knew her dream was a delayed reaction to all the terrifying things she had experienced last night. Other than a brief moment when she almost fainted, she had taken it all in stride—almost cheerfully. How strong she must appear! The truth was, she hadn't reacted because none of it seemed real to her. Her vandalized home, the struggles with the two men, the knife; how could any of that have happened to her? She was just a hardworking scientist. The most danger she had faced was a small fire in her lab. She felt proud to have handled herself so well, but she still had the lingering feeling that this was happening to someone else.

Like a scolding parent her mind put it all together in a dream, forcing her to come to grips with the whole situation. It *had* happened. Her house had been torn up because of something those people thought she had hidden there. She had nearly been kidnapped, had been coarsely groped in the process, and had been threatened with a knife because she had resisted. This was real, it was dangerous, and she was right in the middle of it all. A man she couldn't bring herself to trust had control over her, was restricting her movements and was slowly gaining a hold on her emotions as well. And Erin didn't think she could stand it anymore.

Oh, Logan was extremely capable of protecting her. And of keeping her under his control.

That was what bothered her. His increasingly possessive influence was at once deliciously seductive and smothering, the world in which he held her captive hypnotizing as well as impossible. Erin couldn't help wondering when it all would end.

As it was in her dream, Logan wanted something from her, but if he didn't get it, he would do a lot more than just turn and walk away. He may be infatuated with her at the moment, but if she refused to produce his precious enzyme, she was certain his infatuation would turn to fury, and that was a terrifying prospect.

Logan was an enigmatic man, full of secrets and schemes, eminently capable of playing both ends against the middle. He easily handled the nefarious characters who tried to take her last night, had even seemed to enjoy the danger and intrigue. He had proved to her he could be just as dangerous as the people he was protecting her from. Might he be just as unscrupulous as well?

With a final, resigned sigh, Erin turned and went back to her room. This line of thinking wasn't getting her anywhere. Whatever Logan's plans, she would just have to stick close to him until he trusted her enough to confide in her. That task was tricky enough. He was increasingly possessive of her and not just because of her scientific ability. He coveted her enzyme process, but it was very obvious that he coveted her body too.

Too wound up to sleep but too drowsy to function well, Erin decided to take a hot shower, hoping it would either wake her up or help her drift off again. She went into the bathroom, being as quiet as possible so as not to wake Logan in the other room. Taking off her robe and nightgown, she turned on the water and stepped beneath the soothing spray.

With an elaborate amount of noise, Logan emerged from his room into the bathroom. "Couldn't sleep?"

"What? Get out of here!" Erin cried.

Logan ignored her protest. "I couldn't sleep, either. A nice hot shower sounds like just the ticket," he replied happily.

Through the frosted glass of the shower door, Erin watched his movements, her body pressed as far into the corner of the cubicle as she could get. He was taking off his robe! "What are you doing? I told you to get—"

The door opened and he stepped in with her. "Hi!" He was grinning from ear to ear. "Boy," he said, trying to get used to the temperature of the water cascading over them both, "you like *really* hot showers, don't you?"

"I . . . you . . . get out," Erin sputtered, covering herself as best she could with a washcloth and her hands. She tried to avert her eyes from his body but found that her traitorous mind wouldn't let her. He was tanned all over, except for a thin band from low on his waist to the tops of his muscular thighs. He was obviously very proud of his body, standing unashamed before her. Erin blushed from head to toe.

"Ha!" His eyes gleamed with pleasure. "Where's the soap? Ah, here it is." He picked it up and tried to hand it to her, his gaze raking up and down her glistening body. "Come on. Wash my back," he coaxed, forcing the soap into her hand and turning around. "And hurry up before the hot water runs out."

"I will not!" she exclaimed in outrage.

"Okay," Logan said agreeably. "Then I'll wash yours." He turned, grabbed her by the arms, and spun her around with her back to him. Then he picked up the soap from where she had dropped it and began soaping her back.

With long, slow strokes, he worked his way down to her buttocks, his strong hands caressing and coveting her rounded curves. "Mmm," he said hoarsely. "Very nice."

"Stop that!"

"I don't want to," he replied merrily, wrapping his arms around her and pulling her against his hard, masculine form. One hand wandered over her rib cage to mold and shape each breast, while the other slid down her stomach to the damp, feminine curls below. She was struggling, but he could tell her heart wasn't in it.

"Stop . . . that," she repeated weakly, her own voice growing husky. She groaned and leaned back against him, dizzy from the pleasure he was giving her. "Logan . . ."

He moved his hips suggestively against her, delighting in the slippery feel of her skin. "The water's getting cold," he whispered in her ear, pausing to nibble on the sensitive lobe. "Let's adjourn to my stateroom."

Erin wasn't in any doubt about the throbbing state of his arousal. Her own senses were exquisitely alive as well, and she let him draw her from the shower, supporting herself against his strong, well-muscled body. They stood there for a moment, dripping wet, then Logan lowered his head to savor the taut tips of her breasts, licking the drops from their soft curves with his tongue. She shivered, and a moan escaped her throat, her knees weakening beneath her.

But when he pulled her toward his room, she resisted, trying to regain control of herself and this crazy, tempting situation. "No, I—"

"Your eyes say yes," Logan murmured softly, pulling her into his arms and against his every pulsing inch, trapping her within the powerful strength of his arms. "And your body does too."

He was very strong, and suddenly his strength became a frightening force to her. She struggled against him to no avail, succeeding only in arousing him—and herself—all the more. "Logan," she moaned. "No! Please. Let me go!"

Her struggles were becoming more insistent, almost mindless, and she sounded on the verge of tears. "Erin, I'm not going to hurt you. Relax."

"No!" She pushed against him with all her strength, only the slickness of her body allowing her to escape his grasp. She hesitated a moment, glaring at him, her eyes wide. Then she spun around and fled, locking the door to her room behind her.

A soft knock sounded. "Erin? Are you all right?" Logan's concerned voice was muffled through the door.

"Yes! Just . . . just leave me alone!" She could almost feel him trying to decide what to do, then heard the slam of his door into the adjoining bathroom.

Her breathing coming in shaky gasps, relief washed over her, and she sat down on her bed, her face in her hands. How could she stay here, trapped within the web of Logan and his beguiling masculine ways? She was supposed to be getting to know him but not *that* well. The only thing she could think about was what would happen in the future. If the sexual tension between them kept growing, Erin would soon be unable to prevent the inevitable. Their relationship could, at any weak moment, become very, very serious. How could she possibly allow herself to become any more involved with him and still keep her objectivity?

If she was going to keep the enzyme under her control until she could be sure both she and it were used correctly, then she had to get out of here, away from the mesmerizing lure of his indomitable will. She had to gain her freedom from his tempting offer of shared ecstasy before it consumed her, drove her beyond the point of caring about anything but being in his arms. She had to put some distance between her confused emotions and Logan's world.

"Erin, my dear," she muttered to herself, "you've got to get away from that man!"

With the dawn the gray cloud cover finally parted over the Gulf of Mexico, revealing blue sky and allowing the sun to shine through. In the warm early-morning sunlight, Logan and Stephanos met on deck for their workout.

157

"Erin still asleep?" Stephanos asked as he set up the weight bench.

"She's still in her cabin. Whether she's asleep or not is anybody's guess," Logan replied in a surly voice.

His friend looked at him speculatively. "You look . . . how can I put this diplomatically? Bewildered, that's it. You look very bewildered this morning."

"I *am* bewildered," Logan said with a sigh. He lifted first, then spoke while Stephanos took his turn at the weights. "That woman has me so confused. She's driving me crazy, old friend, and I'm not kidding."

"That's funny," he said, breathing rhythmically. "I'm sure I detect a certain, um . . . fondness developing between you two."

"Fondness? I suppose you could call it that."

Stephanos chuckled, a deep, booming sound in the still morning air. "To hell with diplomacy. What you have is the hots for each other, and don't bother denying it."

"That's part of it," Logan agreed in frustration. "But Erin can be so clinical at times, thinking of everything in terms of consequences, planning her moves so carefully. I know there's a fire burning in her somewhere, but I can't see to get at it."

"Look who's talking. This company didn't get where it is without thinking ahead. You're pretty clinical yourself, Logan."

"It's not the same thing."

"To her it probably is." He stood up from the bench and let Logan take his place. "You're her

158

employer. Even under the best circumstances relationships like that can be touchy. She likes her job, she likes her profession, and both could be in jeopardy if this enzyme thing doesn't work out right."

Logan nodded impatiently. "I understand that. But you and I both know there's more to it than that."

"Sure there is. You don't trust each other."

"What has she done to show she deserves my trust?"

Stephanos slapped his forehead with one big hand. "Sometimes I wonder about you, Logan. Just because she doesn't trust *you* doesn't prove you can't trust *her*."

"I suppose you're right." He thought of Erin's odd behavior earlier that morning. "Maybe it is time I started explaining things to her," Logan said begrudgingly.

"Good. Maybe the breakfast conversations will return to normal around here then." He changed the amount of weight on the barbell and assisted Logan in getting it off the supports. "We're nearly done crating up the machinery from the lab, and pretty soon you're going to have to decide where and when we make our next move."

"I'm working on it," Logan said, his voice strained with the effort of holding the bar steady. "And I take your point. It'll be easier on all of us if I smooth things out with Erin before then. Okay?"

"Okay," Stephanos replied amiably. "I'll change the subject. Those guys last night—at least the two you had problems with—they're probably the ones who threatened her. Don't you agree?"

"I've come to that conclusion, yes. The other two don't seem very well organized."

"What was your assessment of them?"

Logan thought while he did his bench presses. "I think they were in too much of a hurry for some reason. I think they underestimated their opposition—both me and Erin." He grinned as he pressed the bar off his chest one last time and set it back in place. "She has lovely knees and obviously knows how to use them effectively."

"In other words, you took them by surprise."

His expression sobering suddenly, Logan slowly nodded his head. "Yeah. Neither of them were petunias, that's for sure. She got the one pretty good from the way she described it, and yet he was still able to run. I was lucky enough to catch the other from behind." He stood up, wiping perspiration from his face. He looked grim. "They won't be so easy the next time."

"Who won't be so easy the next time?" Erin strolled out on deck, wearing her most worn pair of jeans and a worse-for-wear T-shirt. She looked at Logan pointedly, then sat down on a deck chair. Her skin showed through the holes in the knees of her jeans. She'd brought them with her to make cut-offs for the beach. Now they were serving a much better purpose.

"A real fashion plate today, aren't you?" he observed.

"I think," Stephanos interjected, "that we are being treated to some very heavy sarcasm here."

"You betcha," Erin said, picking absentmindedly at the unraveling hem of her shirt.

"All right!" Logan cried. "We'll go shopping right after breakfast. Now get below and change before I'm accused of harboring a fugitive from the flower-child era."

"Are you calling me a hippie?"

"Why, no, dear," Logan replied sweetly. He looked her up and down, pleased with the contents if not the wrapper. "You are leggy, and you almost qualify for busty. But your hips are just right."

Erin almost chickened out. It wasn't that she hadn't convinced herself that getting away from Logan's influence was the right thing to do. Nor was it any fear of being caught by him or anyone else. For some reason she felt more capable now of keeping a low profile. It was just that she was having so much fun with him today.

Stephanos had again disappeared on company business, so, even though he didn't look too thrilled by the whole affair, Logan drove her to Houston and she went through a considerable amount of money in the high-tone shops of the Galleria. Logan started to enjoy himself the minute Erin began modeling clothes for him and soon fell into the spirit, choosing things he thought she'd look good in. They laughed, walked arm in arm through the myriad of stores, and had a wonderful lunch. For a moment Erin almost decided to forget her plans and remain with him.

Then she thought about what that meant.

There were more dangerous involvements to consider here than mere physical attraction. She was getting attached to Logan, was going beyond desire and beginning to think of him as a friend. She couldn't take a long, hard, objective look at his plans if that happened. And that meant it was more important than ever that she get away from him.

There was a flea market in Houston that almost defied description, a collection of permanent and semipermanent shops and open-air stands selling everything from used clothing to antique furniture. Today it was jammed with people—squirming-room only, as Logan remarked when they went in the main gate—all of them jostling and pushing and spending their money under the sweltering sun. Judging from the noise, everyone was having a wonderful time.

For Erin, her reasons for asking Logan to bring her here were twofold. Though she had taken some of her purchases with her, most of what she had bought today was being sent either to the *Tempete* or to her home in Dallas. Since she had no intention of returning with Logan, she needed to have some clothes to take with her when she made good her escape. Here she could buy what she needed and felt it wouldn't be too much trouble to disappear among this throng of people.

Logan tried to stay close by her side but found it all but impossible. He would stop to look at something, and when he looked up, Erin would be wandering along ahead, nearly out of sight. She did this several times, so he wouldn't become alarmed if he lost her for a few minutes. Nor did he think it odd when she bought a large canvas shoulder bag to hold all her purchases. He was having a good time, and though he thought he detected a certain amount of strain in her eyes, he decided Erin was enjoying herself as well. Who wouldn't be a bit nervous with all she'd been through lately?

It therefore came as no surprise to him when he stopped to buy a large bundle of Tyler roses for her, only to find her missing. Forging ahead through the bustling mass of people, he scanned the crowd for her. He had had no trouble spotting her before. She was wearing a pair of close-fitting designer jeans and the plum-colored silk blouse she had purchased at their last stop at the Galleria. But her long-legged form and that distinctive blouse were nowhere in sight.

Logan searched for a while longer, then gave it up as futile. There were too many people. He started giving her description to shop clerks along the route he supposed she had taken, asking if they'd seen her. After some very strange looks and negative answers, a young man running a used clothing stand nodded his head.

"Well, man, I don't really look at faces, you know? But the clothes I recognize real well." He smiled, then pulled a pair of designer jeans from a grocery bag underneath his table. "She traded me these for a couple pairs of faded size nines and an old chambray work shirt. I tried to make her a deal on the blouse . . . real flossy top, you know? But she seemed in kind of a hurry, so—"

"Which way did she go?" Logan asked. If he had been bewildered this morning, he was positively befuddled by now.

The boy pointed at a cubicle of blankets rigged up on a wire. "She changed into the used stuff in our dressing room back there and took off." He looked at Logan appraisingly. "If you want to buy the jeans back, you'll have to wait till tomorrow. Law says I can't sell them until I wash—"

"Which way did she go?" Logan repeated sharply.

"Hey, don't be mad with her, man. Chicks do it all the time. They get here and see that the stuff I'm selling is what everybody else here is wearing and just want to blend in with the crowd, you know?"

Logan looked around and saw that he was right. As hard as it would have been to pick Erin out of the casually dressed crowd before, it would be impossible now. And that was when he realized that he'd been had.

CHAPTER EIGHT

Freedom! No one telling her what to do, where to go. Erin luxuriated in the feeling as she walked along the back road from the flea market, marveling at the almost rural atmosphere of this part of Houston. And then she noticed something distressing. Walking in Houston didn't seem to be an acceptable means of travel.

After fifteen minutes of cars slowing down as they passed by as if she was some sort of major attraction, Erin decided she stuck out like a sore thumb. First she had to get off the street, and then she had to figure out where to go. The heat didn't really bother her, but the air-conditioned comfort of a roadside ice cream stand still felt relaxing, calming nerves that had started to fray. She ordered an iced tea and sat down to think.

One way or another, Logan had probably figured out by now that she had flown the coop. He might possibly think she'd been kidnapped, and that didn't make her feel too proud of herself. Nor did she feel especially good about leaving him at the market after he had been so nice to her today. They'd been having such a wonderful time. But this course of action was necessary, so she steeled herself to feeling free *and* miserable.

The trouble was, she hadn't thought too much about what to do with her freedom once she had acquired it. Now, out of Logan's protective custody, Erin was just beginning to fully realize how perilous her once-calm life had become. Going back home was out of the question. Besides the mess—and the crew Logan said he would have there today to clean it up—it would be the first place both he and the others would look.

Even here, in this little out-of-the-way place, wearing her hastily thrown together disguise and a pair of dark sunglasses, she felt paranoid. Was her every move under some kind of surveillance? She looked furtively around the restaurant's small seating area and sighed. She was alone.

Erin knew it was only a matter of time before Logan caught up with her. Somehow between now and then she would busy herself gathering needed information on the company she worked for but had recently come to realize she knew so little about. Much of that would simply be a matter of putting two and two together, of doing some research at the library, and of thinking things through. Being able to think clearly was the reason she had decided to take off like this in the first place, to escape the sensual feelings Logan awakened in her. He had been controlling her mind—and her body.

But she needed more than just thinking room;

she needed some kind of inside track on the mess she was involved in, and that brought to mind only one source: David Turner. He was the key. On that point she and Logan were in agreement.

But there was something Logan didn't know about David, something Erin had nearly forgotten herself until last night. She hadn't known the man that well, but at the club, being around his friends, she had remembered that Turner was a gambler and could conceivably have sold company secrets in order to pay off debts. Considering the profit potential of the enzyme, he probably ended up with some extra money. And that gave her an idea.

Erin finished her tea and went back out into the heat, buying a newspaper from one of the machines near the front door. Turner would need a place with less exposure than the usual gambling meccas, a place he could get to quickly without leaving a trail. And there it was, in the entertainment section. The horses were running at Louisiana Downs, just a short hop over the Texas border. She felt certain she would find him there, but even if she didn't, it would be somewhere no one would think to look for her, either.

Tucking the paper into her canvas bag, Erin went to the pay phone bolted to the south wall of the restaurant. Some enterprising company had pasted an advertisement for their cab service to the wall above the phone, which was good, because the phone book had been torn from its metal binding. She dialed the number.

"Swift cab."

"Please send a cab to . . ." Erin trailed off and turned to look at the street sign on the corner. Instead she looked into—down into—the brown eyes of Armando.

"No need for a cab, Dr. Barclay. Carlos and I will be more than happy to give you a lift."

The blue car pulled swiftly up beside them, and the back door swung open. Before Erin realized what was happening, Armando shoved her through the door and followed her in, nearly knocking himself out on the doorjamb in the process. Carlos gunned the throttle, the momentum of the car slamming the door on his partner's foot, and swerved out into traffic amid angry shouts and blowing horns.

The small man lying half on top of her in the narrow backseat was cursing, too, in pain, and in Spanish. He was nearly crushing Erin in his attempts to rub both his bumped head and sore foot at once.

"Get off me!" Erin yelled, then cried out anew when Armando's elbow jabbed her in the stomach.

"Oh, my head! My foot! Carlos, you stupid idiot!"

"What are you yelling at me for?" Carlos gestured wildly with one hand, trying to watch the traffic, his rearview mirror, and his partner's antics in the backseat at the same time. "You're the fool who decided we had to grab her like some back-street thugs!"

Armando seemed to be regaining his composure, for he got off Erin, murmuring apologies, and sat up straight in the seat. "She wouldn't have come quietly otherwise, would you, Dr. Barclay?" he asked, gingerly touching the knot on his forehead.

Erin had news for them. She wasn't coming quietly now. But as she opened her mouth to scream, Armando slapped his hand over her mouth. She bit him, and *he* screamed. The small car swerved back and forth in its lane as Carlos tried to see what was going on behind him.

"Armando, be a man!" he yelled.

"I'll be a man when you act like a driver. You'll kill us all!" He screamed again when Erin bit him harder.

Erin clapped her hands over her ears while the two men yelled, her eyes wide with terror as they narrowly missed an oncoming car. She stopped biting Armando and nodded her head in agreement. If these two didn't calm down, they'd all end up in the hospital. He removed his hand, shaking it in anguish before examining it for damage.

"All right," Erin said in as calm a voice as she could. "All right. Let's just take it easy, okay?"

"Okay," they both agreed.

Carlos settled down and drove; Armando sat back in the seat, watching Erin with suspicious brown eyes. Erin sighed in relief. "Okay. Now, if you'll just pull over and let me out, we'll forget the whole thing."

"No!" Carlos cried.

Erin rubbed her temples in anguish, feeling the start of a headache. "Please, no more yelling."

"You must stay with us," Armando pleaded quietly.

"Yes. You must."

Erin looked from one to the other of the men. They weren't threatening her, they were *begging* her. What kind of lunatics had she fallen in with now? "Um, have you two been doing this sort of thing long?" she asked.

"We are businessmen, Dr. Barclay. All we want to do is talk with you."

"Businessmen," Erin repeated doubtfully.

"Yes. Oh, excuse me. I am Armando," the one beside her said, then pointed at the driver. "And this is Carlos." He held out his hand to her.

Erin took it tentatively, and he kissed her on the knuckle. It was such a charming gesture, Erin almost smiled. "Uh . . . yes, well, I'm Erin Barclay. But I guess you already know that." She felt incredibly foolish, calmly chatting with kidnappers. But, as at the airport, she sensed no immediate threat from this odd pair. Actually she doubted that they could agree on anything long enough to do her harm.

"Of course we know you," Armando replied. He smiled and then continued. "You are Dr. Erin Barclay. You have developed an enzyme that will revolutionize the deep-sea mining industry." Suddenly his expression turned unsure. "Haven't you?"

"No," Erin answered.

He looked shocked for a moment, and Erin heard Carlos gasp, but then he smiled and shook his finger at her. "With all the time I have spent

170

in your country, I should by now be used to the American sense of humor."

Her country? "Where are you from?" Erin asked.

"We are Chilean nationals," Armando replied proudly. "We represent a group of people in Chile who are very concerned about the consequences of your discovery."

"And who might this group be?"

"At the moment they wish to remain anonymous."

"Tell her the truth," Carlos chimed in. "You see, Dr. Barclay, at the moment our link with this group is very tenuous. Unofficial. But, if we succeed, they will welcome us with open arms."

Erin could see his smiling face reflected in the rearview mirror. Obviously acceptance by this group was very important to them. Suddenly she didn't feel quite as at ease as she had before. "And what must you do to succeed?"

Armando looked less than overjoyed with his companion's confession but went on with his explanation. "For now we wish only to talk with you, tell you of our position in this matter. We are certain that once you are fully informed, our success will be assured."

"But—"

He held up his hand. "Please. This is no place for civilized people to have such an important discussion. To make amends for treating you so badly, you must let us buy you dinner. And then we will talk."

Erin shrugged helplessly and nodded her acceptance. Short of making a scene—to which

171

she didn't know how these volatile gentlemen would react—Erin wasn't quite sure how to go about getting away from them. She *was* sure it would be safer to wait until after they all arrived safely at their destination.

In addition they seemed to be seeking only information, a goal she shared. She would talk, but she would listen too. Perhaps they could help her understand the situation better. She indicated her attire with a wave of her hand. "Can you take me somewhere I can change first?"

"Certainly. We are on our way to the hotel now."

The hotel was the Hilton, and dinner was a delicious French meal catered in their room. It was obvious to Erin that Carlos and Armando didn't trust her very much in spite of their confidence in their powers of persuasion. While she was changing into the embroidered cotton skirt and blouse she had bought at the flea market, they kept knocking on the bathroom door to make sure she was still there, as if she could escape out a window on the seventh floor!

During the meal they told her of their country, describing in glowing terms the vast coastline, the widely varying climate, and the majestic Andes they shared as a border with their neighbors, Peru, Bolivia, and Argentina. Their patriotic fervor was evident to Erin, as were their manners and social grace. She found that she was enjoying their company but at the same time remained skeptical about their motives.

The more they talked, the more certain she

became that whatever information she might gain from Armando and Carlos would most likely be one-sided. Still, Erin listened intently when they finally finished their travelogue and got down to business.

"You have heard of the common heritage of mankind?" Armando was asking her. Seeing the confusion on Erin's face, he continued in a polite, but cool, manner. "Do not feel badly. I have found that few Americans concern themselves with the desperate plight of the so-called developing states of the world."

"Now just a minute!" Erin replied heatedly.

Armando held up his hand in a placating gesture. "Ah! I see that you do not like to hear such things. That is good."

"Yes. Very good," Carlos agreed.

"Just because I've never heard of the common heritage of mankind doesn't mean I don't care about Third World countries," Erin interjected. "No one likes to think about starvation or poverty."

"Indeed not." Armando poured Erin another glass of wine before he went on. "And yet one *must* think about it. That is why I say it is good to hear anger in your voice. It proves to me that you *do* care."

Erin leaned back in her chair and sipped at her wine, looking at the two men warily. Whatever else this pair might be, and no matter how inept they were at strong-arm tactics, they were quite good at manipulating emotions. She realized that she was more in the company of diplomats than kidnappers. It didn't comfort her much. "So tell me. What *is* the common heritage of mankind?"

"It means many things, of course, but the United Nations has generally defined it as the riches bestowed upon mankind as a whole. When you really think about how hard some of those riches are to acquire, you begin to look at it as the redistribution of wealth."

"What wealth?"

Armando spread his hands and shrugged. "All wealth."

Erin couldn't help a small smile from tugging at the corners of her mouth. "I think, gentlemen, that we are headed for a confrontation here. As you pointed out, I'm an American. And a believer in the capitalist system. I may not be very politically oriented, but I recognize socialism when I hear it."

Again Armando shrugged. "A great deal of the world is socialist, Dr. Barclay, but let us not get bogged down in political jargon. Just answer this question for me if you can. Who owns the moon?"

Erin frowned. "The moon? I don't think anyone owns it, or can. We may eventually be able to build on it, use its minerals, but—"

"We?" Carlos asked the question this time, and he looked just as serious as his partner. "Who is *we*, Dr. Barclay?"

Her smile this time was broad as she realized how easily they were directing her thoughts. "Mankind, I suppose," she answered.

"But will mankind really share in that adventure or in the profits to be derived from it?"

174

"I see your point, gentlemen," Erin said, unable to hold back a chuckle. "Actually we are discussing a point of international law, and such things are all but impossible to enforce." Her brow furrowed in thought. "In the end I think it will be the way it has always been with new frontiers. First come, first served. At any rate, such events are quite a bit in the future. We shall just have to wait and see."

"That we shall," Armando agreed ruefully. "I doubt very strongly, however, that Chile will ever have a base on the moon. Don't you?"

"It doesn't seem very likely, no."

"No. There is, however, another element of mankind's common heritage, one much closer to home. And one that can have a great impact on my country's future." He looked at Erin, his brown eyes burning with purpose. "The sea."

Erin nodded slowly, understanding at last where all this was leading. "Manganese nodules."

Armando seemed pleased. He grinned triumphantly. "My country realizes that we do not possess the technology or the financial resources to mine those nodules. We also realize that those who do will not eagerly share the profits simply because the United Nations says they should."

At last they were getting to the heart of the matter, and Erin couldn't say she liked the direction in which her thoughts were taking her. "That, I take it, is where I come in."

"We know that your enzyme can make the mining of manganese nodules profitable—very profitable—for the first time since their discovery over a century ago."

Erin saw her chance and jumped at it. "And just how do you know?"

The two men smiled enigmatically. "The information is, shall we say, making the rounds."

She didn't like the sound of that at all. Just how many people were after her by now? "As informed as you are, then, I can't say I understand what you hope to gain by talking with me. I work for the Scott Corporation."

"Come, come, Dr. Barclay. We know you are on less than happy terms with the Scott Corporation. We know Logan Scott does not let you stray far from his side. Indeed, are you not at this moment absent without leave?"

Erin got up from the table and went to the window, gazing out on the highway and traffic below. "I just needed room to think, that's all," she answered quietly. Carlos and Armando were indeed bringing a point home to her. She had betrayed a trust by escaping Logan. Not only that but in their eyes—and Logan's as well—she was a free agent, a traitor.

"All we are asking you to do is think. Something you say you do better away from Logan Scott's influence," Armando said with a sympathetic smile. "Figuratively speaking you hold in your hands a marvelous opportunity. Now, with the nodules, the noble idea of the common heritage of mankind truly will be tested."

Erin turned and looked at the pair, her expression guarded. "My doubts about the Scott Corporation notwithstanding, I've been involved in private American industry too long to be very optimistic about such an idealistic principle."

"It is within your power to make a grand gesture, Dr. Barclay. You are a scientist, supposedly working toward the betterment of mankind. And now you are faced with a decision. Do you want your discovery to increase the wealth of one man or of the world?"

Erin couldn't believe what she was hearing. She didn't know if they were aware of it or not, but they were voicing questions she had been asking herself from the moment she had made the breakthrough. Just what *was* the best use of the process she had discovered?

At the same time, suspicions were growing within her, about these men, their true motives, and her place in their plans. She walked back to the table and sat down, regarding them suspiciously. "We have a saying in America. If something looks too good to be true, it probably is."

"Meaning?"

"Meaning, what's in it for you?" Erin countered.

"Chile is one of the world's largest producers of copper. Indeed, we produce some of the highest grade ores in the world," Armando explained with quiet intensity and pride. "We can stand normal competition and have done so for quite some time. But your enzyme could break us. It is just that simple, Dr. Barclay. You hold the future of my country in your hands."

Erin shook her head doubtfully. "I don't see how that could be. It would take a very concentrated effort on someone's part to glut the market of any one metal found in the nodules."

"Perhaps. But we have suffered at the hands

177

of American mining interests before and have no reason to believe that the situation will change."

Erin closed her eyes and sighed. When she opened them again, she was seeing things much more clearly than before. "Now I understand. You're not asking me to guide the development of the enzyme in a fair fashion, or even to make the discovery public, so the world can take part in its development. You want me to give it to you."

Obviously Carlos and Armando didn't see what she found so disturbing about that. "To us, yes. To Chile. Then through us it will go to the world."

"And the president wears purple pantaloons."

"What?"

Erin stood up, leaning with her hands on the table and glaring first at one then the other of the two men. "Thank you for the dinner. Thank you for the conversation. You have indeed given me much to think about, and I really mean that. Rest assured that the best use of my enzyme is uppermost in my mind too."

"You sound as if you are saying good-bye, Dr. Barclay," Armando said quietly. He rose to his feet, as did Carlos.

"I am," she replied. "Something wrong?" With an airy manner she didn't really feel, Erin went to the couch where she had left her bag and slung the strap over her shoulder.

They watched her every move. "Dr. Barclay. Must we remind you of how much information we have? There are many international organizations and even segments of your own government that would be most interested in your little secret," Armando said. He continued in a quiet, threatening tone. "If you will not help us, you force us to find someone who will. And that could have serious complications for you."

Carlos came slowly around the table toward her. "You cannot leave," he added in a chilling voice.

Her hand on the doorknob, Erin turned and pinned them with a threatening stare of her own. "I can, and will. If you try to stop me, I'll have everyone on this floor convinced that you're a couple of perverts in six seconds flat." She opened the door for emphasis, stepped into the hallway, then poked her head back in and smiled. "I'll give your regards to Stephanos. He's just dying to meet you again!"

With the satisfaction of their faces going pale right before her eyes, Erin closed the door quietly, took three or four steps with calm self-assurance, then made an undignified dash for the elevator.

When she emerged from the Hilton, Erin frantically looked around for a cab. She saw one and hurried toward it, unaware of the eyes following her from within a nondescript car parked across the street from the hotel.

"There she is."

"I see her. Boy, do I have a score to settle with that broad." Robert Johnson smiled in anticipation, but the hair on his face hid any trace of happiness.

His brother, Brian, was not a twin. It was just

the penchant they each shared for beards that made them look so much alike. "You got what you deserved. And you'd better remember who you work for. Reynolds isn't kidding when he says he'll have us shot if we don't bring her to him unharmed."

They watched Erin get into the cab, then started their car and followed, blending into traffic a discreet distance behind.

"Yeah, yeah," his brother said in disgust. "Look who's playing high and mighty. You like her looks as much as I do, and it's not as if you don't have something to remember last night by." He chuckled, then wheezed with the cold still plaguing him.

Brian held up his bandaged wrist, a reminder of Logan Scott's strength. His eyes narrowed, and his mouth drew into a thin, vindictive line. "I'm not saying there aren't scores to be settled. But there's a time and a place for everything. Dr. Barclay made a real bad move when she took off on her own, and her time's about up. Scott'll get his clock punched soon enough too." He changed lanes when the cab did but stayed a few cars behind, trying to remain as inconspicuous as possible. "Patience, brother. Good things come to those who wait."

In the cab Erin was coming to grips with reality. She had been lucky. If it hadn't been Armando and Carlos who had found her first, or if they had been more inclined to force her to their will . . .

Her mind clamped down on her fear. Though her heart pounded in her chest and she had to

180

hold her hands in her lap to keep them from shaking, her thoughts were still proceeding in a relatively normal fashion.

Or were they? She had told the cabdriver to take her to the airport but now realized that was a poor idea. She had been caught there before. If she wanted to get out of Houston, to go to Louisiana Downs in search of David Turner, she would have to find some other means of transportation.

"Leave the driving to us," Erin said, thinking out loud.

"What'd you say, lady?" the cabdriver asked.

"I've changed my mind. Take me to the nearest bus terminal, please."

The driver shrugged, pulled over to the side of the road, then made a U-turn when it was clear. "It's your money, lady. Me, I don't like buses. Take forever to get anywhere."

The move took the Johnson brothers by surprise. They whizzed by Erin before they knew it, then watched in shocked amazement as the cab turned behind them and went back the way it had come.

"Hold on!" Brian slammed on his brakes, narrowly escaping a rear-end collision and pitching his unprepared companion into the dashboard. He quickly whipped the car around and floored the accelerator in pursuit of the rapidly disappearing cab.

"I think my nose is broken," Robert Johnson said with a moan.

"I told you to hang on!"

"And I told you I should drive. With that

wrist of yours we just missed getting creamed back there!"

Yelling and making obscene gestures, his brother wove his way through traffic in an effort to catch up with Erin's cab. "Can I help it if some people don't know enough to stay out of the way?"

"Listen. I can hear it click," Robert said, tenderly moving his nose back and forth with a thumb and forefinger.

"I don't want to hear your nose click. Just keep your eye on that cab." He cursed under his breath. He couldn't believe the run of bad luck they'd been having. He knew Reynolds wouldn't, either. "I am *not* going to lose her again!"

Both cars got on the freeway, the cabdriver moving expertly through traffic and the Johnsons trying to stay about five cars behind him. Blissfully unaware of the men following her, Erin sat back and smiled. This was a really good idea.

At the bus terminal she could change back into some less conspicuous clothes, even give a false name and pay cash so as not to leave a trail like last time. Wouldn't Logan be proud of her! She was learning, after all.

With that thought her smile disappeared. No, Logan wouldn't be proud of her. She had convinced herself she was trying to find David, to get to the bottom of things. But all she was really doing was running away, trying to escape Logan, the powerful feelings he created within her, and her own fear of losing control. She was taking matters into her own hands, and that was exactly what had gotten her into trouble the last time. It was also what had made Logan so suspicious of her in the first place.

He had started to trust her—just a small amount, it was true—but she had betrayed that trust. The answers she was looking for didn't lie on some library shelf, in newspaper microfilm files, or even with some elusive lab-assistant-turned-informant. Only Logan had the answers, and there was only one way she had a chance of getting them.

"I've changed my mind again," Erin told the driver. "Take me somewhere I can rent a car."

The cabdriver stiffened visibly, all but certain that he had a crazy woman for a passenger. "What?"

"I want to rent a car," she repeated with determination.

"So you *do* want to go to the airport."

"No," Erin replied quickly. That was where she had first run into the two strange men from Chile. "Not the airport. There must be some-where else."

The driver gave a deep, long-suffering sigh. "Yeah. There is." He jerked his thumb over his shoulder. "Back the other way."

"Fine."

"Fine, she says," he muttered under his breath. Shaking his head and continuing his soft cursing, he stepped on the gas and crossed four lanes of traffic in the space of a hundred or so feet. He just barely made it in time to get off at the next exit, turned under the highway and got back on, going in the other direction. Then he looked at Erin in the rearview mirror.

"You sure this time? Or are we going to go around in circles all evening?"

Erin ignored his sarcasm. "I'm sure."

Absorbed in her thoughts, Erin barely looked up when the cabdriver exclaimed, "Hey! Some wreck over there." He shook his head in amazement as he looked at the chaos on the opposite side of the highway. "You never can tell. That's just where we were a second ago. If we had been about five cars behind where we were, whamo!"

CHAPTER NINE

It was enough to drive a man to drink.

Logan poured a shot of tequila into an ornate glass and tossed the fiery liquor down his throat, following it with a bite on a salted lime. He wasn't getting drunk. At two hundred and twenty-five pounds it took quite a bit, anyway, but such was the power of his rage that he couldn't even feel the effects of the alcohol. It was just something to pass the time while he watched the sunset from aboard the *Tempete* and waited.

Stephanos was at Houston Hobby airport, waiting to see if Erin would try to return to Dallas. If anyone could catch her, he could. But she had to show up there before the big man could do anything, and so far his reports had been negative.

Logan knew it was futile, but he had searched the flea market for Erin, anyway. He'd even had her paged. Then he had driven around in ever widening circles looking for any sign of her, the munchkins, or suspicious hairy characters. Even though her sneaky change of clothes and sudden disappearance made it obvious that she had planned to escape all along, it was still possible she had been kidnapped instead.

But somehow, deep down, Logan felt he hadn't found her because she didn't want to be found. And that brought all kinds of questions to mind. Where was she? Who had she escaped to see? He wasn't naive enough to think that her notebook, locked in his safe, was any kind of guarantee that she couldn't easily reproduce the enzyme—with time and the proper equipment. And to think he had been on the verge of taking her into his confidence, of at last treating her like a partner instead of a prisoner! What a fool he'd been!

Still, somewhere in the back of his mind he had hope. Perhaps she had just needed time to think. He considered the events of the past few days to be excitement, but to Erin it probably had been a nightmare. Maybe she would come back once she had realized she had nowhere to go. Maybe she would come back to see him.

"Lord," he muttered to himself, "now I'm getting maudlin." But that was why he was here instead of out scouring the countryside looking for her. His information network was a good one, and he could sit here like a spider in the middle of that web. But what he really wanted was to be here if she returned. He wanted to see her face and hear her voice, even feel the cut of her sarcastic tongue.

He *did* want the enzyme. He also wanted her safe, sound, and under his control again. But he wanted her in other ways too. He missed her. For some reason he even felt a bit lost without her around.

"Fool," he muttered again. He poured another shot of tequila and stared at it, greatly disturbed by the strange, uncharacteristic emotions his thoughts were creating in him.

A tired, feminine voice roused him from his reverie. "I'd kick myself if I missed the opportunity to say this," Erin said, sitting down beside him at the table. "Buy me a drink, sailor?"

For a moment Logan just sat and stared at Erin, stunned into silence, watching the light breeze from the bay gently tousle her hair. If anyone had asked him to describe his emotions at seeing her, he would have been hard-pressed to do so. Something like a mixture of relief, gratitude, and wildly possessive lust. She'd come back. She was his.

Then his mind lowered a curtain on those feelings, and in their place came outrage and ferocious anger. "Where the hell have you been!" he yelled.

"Please," Erin replied, wincing in anguish. "Don't yell. I've had all the yelling I can stand for one day."

Logan stood up and hauled her from her chair, shaking her at arm's length. "Tough! Too damn bad! I've got people working overtime looking for you, and here you saunter in like . . ." He trailed off, so mad he couldn't speak.

"Nice to see you too," Erin said sarcastically.

A bell sounded in the wheelhouse, and Logan let her go. "Stay put!" He went to answer the phone, and Erin could hear his strident voice.

"Yeah, she's here. Of course you should have let her in! But don't you dare let her walk back out that gate, understand?" He hung up violently, then called Stephanos. "She's back." Silence. "How the hell would I know?" More silence. "I'm sorry, old friend. I'll do my best."

When he came back, he seemed to have calmed down a bit. He sat down across from her, looking at her through narrowed eyes. "So, did you have a nice day?" he asked bitterly.

"Oh, yes," she shot back. "I had a lovely walk, then was invited to dine with some diminutive gentlemen from South America who can't decide whether they're humanitarians or terrorists." Logan was glaring at her, so she leaned toward him and glared back. "I was nearly in two car wrecks, irritated a cabdriver to the point that he didn't complain about his tip, then came within an inch of drowning myself three times on the way back here." Erin poured herself a shot of tequila, then downed it.

"You expect me to believe any of that?"

She stood up. "Frankly, Logan, I don't care what you believe. At the moment all I want from you is a shower and eight hours sleep. You can yell at me tomorrow."

Logan caught her by the arm as she turned to leave. "You bet your pretty backside I'll yell at you tomorrow! But what *I* want from *you* is an explanation. Why did you take off like that?"

This was worse than Erin had thought it would be. She had expected him to be angry. She could deal with his anger, could accept the mistrust she saw in his eyes. What she hadn't expected was her reaction to being near him again. His touch wasn't gentle, but it thrilled her all the same. Though he was being loud and sarcastic, it was still good to hear his voice. His presence wrapped around her like a cloak, protective, dangerous, and powerfully intoxicating.

"I just needed some space," Erin said at last. "Some time by myself to think." Lord, how lame that excuse sounded, even to her!

"Of all the stupid, irresponsible . . ." he ground out through clenched teeth. "Didn't you even think about what might happen to you?"

Erin stared into his cold cobalt eyes, a grim, thin-lipped smile on her face. "You can interrogate me in the morning, Logan. Here I am, all safe and sound, and nobody pried the secret for your precious enzyme from my head. That's all you're worried about, so why don't you just let me get some sleep?"

Logan grabbed her other arm and jerked her around, his face inches from hers. He continued to broil her beneath his outraged gaze, and for a moment Erin thought his fury would explode in her direction.

Then his grasp softened. He slowly pulled her into his arms, held her tightly against his chest. "That's not *all* I was worried about, you little idiot," he said, the softness of his voice taking the string from his words. "I was afraid you might have—"

"Sold out?" Erin interrupted, her voice muffled against his chest. She could feel the heat of his body next to hers, and it started a fire within her. Despite the antagonism between them, she felt herself relaxing beneath his touch.

Logan groaned in exasperation. "What's the use?" he muttered. He roughly tilted her face to his with a hand under her chin and took possession of her lips, kissing her with a harsh, demanding ferocity. His tongue entered her mouth when she gasped, making the warm cavern his, plundering the sweetness within until he felt her body go soft in his arms.

Their lips parted, and she looked at him, murmuring a desperate entreaty. "Logan—"

"Oh, shut up," he said softly. "I know it isn't wise, but I just don't care anymore." Burying his face in the dark softness of her hair, he nipped gently at her earlobe before caressing her neck from nape to collarbone with his tongue, leaving a trail of fire that set her senses burning.

Her arms wandered around the broad expanse of his chest, taking all the warmth his body had to offer and drawing it within her, pulling him against her breasts, her hands splayed on his back. It made no sense, and it wasn't wise, but she didn't care anymore, either. She only knew how good his body felt against hers, how impossibly exciting his hands were as they found the bottom edge of her blouse and glided beneath to massage the bare skin of her back.

"Oh, Erin," Logan moaned. "Why are you such a pain in the—"

Erin interrupted him with her mouth on his, finding her own desire to be just as rough and angry. She pulled his shirt loose from his slacks, just as eager to feel his skin beneath her fingers. The strong muscles of his back grew taut under her touch, and her mind filled with such overwhelming erotic images, she thought she would burst. Such was the strength of their mutual need that it felt more like an unquenchable thirst than mere passion.

When he felt her fingernails dig lightly into the skin of his back, Logan swept her into his arms, holding her as easily as he would a child. "You want to go to bed? I'll take you to bed, all right," he said in a voice full of sensual promise.

With her feet on the ground Erin had felt in control, confident in the power of her own body and reveling in the effect she was having on him. But, cradled in his arms, she realized who was really in control. With his strength and possessive, burning gaze Logan was letting her know he could take her anytime he wanted her— and he wanted her right now.

Erin was suddenly terrified and knew without a doubt that if he did as promised and took her to bed, nothing could stop him from finishing what they had both started here on deck. She stiffened as he carried her below, struggling to find some way, some argument that would cool his ardor. It was useless, because her own blood was running just as hot in her veins.

When he got to her stateroom door, he paused to look at her face, and his eyes narrowed. "What's wrong? Up there you acted like a lioness, and now you look like a scared kitten."

"Just . . . just put me down. Please."

He did so, concern suddenly overriding his

suspicion that he was being sexually teased. "You're as white as a sheet! Are you ill?"

She was. When she was in control, his touch had thrilled her, had driven her to explorations of her own. Then he had seized that control from her, and she was so frightened, her stomach felt tied in a knot. But how could she explain? It wasn't him; she wanted him, felt starved for his touch. It was the situation, the way all of it was happening. How could she explain what she didn't understand herself?

"I can't, Logan. I just can't." She couldn't seem to catch her breath, and it was making her dizzy. What was happening to her?

Logan tenderly touched her shoulder. "Hey," he said softly. "Take it easy. I'm not a beast." He felt like one, though. A randy, sex-starved beast. Her rapid breathing swelled her breasts against her blouse, and he wanted nothing more than to tear away the cloth and take possession of the soft flesh underneath. He wasn't the kind of man who could turn his desire on and off like a water faucet. But neither was he the kind of man who would take advantage of a woman who was obviously beside herself with anxiety.

Erin finally managed to look up and into his eyes, knowing he wouldn't like what she was going to say. "Logan, I really am exhausted. This is all too much for me to handle right now," she explained softly. "Do you understand?"

For a second he looked angry, suspicious. Whatever was going on here, it was more serious than exhaustion. But then he nodded. His voice was not quite compassionate but accepting, sympathetic. "Yes. I understand. We can—"

Behind him, in his office, the phone rang, vying imperiously for his attention. "Could you hold that thought for a moment?"

Erin breathed an inner sigh of relief. That was it. The crisis had been averted, and Logan would have to return to business. "Go ahead. I'm going to take a shower and go to bed."

He looked at Erin and saw that color was already returning to her face. "All right," he said. "We'll let it go at that—for now. Sleep well."

When Erin woke up the next morning, the first thing she noticed was a vibration, a kind of hum throughout her whole body. She jumped out of bed and realized it wasn't her body humming, it was the *Tempete*.

She dressed quickly in a pair of khaki shorts and a short-sleeved shirt of blue oxford cloth that she'd bought the day before. It felt good to have something different to wear, but her mind didn't dwell on it long; the steady rhythm beneath her feet prodded her onward. In the bright sunlight up on deck she found herself surrounded by activity.

A large truck had pulled up next to the *Tempete* at the marina dock, and men were carrying boxes aboard, taking them below to the yacht's cargo hold. Erin made her way forward to the wheelhouse, carefully keeping out of everyone's way.

In the control room she found Stephanos

seated before the radio, headphones on and a microphone in his hand. He waved when he saw her, but there was something in his eyes Erin didn't like. He was looking at her with detachment, as if she had changed since he'd seen her last. He smiled at her, but it wasn't the full-blown smile she was used to.

Logan was across the way at a large, flat table, making marks on a map spread out before him and occasionally referring to a pile of leather-bound books off to one side. As she approached he looked up, eyes cold and face grim.

"Good morning, Miss Arnold," he said flatly.

"Arnold?"

"As in Benedict." He put down his pencil and stared at her intently. She almost squirmed under his direct gaze. "You must have been very busy yesterday," he said at last.

"I don't know what you mean."

Logan shook his head contemptuously. "How long did it take you to perfect that look of confused innocence?"

With angry movements he reached for a stainless steel carafe on a counter behind him, pouring coffee into first his mug and then Stephanos's. His friend nodded his thanks, then went back to listening and speaking quietly into the microphone in turn, though his eyes followed Logan as he filled a cup for Erin and brought it to her.

"Are those the engines I feel?" Erin asked.

"No. Auxiliary generator. We're disconnected from the marina's power lines."

"Why?"

194

Logan sighed. "Because we're preparing to get under way, that's why," he answered brusquely.

A slightly built, but wiry-looking man entered the room, handing Logan a clipboard. As he spoke he stole an appreciative glance at Erin's tanned legs. "All loaded and secured, Mr. Scott."

Logan leafed through the pages, then signed his name to the last one. "Thanks. Tell Jim he can haul the gangway off now."

"Right. See you in a few weeks?"

Logan shrugged. The man smiled, winked in Erin's general direction, then left the control room. Logan sat down in a large swivel chair mounted at the *Tempete*'s helm, turning to face Erin. He jerked his head in an indication that she should sit in the similar chair beside him. He took a sip of his coffee, then looked at her seriously but didn't say anything.

"You mean you're leaving?" Erin asked, uncomfortable with the silence.

"*We're* leaving," he corrected.

She cleared her throat nervously. "Where are *we* going?"

Logan pursed his lips, continuing to hold her eyes with his. "From now on, Erin, any information you receive will be on a need-to-know basis."

Erin blew out the tense, exasperated breath she'd been holding. "Logan," she said, bewildered, "what is going on?"

"That's a very good question, one I'd like an answer to myself."

Stephanos caught Logan's attention, and he released Erin from his scrutinizing gaze. The

195

big man took off the headphones. "All set," he said.

Logan nodded. "Good." He turned back to Erin. In fact, both men focused questioning eyes upon her. "I think it's time we finished our discussion of last night."

Erin knew he didn't mean their interrupted lovemaking. "You mean, about where I went yesterday?"

"Yes," Logan replied with a sarcastic smile. "The other discussion can wait."

His bitter tone brought her temper to a slow boil. "You obviously weren't listening," she returned, her voice matching the acidity of his. "I told you I just wanted some time to think, then I fell into the hands of our munchkin friends. I got away from them by threatening to yell rape, then finally made my way back here. Simple."

"You said South Americans."

So he *had* been listening. What was this all about? "Right. Chile. Their names, by the way, are Armando and Carlos." She looked at Stephanos, a man she considered her friend. "They're very anxious to see you again, Stephanos," she said, trying to lighten the mood.

He smiled broadly, but his eyes still looked troubled.

"These men are your partners?" Logan interjected.

"What?" Erin exclaimed, nearly spilling her coffee. "Where did you get that idea?"

"Then what were you doing with them?"

"I told you," she ground out. "They abducted

196

me. Sort of." Confusion returned to her face. "I'm not entirely sure what they were after. I don't think *they're* sure. Mostly they spouted socialist theories, but they seem to have greed on their minds concerning the enzyme as well." She shrugged. "Beats me how they got so much information. Their lips were sealed on that particular subject, as well as who they work for."

"Sounds like you were doing some investigating as well as thinking, Erin," Stephanos offered. Logan looked at him with raised eyebrows, and he shrugged helplessly. "Just trying to help."

"Thank you, Stephanos," Erin said, interrupting Logan before he could open his mouth. "I was trying to help too. Armando and Carlos didn't get anything from me," she added, looking pointedly at Logan, "and I didn't get much from them, either." Now, she decided, was not the time to grill Logan about *his* thoughts on the common heritage of mankind. He'd already made it plain that he wasn't predisposed to tell her anything. "But I *was* trying to think about our investigation as well as gain a bit of breathing room. And I think I may have come up with a pretty good idea of where we might find David Turner." Her chin tilted defiantly, she looked at Logan, expecting him to be surprised, maybe even pleased.

He simply continued to glare at her. "That's all academic now," he said quietly.

"What's that supposed to mean?" Erin asked.

"Things have changed, Erin," Stephanos said. "Changed drastically and literally overnight. From your description of your actions yesterday,

I just can't see the connection." He looked at her, his black eyes baleful. There was something in his expression that told Erin he believed her but that there was nothing he could do to change Logan's mind. "It sure is a big coincidence."

"What I told you is the truth!" Erin cried in outrage. She calmed herself. "What do you mean, things have changed?"

"He means," Logan said, his words edged with steel, "that your little solo investigative foray—if that's what it was—has stirred up a hornet's nest of sudden interest in the enzyme." He got up irritably and leaned over her, supporting himself with his hands on the padded armrests of her chair, confronting her face-to-face. "I fended off phone calls all night long. This morning the radio calls started coming in. Coincidence, my eye!" he finished, pushing away from her and going to stand at the window.

"What calls? What are you talking about?"

Logan stood with his back to her, looking out to sea. "Tell her!" he said, too angry to explain himself.

Stephanos leaned forward in his chair by the radio, resting his forearms on his knees, his big hands moving restlessly in front of him as he spoke. "All of a sudden everybody knows, Erin. We've been getting calls from deep-sea mining consortiums, land-based mineral producers, anybody and everybody the enzyme could affect. And from all over. The States, Great Britain, Africa."

Logan finally found his tongue. "And that's

not the worst of it." He spat the words out as he turned to face her. "The competition is getting edgy, and that's just fine with me. Let 'em stew. But I'm getting governmental heat now."

"*Our* government?" Erin asked, her voice a bit weak. She was getting a queasy feeling, and she didn't think it was from coffee on an empty stomach.

"Everybody's government!" Logan yelled. "The International Maritime Bureau, the United Nations Conference on Trade and Development. Even the damned IRS called, wanting to make sure I was planning on divulging full information on profits from an enzyme I don't even have yet!" He pinned her to her chair with the searing anger of his eyes. "And just where do you suppose *they* found out? I doubt David Turner or any of your kidnapping friends would have told them."

So that's what this inquisition was all about. He thought she had been leaking secrets. "You're wrong," Erin countered quietly.

"What?"

"Carlos and Armando. I—I thought they were just bluffing," Erin began hesitantly. "They wanted the enzyme 'for Chile and the world.' When I told them I wouldn't help them, they threatened to find someone who would." She looked at Logan apologetically. "I guess they did, huh?"

Logan stared at her in shock for a moment, then sat down heavily in his chair, his anger toward her visibly dissipating. "Yeah. I guess they did." He looked lost in thought.

"So that's why we're leaving?" Erin asked.

Logan nodded distractedly. "A total communications blackout," he said. "My business is just that. *My* business. None of these yahoos has any right to know what I'm up to until I decide to tell them." He looked at Erin, suddenly aware that he had been thinking out loud. "And that, Erin, is as much as you have a need to know at the moment."

"Yes, sir, Captain Scott," she said sarcastically, giving him an elaborate salute. She heard a choking sound and turned just in time to see Stephanos hide a grin behind his hand.

Logan ignored them both. "Let's get out of here before the SPCA decides I'm being cruel to bacteria or something."

"Come on, Erin," Stephanos said, getting up and holding out his hand. "I'll show you how to cast off."

When they had left, Logan allowed himself a moment to contemplate the situation as it stood now. Once again Erin had managed to slip away from him when he thought he had her number. Damn! This whole mess was getting too complicated. He wanted to leave all right but not to run from the heat he was getting from all sides. It was necessary to do so, he supposed, but he would personally rather stand and fight.

But he couldn't fight, keep a suspicious eye on Erin, and oversee the production of the enzyme at the same time, at least not here. But at his retreat on the southern tip of the Texas coast he could. And there, perhaps he could finally unravel the puzzle that was Erin Barclay.

So much woman, so much passion. And yet a gate holding everything in check. He'd find the key to that gate and be waiting when the waters of her desire at last flowed unhampered in his direction. To hell with business! He just wanted to get her alone, away from all these interruptions!

Under Stephanos's expert tutelage Erin and he cast off the lines holding the *Tempete* to the dock. Under Logan's expert pilotage the boat swung about as it left its slip, engines throbbing with a power that sent a shiver up and down Erin's spine. As they motored slowly out of the marina's safe harbor, Erin looked back to the spot where she had spent the last four days.

Then she turned her face in the direction of the sea, feeling a freedom she hadn't known existed. It was perfect, a breaking with the past and with the land that held so many problems. Then they pulled out into the ship channel, picking up speed, the land behind looking all the same to Erin's untrained eyes. She didn't know where she was going and probably wouldn't know even when she got there.

But as perfect as it all seemed, she knew she still had problems. Logan was at the helm, taking her heaven-knew-where. If she thought she had been under his control before, she hadn't known what control was. A curious mixture of fear and anticipation filled her. Would it really be so bad to lose control, as long as she was in Logan's arms at the time? One way or another, she felt she would soon know the answer.

CHAPTER TEN

With evening closing in around them Logan and Stephanos set up the system of anchors that would keep the *Tempete* safe and secure until morning. Then, with all engines stopped, quiet descended upon the placid waters around them like a tranquil blanket. Sipping beer, they both relaxed in their chairs in the wheelhouse and breathed a sigh of contentment.

"I think we made it," Logan said.

Stephanos leaned over to peer at the radar screen set into the control panel and nodded, his face bathed in an eerie green glow. "No suspicious contacts. We're as alone as one can get in this part of the Gulf."

"Where's Erin?"

"She was on the forward deck the last time I saw her, which was a while ago," Stephanos replied, easing back into his chair. "While you were in your office earlier I let her take the helm for a few miles. I think it bored her."

"Bored her?" Logan inquired with a grin.

"She said she's done some sailing. I guess she prefers hauling lines and trimming sail to diesel power."

"So do I, under the right circumstances. Where did she do her sailing?"

"California. Catalina, I believe. Fair-weather stuff."

"Ah," Logan said, understanding. "She'd change her mind about motors if she had to beat a tack against the wind all day or in a rough sea."

The two men were silent for a while, enjoying the slight breeze drifting in through the open doors and the motion of the gentle swell beneath the *Tempete*'s hull.

"You plan on making landfall early in the morning, right?" Stephanos asked at last.

"Very early morning. The fact that I have a retreat down here isn't totally unknown, so I'm sure someone's bound to figure out where we've gone sooner or later. But I'd rather it be later." Logan stood up, stretched, and finished his beer. "We'll lay at anchor here till before dawn, just to see if anybody shows up. Then sneak in."

"Anybody cruising down the coast with a good pair of binoculars will be sure to spot the *Tempete*, even in that sheltered bay," Stephanos observed. "Still, I suppose there's no reason to make it easy for them."

"Nope," Logan agreed. "Well, I think I'll go find Erin, see how she feels after her first day out."

On deck all was quiet. Erin leaned on the afterdeck railing, marveling at the solitude she found under the full moon. Dinner would be on the table soon, and she was hungry. But her stomach could wait, as could seeking out Logan and Stephanos.

Erin had no idea what was going through Logan's mind or what his plans were, and she didn't think she would find out anytime soon. He had said a total communications blackout, so that meant he was keeping a secret from the whole world—or nearly so.

And there wasn't a thing she could do about it except stay close and keep her ears open— and that was something else she didn't have any choice about. Logan was in control, and she had finally resigned herself to that fact. She was with him, under his suspicious, watchful gaze, and would remain that way for the foreseeable future.

The surprising thing was that for all the uncertainty of her present predicament, she felt at ease—almost peaceful. "If there isn't anything you can do," she murmured to the dark, quiet sea, "then don't do anything." The ocean, with all its might, was a good teacher. Go with the flow. If she didn't, she would be battered to pieces by the force of Logan's will just as surely as would a boat trying to sail in winds too violent for its design.

Logan stopped abruptly as he crested the afterdeck ladder. He had found Erin. Pausing for a moment, he let his eyes feast on the sight before him. Erin's hair was flying in the breeze, revealing the gentle arch of her delicate neck. She wasn't wearing a brassiere under her thin cotton shirt, he noted, and he felt his body jump in response to the thought of touching, kissing, tasting her breasts. How much more of this torture could he take?

Since he had first met her, he had been dreaming of her, at least when his thoughts had let him sleep. The dreams were of such erotic content that they had caused him to toss and turn in his bed, wanting to go to her cabin and take her, but knowing that she wouldn't accept his advances. She wanted him too. He knew that, could feel it in her response on those occasions when he had gotten close enough to her to touch her. But there was something standing in his way, something more than this idiotic problem with the enzyme.

How he wished he had met her before all this had started! Perhaps now that they had this breathing space from all the interruptions and complexities of the world of ocean mining, they could get to know each other. *Really* get to know each other.

Her shorts rode low on her hips, revealing a tantalizing sliver of her bare waist below her top before flowing into rounded hips. And her legs, those marvelous, sleek, tantalizing thighs. Lord, how he wanted to kiss every inch of them!

Logan's own white shorts were becoming uncomfortably tight, but he continued his unnoticed perusal of Erin's moonlit form. Her buttocks were firm, well rounded, and full. He ached to caress them. Long, shapely legs just made to wrap themselves around his hips. The ache in him had become a nearly unbearable pain, and Erin wasn't even aware of his presence.

She was still standing exactly as he'd come

upon her, a dreamy expression on her face, her hips thrust forward as she looked out to sea. Her long-fingered hands were gripping the deck railing against the gentle roll of the boat in the soft swell. Logan imagined her rocking against him with the same motion, and the image made him leave his shadowy hiding spot.

Erin didn't turn around when she heard footsteps behind her. She knew it was Logan. So acute was her awareness of him that she had felt his presence at her back, wondering if he were going to leave her alone or join her. She could feel the heat of his body as he came up to stand so close to her. And yet he didn't touch her. The hair on the back of her neck tickled in response.

"Logan?" she whispered.

"Yes."

"I . . ." She shivered suddenly, and the words wouldn't come.

"Are you cold? The wind is fairly brisk."

"Yes," she answered, wanting to feel his arms around her, to have the heat of his body joining with hers. She shivered again as she realized how little control she had of even her own body, let alone that of such a powerful man.

"You *are* cold," Logan murmured in her ear. His arms wrapped around her, pulling her close to his warmth. Her skin was indeed cool beneath his touch. In these latitudes even a brisk wind was warm and humid at this time of year, so he knew she wasn't really shivering with cold. Was he in for a repeat of the other night when he had felt her stiffen in his arms outside her cabin door?

Erin didn't know what frightened her more: Logan, her own desire, or the insane anxiety welling up within her as she felt control over her emotions slip away. She only knew she couldn't fight her feelings anymore. Her body seemed to melt into his waiting warmth. With her back pressed tightly against his broad chest and her buttocks fitted snugly to his hips, she felt his arousal and realized that she did have some control over him after all.

She was the cause of that delicious pressure against the base of her spine. She moved her pelvis slightly and heard his soft moan of need in reply. His lips traced the line of her neck, and she heard her own sharp intake of breath. They held equal power here like this, the power to fulfill each other. Why hadn't she understood that before?

"Better?" Logan murmured. He moved the silken mane of her hair aside and stroked the back of her neck with his cheek.

"Mmm," she hummed, unable to describe her feelings coherently. Her insides were quivering, her emotions taking possession of her mind. She let them, bone-tired of analyzing what was happening to her. Only one thought could penetrate the delicious fog. *I am losing control. And I like it!*

Logan moved his hips suggestively, the hair on his legs feathery on the backs of her thighs. Resting just below her breasts, his strong, bare arm moved higher until he could feel their weight. She wasn't fighting him, she was melting against him, and he gave in to temptation. His other hand traced the curve of her neck, moving down over her collarbone until he found the softness he sought, feeling her nipples harden beneath his touch. He heard her gasp.

"Don't be afraid of me, sweet Erin."

"I—I'm not. It's just . . ."

"I'm not taking, Erin, I'm giving," he whispered. His hands slid inside her shirt, caressing her waist and gliding up across the gentle slope of her stomach to cup her breasts. "Giving pleasure. I would never force you. Do you believe that?"

"Yes," she moaned as he gently savored the weight lying in each of his hands. He moved his thumbs and felt her responsiveness, small buds waiting to flower beneath his touch, his kiss. She leaned heavily against him, wanting to feel his full length touching her. Her hands slipped behind her to caress his waist beneath his shirt, errant fingers dipping into the waistband of his shorts, feeling his muscles jump and tighten in response to her touch. She wanted to give pleasure, too, more aware of her power to do so than she had ever been in her life.

The movement of his hands on her breasts was covetous and possessive, and she never wanted the feeling to stop. But she also wanted to press their fullness against his chest without any interference from their shirts, and yet she knew that this was not the place for such indulgence. She turned around and looked at him, her eyes communicating her thoughts without the need for words.

Logan brushed her lips with his, then returned for a second, deeper taste of her sweetness. He separated from her slightly and almost lifted her into his arms but remembered how strongly she had reacted last time and stopped himself. The last thing he wanted was to move too fast, but he didn't know how long he could wait, especially when Erin looked at him as she was now. Her eyes were liquid desire.

Soft, gentle music started playing from somewhere, drifting around them on the summer breeze. A quiet, soothing voice joined the poignant melody: "Hello, young lovers, wherever you are." It was Stephanos, deftly using the *Tempete*'s public address system. "I have been slaving over a hot microwave for at least ten minutes. If you are at all interested in food, I suggest you join me in the forward saloon or I'll eat it all myself."

"Are you hungry?" Logan asked.

"Yes," she answered. "I guess I am." In truth she was hungry for his touch, the taste of his lips. But something inside cautioned her to go slowly with this newfound willingness to surrender.

The music stopped. They seemed suspended in time for a moment, lost in each other's eyes. Then the strains of a German polka band filled the night air.

"Oh, no," Logan moaned.

"What?" Erin murmured, part of her not wanting to let the moment slip away, another part glad for the interruption.

"That music. It means hot dogs and sauerkraut."

"You're kidding! From a cordon bleu chef?"

Logan nodded. "Hard to believe, isn't it? And he complains about *my* tuna casserole! It's disgusting."

"I happen to like hot dogs and sauerkraut!" Erin exclaimed.

He looked at her as if she were out of her mind. "With hot mustard and mashed potatoes, I suppose?"

"Yum, yum!"

"Oh, Lord. I'm in the hands of barbarians!"

By the time day broke over the Gulf of Mexico, the *Tempete* was lying at anchor toward the center of a small, secluded bay. Erin had come up on deck earlier, peering through the mist as Logan and Stephanos made their painstakingly cautious approach to land. It was a mystery to her how they found their way, and she had given up and gone back to bed for lack of anything to look at.

Last night was a happy memory of German music; rich, dark beer from the yacht's stores; and Logan's possessive eyes. But it was obvious that he was biding his time, and her own caution had returned as well. Both men had asked her to dance, though, taking turns twirling her around the deck until they all retired in a state of pleasant exhaustion.

Now a stillness had descended around them.

Wherever they were, it was warm, humid, and very quiet except for the calls of unidentifiable birds from the palm-crowded shore. It was all quite tropical, and Erin felt as if they were in the Caribbean. But even the powerful *Tempete* wasn't that fast, and from the time and distance traveled she knew this had to be either Texas or Mexico.

Her first view of the shore in the near distance seemed like a foggy dream. But the mist slowly cleared as they were having a light breakfast on deck, listening to the soft murmur and hiss of waves against the beach. Then Erin finally got a good look at Logan's hideaway.

It was a rambling, white stucco construction with a red tile roof, shaped to conform with the contours of the land and private beach. It nestled there, a peaceful addition to the tropical ambience of the place, a pristine blend of modern glassed-in comfort and Old World charm.

"Good Lord!" Erin gasped. "The playgrounds of the very rich!"

"Just my little cabin in the jungle," Logan demurred. But his eyes told her he was well aware of the quiet decadence of this little bit of private paradise, and his smile bespoke of his pride in ownership. "A man can't spend his whole life living on a boat, not even the *Tempete*."

Erin immediately began clearing the breakfast dishes, anxious to wiggle her toes in the sand and see the inside of Logan's "little cabin." "I don't know about you two, but I'm for solid land beneath my feet and a quick dip in the ocean."

Logan looked at her and laughed, one eyebrow lifted in surprise. "I would have thought you'd have some comment about this just being another prison."

"Prison? No way! You promised me a vacation not too long ago if I remember correctly, and I intend to start right now."

Erin was the first one into the dinghy when Stephanos lowered it into the water. She had put her swimsuit on under her jeans and shirt, so while Logan and Stephanos made several trips bringing luggage and boxes to the beach, she peeled them off and frolicked in the surf. She could feel Logan's eyes on her almost constantly and found herself behaving shamelessly provocative in spite of the consequences that would doubtless follow. She couldn't help herself. This place made her feel wanton, teasing. She had never been so aware of her femininity in her life.

Leaving Stephanos to happily exercise his considerable strength lugging things into the house, Logan strolled down the beach. Erin lay on her back, propped up on her elbows, looking out at the bay and the sea beyond. She smiled up at him when he joined her. "It's like a dream."

"That it is," he agreed. *She* was like a dream, a nymph from the sea, her skin still covered with glistening drops of salt water. "I think this place likes you. I've never seen it more beautiful." He gazed at her lovingly. "I've never seen *you* looking more beautiful, either." He bent down and ran a finger along her shoulder, feeling her shivering response. A shot of fire ran through him as he looked into her soft gray eyes. "But you'd better take it easy. We're not that far from the Tropic of Cancer here, and the sun will teach you a lesson you won't soon forget if you're not careful."

Erin got up, suddenly shy under his appreciative gaze. "Yes . . . well, I'd like to see the inside of the house now, anyway."

Logan helped her brush the sand from her body, her skin burning beneath his touch. She turned skittish and ran the rest of the way to the house. Logan followed at a leisurely pace, enjoying her lithe movements and the gentle bounce of her breasts as she ran. An ache had lodged itself firmly in him last night as he held her in his arms on deck, and now that ache grew stronger. At the risk of rushing her, he would have to do something about it—and soon.

He didn't know if she was aware of what her on-again, off-again sensuality was doing to him. But whether she was aware and prepared for the unleashing of the forces she was building inside him or not, he couldn't stand much more. Today, tonight, tomorrow at the most, Erin would have to pay the price for her hesitancy, her seemingly deliberate teasing. Logan's patience only stretched so far, and it was at the breaking point.

The house inside was just as dazzling, geared toward a casual beachfront life-style, yet with a touch of elegant formality. The colors reflected the outdoor surroundings, stark white and cream, with blues, sandy browns, and green as predominant counterpoints. Erin settled in her room

213

overlooking the bay, showered off the salt and sand from her ocean dip, then changed into a blouse and wraparound skirt of cool, pale blue silk.

When she rejoined the men, it was with surprise and some suspicion that she noted that Stephanos was preparing to leave. "Where are you off to?" she asked him.

He glanced at Logan out of the corner of his eye before answering. "I have to go into town to wait for some supplies that should be arriving soon," he said hesitantly, then, changing the subject, "It looks like you'll either have to take over the cooking for a while or prepare yourself for the likes of Logan's tuna casserole."

"At least we're out of hot dogs," Logan said thankfully.

Erin wasn't being misdirected. "What town?"

"You're on a need-to-know basis, remember, Erin?" he reminded her.

She shrugged as if it didn't matter to her. "It's just that I thought we were in the middle of nowhere."

"For all intents and purposes we are," Logan replied, his tone telling her he considered that the last word on the subject.

Stephanos slung the strap of his leather bag over his shoulder and headed for the door. "The sunscreen is in the top drawer of the master bathroom, Erin. Remember to use it." He turned to Logan. "I'll give you a call on the radio if anything unusual comes up." Erin held the door for him, and he leaned close to her on his way out. "Just hide the tuna fish and you'll

214

survive. The only other thing he tries to cook is bacon and eggs." Stephanos frowned. "On second thought you'd better hide them too."

He left, and a moment later Erin heard the roar of an engine. She looked out a side window just in time to see a rather mean-looking truck with big fat tires disappear into the palms behind the house. "He sure likes trucks," Erin observed.

Logan grinned. "They're the only things that fit him."

He was standing right behind her, and she turned, unprepared for the blatant desire she saw in his eyes. She moved away and said nonchalantly, "He's not really going for supplies, is he?"

"What?" Logan asked, taken by surprise. His mind had been on a completely different tack.

"It doesn't take a genius to see how secluded this place is. I imagine there are only three ways to get here." She counted them off on her fingers. "By boat, helicopter, or by what I imagine is the only road. I figure Stephanos is our rear guard. Right?"

Logan simply shrugged, his expression unreadable.

"Just what are we doing here, Logan?"

Logan strolled back to the living room and took a seat on the plush sofa by a window facing the bay. Erin followed but remained standing, looking at him expectantly. He sighed. "Would you believe me if I told you that we really *are* here for a short vacation, a breather from this mess?"

"I don't know what to believe."

Logan looked at her and smiled, then chuckled, then began to laugh. "I can almost hear the gears spinning in your head. You look totally befuddled."

"I am," she replied honestly, starting to smile in spite of herself. She knew the time was coming when he would ask—or try to force—her to reproduce the enzyme. And she also knew that no matter how things were changing between them personally, she still wasn't sure where she should place her loyalties. Why should she complain about the delay?

He patted the cushion beside him. "Come sit down and rest that sharp mind of yours before you blow a fuse." She did so, thinking how handsome he looked when he smiled and how exciting it was to feel his thigh brushing hers. "We both need to recharge our mental batteries for a couple of days. You said it yourself: This place is a playground." He took her hand in his, lifting it to his lips and kissing the sensitive skin of her palm. "Let's play."

"I don't know the rules of the game," she said hesitantly, enjoying the warmth of his hand, the tingling sensation his lips caused.

All the intrigue, the danger, everything that had been happening to Erin lately had afforded her a certain amount of emotional protection from the onslaught of their mutual desires. But this sultry, quiet hideaway stripped her of that protection. She felt open, vulnerable, and very aware of an almost desperate physical need.

216

The last barrier between them was dissolving. She wanted him. Now.

Logan saw the willingness in her eyes. He still held her hand, and with the other he began unbuttoning her blouse. "First," he said, "you were right. This place is secluded. And in this climate the less clothing the better."

"But—"

"Unh-uh." He placed a finger to her lips. "That's another rule. No arguing. Relax," he commanded softly as he finished undoing her buttons. "Ah, good! I see you had already decided not to overdress."

How could she relax with his hand inside her blouse? His fingertips were working a sensuous kind of magic on the soft tips of her breasts. She felt herself come alive under his touch, her nipples growing taut and becoming the center of a warm, tingling sensation that radiated all the way to her toes. She moaned softly and closed her eyes.

"Yes. Moaning is definitely allowed here." Logan's voice was deep and soft. "And you do make such sweet, sweet sounds when I touch you, Erin." He proved it to her by gliding his hand around her breasts and down her side, crossing her stomach, his feathery touch dipping lightly beneath the material of her skirt at her waist.

"Are . . . are there any other rules I should know about?" Erin swayed, engulfed in the warmth that pulsed through her. She felt her face begin to flush, and small moans of pleasure escaped her throat.

"Only one." Logan pulled her against him and buried his tongue in her mouth, kissing her as though trying to commit her to memory. "The golden rule. Do unto others." He took her hands in his and placed them on his chest. "In other words, feel free to participate."

The heat of his chest underneath her hands seemed to burn her palms. She could feel the beat of his heart, felt as though it matched the sound of her own in her ears. Her fingers trembled as she unbuttoned his shirt, then softly traced the contours of his hard muscles.

"Like this?" she asked in a husky voice she barely recognized as her own. Before he could answer, she lowered her head, her lips grazing his chest lightly before her tongue darted out to touch each of his male nipples in turn. His response startled her, a sharp intake of breath that made her look up into his eyes. Burning there she found a desire so strong, it took her breath away.

Logan covered her mouth with his, pressing her back against the sofa, his hands searching for and finding the tie that released her skirt from her waist. But he didn't unwrap it. Instead he followed the golden rule, returning her pleasure, his lips closing around first one rose-tipped breast and then the other. His tongue took exquisite delight in softening each hardened nipple, then the sparsely callused pad of his thumb brought them erect again.

As his cheek caressed her stomach she spoke, surprising even herself with her boldness. "Logan, aren't you breaking one of your own rules?"

"Which one?" he murmured against her softness.

She tugged gently on his shirt. "You have on too many clothes," she scolded with a devilish smile.

She watched as he pulled it off, then did the same with her blouse. Cupping her face in his hands, he ran his tongue over her full lips before plunging into her mouth, and then he followed her urgent, unspoken directions to lie down next to her on the wide couch. Erin pressed her breasts against his chest and sighed. "Better?" he asked tauntingly.

"Much." A wanton flame teased the center of her being, and she rubbed him with her breasts, smiling wickedly at the passion exploding in his eyes. Those deep blue eyes weren't cold now, and neither was any other part of him. He ground his hips into hers as he pressed her against the back of the sofa, and she could feel every inch of him, throbbing, rock-hard and potent. It made her acutely aware of the fire within her, of her own femininity.

Erin's skirt unwrapped as if it had a mind of its own when he rolled her on top of him, allowing his hands to smooth over her hips and under the only filmy garment remaining. His hands molded her buttocks, pressing her against him.

She pushed against his chest, one hand trying to slip between them to the waist of his slacks. "This is one-sided again," she complained.

Logan smiled and brushed her hair from her face, trailing kisses from her neck to the tip of her nose. "And that's very important to you, isn't it?" he asked. His voice was sensuously playful, but his eyes were quite serious.

"Yes," she answered softly, averting her gaze. "Yes, it is." She felt his finger on her chin, and he turned her face to his, kissing her gently on the lips. Then he lifted and returned her to a sitting position, her thighs stretched out across his lap, having used his powerful body in an oddly soft way in doing so. Erin cocked her head and looked at him curiously.

He loosened his pants and slid the rest of his clothing off. "There. Now we're more than equal. In fact," he taunted softly, pulling on the thin elastic band of her panties, "you're overdressed." He ran his hands down her lovely, trim legs, teasing her calves with his fingertips.

Erin felt warm all over. It was as she had thought it would be. Logan was a mixture of rough and gentle, a little bit crazy and very caring. She wanted to touch him everywhere at once, show him how much she appreciated his concern. Her hand slipped beneath her outstretched leg and stroked him gently against the inside of his thigh. "Then you'll have to be compensated for your gallantry," she said in a whisper. She leaned closer to him and kissed his ear, running the tip of her tongue around its edge.

"Oh, Erin," he groaned. He moved almost convulsively beneath her legs, her hand driving him beyond the brink of control. He opened his eyes and looked at her, a smoldering look that made her lashes lower over her eyes, reveling in the feeling of power it gave her. In this, at least, she was just as controlling of him as he was of her.

She was so absorbed in the intoxicating feeling of giving him pleasure, she lost that control before she knew what was happening. His hands deftly removed the last wispy bit of her covering, and he rolled atop her, pinning her beneath his strong, hard body. A cry escaped her lips. "No!"

"I want you, Erin," he said, his voice rough with passion. "If you meant to just tease me, you've gone too far."

"I want you too," she moaned, struggling beneath him. "But not this way . . . not . . ." She trailed off, her fingernails digging into the flesh of his back. "Don't dominate me!"

Logan took his weight from her but kept her trapped beneath him. He was aware now, even through his consuming passion, that she wasn't teasing. This was the problem, the key to the gate behind which Erin had imprisoned herself. He kissed her softly, his voice gentle and compassionate. "I'm not dominating you, Erin. I'm loving you." He kissed her again, his tongue probing easily between her parted lips. "I want you. I need you. I wouldn't hurt you for anything in the world."

Erin's struggles weakened, and she began to respond to his gentle words. Her mouth opened, and her breathing started to quicken beneath his lips. "Please . . ."

"Yes," he answered. "Please. I want you, Erin." His lips trailed a path of fire across her cheek and down her neck, feeling the pulse in the hollow of her throat, which was warm at the touch of his tongue. "Do you want me?"

"Yes," she moaned. Her hands wandered to his hips, down over strong, muscular buttocks. She shivered. "I do."

"I know you do. I can feel that you do." He felt her body relax again, and he entered her, expertly and slowly, trying not to let her shuddering response drive the tenderness from him. Her muscles gripped him, and he smiled at her, gradually allowing his weight to press upon her.

Erin opened her eyes and looked at him, feeling him within her and seeing that possession reflected in his hungry, yet tender, gaze. She smiled back at him, her hands running along the length of his hard, smooth sides. "Love me, Logan."

Even though he had waited so long to hear her say those words and had had such a fierce desire for her bottled up inside him for even longer, Logan took her slowly, matching his rhythm to hers. Only when she began to move beneath him and cry out in joy did he unleash a small measure of the passion clawing to get out of him. They swept over the edge in a torrent, one after the other, driven along by a tension that had been building between them since their first meeting.

Then Logan held her body next to his own, cradling and stroking her with tender reassurance. He had done it. He had finally tapped the fire within this fantastic woman. And this brief, almost restrained, lovemaking was only the beginning. He felt instinctively that there was so much more she had to give, and they would discover the depths of their passion together, searching for the limits of what seemed a limitless desire. She was his. A prized possession. But Logan knew he was possessed as well. Erin had reached out and captured his soul.

CHAPTER ELEVEN

Erin felt suspended in time. A day, then two, passed, sun-filled and carefree. The lovers forgot everything except each other, allowing their intimacy to become everything, delicious and consuming. They ate when they were hungry, slept in each other's arms, made love lazily in the sun and passionately, feverishly beneath the stars.

The first time Logan had made love to her she had been tense, hesitant, frightened of his strength and powerful male dominance. But her fear disappeared under his tender touch and gentle coaxing. In its place came a fierce pride, a certain knowledge in the power of her own femininity that made her bold beyond her wildest fantasy. They *were* equals now, experimenting, pushing at the boundaries of their own sexuality, enjoying each other with an abandon Erin had not thought herself capable of. She had no regrets, no misgivings, only joy. She didn't think about endings, only of beginnings and of the contentment she had found in Logan's arms.

For the first time she resolved that change was necessary and good. The changes in her own life these past few days were proof enough of that. If she had resisted the change in her relationship with Logan, she would never have felt these marvelous feelings in the first place. She wouldn't have discovered such joy and contentment. Most important of all, she would never have found out how much she loved him.

The next morning Erin felt a sharp disappointment as the real world returned to melt her image of paradise, like a sand castle in the tide. Stephanos was back, and he wasn't alone.

She was on the beach enjoying the sun when she heard the sound of engines and the tooting of a horn. Stephanos's pickup roared into view, followed by a large flatbed truck that rolled slowly over the sandy rise behind the house, its driver being very careful on the uneven ground. It pulled up near a building Erin hadn't investigated but had assumed was the garage. It wasn't, or if it had been at one time, it had been recently converted.

Stephanos parked his truck—both trucks were loaded with crates of various sizes—beside the building and swung wide the big double doors. Erin went to see what was going on, but when she looked in the building, she wished she hadn't. It had been converted, all right, into a smaller version of her lab at Scott R and D. And the crates as they were opened didn't contain supplies—or at least not the kind Erin had expected. They held machinery, apparatus, and supplies from her lab. Her time, it seemed, had finally come.

Logan had been on the *Tempete* since early morning, behavior Erin hadn't considered suspicious until now. She watched as he beached the dinghy and strolled purposefully toward her. He looked handsome and relaxed, smiling as he approached. When he reached her, he started to hug her but was warned off by the angry look in her eyes.

"You lied to me," she stated quietly.

"Excuse me?"

"You lied. You said we were here for a vacation."

Logan lifted a brow. "I said we needed a couple of days off to recharge our mental batteries." He ignored her accusing tone and took her in his arms. "I don't know about you, but I'm at full voltage now." He dipped his head to kiss her, but she shied away. He turned her loose.

His touch awakened a smoldering flame in her; his possessive eyes caressed her every curve. Erin didn't know how to deal with the confusion of emotions she was feeling. She had thought him as lost and consumed by their newfound intimacy as she was. But how could he have been if he had been planning this all along? "It—it's been wonderful. I just thought . . ."

"It *has* been wonderful," he said, reaching out a hand to caress her cheek. "But we can't stay on vacation forever. We have work to do."

Was that what these past few days had been to him? A temporary diversion while waiting for his plans to come together? "I see," was all she could say.

Logan put his arm around her waist, giving her a playful shake as he turned her around. Listening numbly to his cheerful voice, she let him lead her back to the building where Stephanos and the driver of the truck were continuing their unpacking.

"Hey! Cheer up, sweetheart," Logan cajoled her. "We have to get moving on this thing. And as long as the work has to be done, I can't think of much nicer surroundings to work in. Can you?" he asked, waving his hand at the beauty around them.

Erin looked at him glumly. For her this paradise had lost some of its beauty. She didn't miss the camaraderie in his voice, nor the casual endearment. Did he think that making love to her had suddenly put an end to all her doubts? If so, perhaps he was ready now to explain himself to her.

Erin halted in her tracks, watching with dismay as the men hurriedly uncrated her equipment. "I don't see what the rush is all about."

"It will take you, what, two or three weeks just to get your experiment rolling again?" Logan asked.

Erin nodded. "About that."

"Then two or three more to actually see any results we can use. Correct?"

Frowning, Erin nodded again. Her mind felt lazy, unwilling to return to this problem. Heaven knew that she hadn't been thinking much about business lately. There had been too many other thrilling, pleasurable things to concentrate on. But deep down inside she had known he hadn't forgotten the enzyme, knew the time was coming when he would ask—or force—her to produce.

Actually, now that the time had come, she didn't think force would be necessary. She felt a kind of relief knowing that Logan was still excited about producing the enzyme. She hadn't forgotten his speculations about there being even more money to be made from *not* putting her process to use as there was in using it. She still didn't know what form his marketing plans would take—or if she would approve—but at least it was better than the "corporate blackmail" he had told her about previously.

"So," Logan continued, taking her thoughtful silence as a good sign that she was following his line of thinking, "we really can't afford to delay another moment in getting back to work. As far as everybody else is concerned, we've already done our testing and are ready to roll."

"I thought you said you didn't care what the competition thought," Erin said.

Logan smiled wryly. "That was a combination of wishful thinking and a bad mood. We have to take them into account, because they all want a piece of the action, and we don't even know how big a pie we're dividing yet," he replied.

"You plan on working with them?" Erin asked with surprise. Logan was being so open with her. She really *was* starting to feel like a part of the team. She would have time to learn the full extent of his plans. And now, perhaps she would even have a say in those plans.

"Indirectly. Like I said, everyone thinks we're ready to roll. When we don't, they'll have to assume we're holding out, pulling a fast one somewhere to manipulate metal prices or some such."

"Then we'll just have to explain, show them—"

Logan interrupted Erin with patient exasperation. "It's much more complicated than that. One hand has to wash the other for the Scott Corporation—or any other diversified company—to survive," he explained. "We're going to irritate a lot of people if we say, 'Hey, guys, just give us a few more months.' Nobody will want to wash their hands with ours because they'll figure the water's dirty."

Erin was reminded then that she was in the presence of the man who had built the Scott Corporation up from a simple shipping company to a powerful industry giant. In the blissful days and nights they had just spent together, she had thought of him only as a man, a man whom she desired and who had treated her with such passionate tenderness. A man she loved.

It was hard for her to think of them as being the same person, but they were, and she supposed it was time to face that fact. Right or wrong, good or bad, Logan held more control over her than she would have thought she ever could allow. He had bound her to him by her every fiber. That thought frightened her more than a little, but it was too late to turn back now.

"Do you think we can pull it off?" she asked. How casually she used the word *we* now!

"I think I can hold things together until we're ready." He looked at Erin and grinned. "As long as someone very close to me gets off her sweet behind and does what she's supposed to do."

Erin stepped away from him and came to attention, displaying only a trace of the sarcasm she had used on other occasions when he had given her orders. "Aye aye, Captain!"

Logan watched her with great interest. How beautiful she was! The ivory maillot she wore displayed her legs at their fetching best. "Perhaps we can turn this into a working vacation," he said, his eyes alive with a wicked gleam.

Erin gazed back at him, licking her lips in a sensuous gesture only he could see. "Well, you know the old saying. All work and no play . . ."

Sluggishly at first, then with renewed dedication, Erin threw herself into the task before her. Once unpacked, her lab equipment and supplies had to be set up, cleaned, and tested. Then there was the struggle of getting her mind back into the work and the time-consuming, meticulous job of beginning each of the interdependent series of steps necessary to produce the enzyme. There wasn't much time for play.

However, even though Logan was busy, too, the nights still belonged to the lovers. Stephanos was staying on the *Tempete*, explaining that he didn't sleep well on dry land, but Erin thought it was out of respect for the very obvious changes that had taken place between her and Logan in his absence. They had the house to themselves, and they made the best of it.

The trio did have a tension-breaking party to

mark their first week at the hideaway, with Stephanos outdoing himself in the kitchen. And occasionally, when the work got to be too much for her, Erin would badger one of the men until they took her out on the bay for a lesson in the sailboat. She was getting fairly adept at handling the small craft, so she knew they went with her more to get away from their own duties than because of any doubts about her seamanship.

Another of the fine mornings Erin was coming to expect from this paradise arrived with its usual beauty, finding her unexplainably restless. Logan had gotten up earlier than usual, then promptly disappeared. After a quick dip in the bay and a shower, Erin went searching for him. It was a good morning for a quick sail before settling down to work.

When she emerged from the house, she saw him with Stephanos, pulling the dinghy up on shore. She waved, then went to meet them. Logan smiled at her as she approached, but she also noticed that he looked irritated.

"Hi!"

"Hi, yourself," Logan replied, giving her a quick hug.

"Something wrong?"

"Yes. I've got to go to Houston and take care of a problem with one of our shipping clients. Guy's threatening to take his business elsewhere unless he can meet with me personally to renegotiate our contract." He sighed, obviously disgusted. "All I need right now is to have to go hold some nervous executive's hand."

Erin intertwined her fingers with his. "You can hold my hand. Take me with you?"

Logan grinned at her. "Stephanos!" he called over his shoulder to his friend standing discreetly in the background. "Get out the whip! We have a rebellious employee on our hands."

"Okay, okay." Erin stuck her tongue out at him. "I'll continue to slave away tirelessly in your absence," she said with melodramatic self-pity. "While you go and have fun."

"I'll be gone two days, half of which I'll spend on planes getting there and back, and the other half in a smoky meeting room." Logan leaned over and kissed her on the tip of the nose. "Some fun."

"Poor baby," Erin commiserated.

Later, looking incongruous to the surroundings in a gray business suit, Logan kissed her fiercely, threw his suitcase into the pickup truck, and took off. She watched and waved until he was out of sight, then tried to push away the depression creeping up on her. She missed him already.

"Take me for a sailing lesson?" Erin asked Stephanos, hoping that a sail would brighten her mood.

"Oh, I'm sorry, Erin. I have the *Tempete*'s auxiliary generator in about fifteen thousand pieces. I have to get back to work on it or I won't have any air conditioning tonight."

"You could sleep on shore."

The idea seemed to make him extremely uncomfortable. "No, I have to get it fixed. But that's no reason you can't go ahead and go. You're good enough to sail that boat alone."

"Well . . ."

The big man grinned broadly. "Go ahead! Solo!"

Erin didn't know what she had been so worried about. It was an easy craft to handle, what was known as a day sailer, made for sheltered waters under calm conditions. She got it away from the small pier and unfurled the single sail and soon was skimming over the surface of the placid bay like a pro.

Sailing gave her such a sense of freedom. And alone, like this, it also appealed to her yearning for control, a control she hadn't had much of lately. She didn't know where she had acquired such a need. She envied Logan's ability to fly a plane. Though she wasn't one of those people who flew from place to place with white knuckles from gripping the armrests, it bothered her more than most to have someone else responsible for keeping her in the air. Were she the pilot, flying wouldn't bother her at all.

The wind was coming from directly behind her as she tacked toward the mouth of the bay, driving her along at a thrilling speed. As she neared the choppier water of the sea beyond, the breeze freshened, and she shortened sail so as not to overshoot her planned turning point. The trip out to this point had been exhilarating and easy, but going back, she would be heading into the wind and would have to do a considerable amount of maneuvering to arrive at the dock.

Erin pushed her tiller and prepared to come around, ducking under the boom as it swung across the narrow deck. But she had forgotten to drop her centerboard, the retractable wooden keel that gave power and control when sailing at angles to the wind. She was struggling to lower it and keep the boat pointed just off the wind at the same time when a violent gust hit her sail. It skewed the craft sideways, and then another gust hit, heeling the boat hard over. Try as she might, Erin couldn't seem to get her weight in the right spot in time, and she found herself in the water, holding on to her over-turned craft.

Half hoping that Stephanos wasn't watching, and half hoping that he was, Erin muttered a few choice epithets and went about trying to right the boat. This had happened before, and Logan had made it look so easy. But once again, she couldn't seem to use her weight efficiently, the waterlogged sail fighting her at every turn. Worse still, she was drifting beyond the mouth of the bay and into open water.

Just as she was starting to panic and hear the opening musical strains of a certain shark movie playing in her head, she heard another sound. A motor! She turned around and saw a long, sleek pleasure craft bearing down on her.

"Need some help?" one of the two tall men aboard asked when they pulled up alongside.

"Uh, you might say that, yes," Erin replied with chagrin. The two men were jostling each other with their elbows and grinning from ear to ear. She was glad she had decided to wear jeans and a T-shirt today instead of her usual swimsuit. That would probably have given them even more enjoyment.

With their help and a line from their boat, the little day sailer was soon upright again. Then they pulled Erin onto their own craft and handed her a towel.

"Hey, listen," one of the men said. "Our yacht is anchored just on the other side of that finger of land over here. Why don't we tow you over, and you can let yourself and your sail dry out before you head back?"

Erin did feel a slight chill, even in the warm breeze. A shiver ran down her spine. "Okay." She looked at them, a frown creasing her brow. "Have we met somewhere before?" she asked.

The other man, who hadn't said a word as of yet, had a strip of tape across the bridge of his nose. He opened his mouth to speak, but his companion gave him a vicious jab in the ribs with his elbow. "Oof!"

"Pay no attention to Robert, here. He's had too much beer." He regaled her with tales of their fishing exploits while piloting the boat around a little grassy mound of land toward a yacht just slightly smaller than the *Tempete*. As he talked he waved one hand in the air. It was bandaged from fingertips to just below the wrist. Erin couldn't get over the eerie feeling of familiarity she had when looking at the odd disheveled pair.

The yacht was very nice, though Erin personally preferred the *Tempete*. A cabin boy in a white jacket brought her some lemonade and another towel, then went away. The two men had disappeared as well, so Erin sat alone in a chair on deck, fluffing her hair with her fingers. Under the hot sun her clothes were almost dry again.

Just as she was about to search out her rescuers to tell them she had to be on her way, a very distinguished-looking man in an impeccably tailored tropical suit stepped out on deck. He strolled over, pulled up a chair, and joined her.

"Well, you look as if you might pull through," he said in a cultured voice. He smiled, showing brilliant white teeth.

Erin cocked her head curiously. The other two men had said this was their yacht, but this looked more like a man who had the wherewithal to own such a craft. He was quite handsome. Too handsome for Erin's taste. She had never trusted pretty men. "I'm fine. I was just about to try to find the other two—"

"My employees. Brian and Robert. They'll join us in a moment."

"As I was saying," Erin continued, "I really must be going now. I have a lot to do today."

The man's smile broadened, and he chuckled. "Yes. I imagine you do. But please. Stay and talk for a while."

Erin started to get up. "No, really . . ."

"I insist, Dr. Barclay." His voice was polite but firm. "We have much to discuss, you and I."

Erin sat back, wide-eyed with shock. Her throat tightened, and a restless fear started churning in her stomach. "W-who are you?"

"Ah, where have my manners gone?" he replied pleasantly. "My name is Reynolds. Seth Reynolds. My friends call me Seth, and I do so hope that we shall become friends, Erin."

Her mind reeling in confusion, Erin continued to stare with alarm at the man seated before her. "I don't understand."

He leaned toward her, looking at her intently. "Come now, Erin. I think we can skip all this, don't you? I know who you are and what you have discovered. I am a businessman, with interests not at all unlike those of Logan Scott. What I have for you is a business proposition, and you would do well to consider it."

Erin frowned. She was beginning to recover some of her wits. "What kind of proposition?"

"It's very simple. I want you to produce the enzyme for my company instead of for the Scott Corporation," he said.

"Or else, right?" Erin asked sardonically.

"What?" Seth exclaimed. "You do me an injustice, Erin. This is a business discussion, not a laying down of ultimatums!"

"Uh-huh. And you just happened to be in the area, so you thought you'd invite me to a meeting."

He smiled ingratiatingly. "I admit that I've been looking for you. It was just a happy circumstance that I was able to be of service this morning. We have all been quite concerned as to your welfare."

"We?"

"The industry. We were very worried when you dropped out of sight a week ago."

Slowly Erin's fear was dissipating. She was

still very suspicious, but her curiosity was getting the better of her. "I can imagine. But, as you can see, I'm fine." She sipped casually at her lemonade, trying to appear calm.

"You've been treated well?" Seth asked solicitously.

Erin smiled, remembering the glorious days of love she had spent with Logan. "Very well."

"Good, good. And work on the enzyme? It is progressing satisfactorily?"

Her smile disappeared. "Look, Mr. Reynolds. I am an employee of the Scott Corporation. I will not discuss a classified project with a competitor. *If* that's what you are," she said with more panache than her present situation made her feel. Where was Stephanos? Hadn't he missed her yet?

Reynolds put his hands up in a pacifying gesture and assured her, "Competitor is a fair, albeit simplistic, description. And, of course, I respect your loyalty. I believe that loyalty to be misplaced, but then that is why we are having this discussion. It is my duty to clarify the position of my company and that of the industry as a whole."

That made Erin's ears prick up. Her romantic interests and personal feelings aside, she was still a scientist with an important discovery and still sadly lacking in information. "A little clarity would be much appreciated, Mr. Reynolds." She glanced at her wristwatch, glad to see it still running after her unexpected dip in the ocean. "As well as brevity."

"I see by the look on your face that you are

interested in the information I have to give," he began, getting right to the heart of her thoughts with frightening accuracy. "To me that means you are as in the dark concerning Logan Scott's plans as is the rest of the world. Am I correct?"

Erin tried not to let her surprise show on her face. "Please continue," she prompted, ignoring his question.

He smiled. It was a rather reptilian smile in Erin's opinion. "Yes. Perhaps it would be better if I simply asked you the questions running through all our minds as of late." He looked at her with pursed lips for a moment, then continued. "Why is Logan Scott being so secretive?"

"I—"

"No need to answer, Erin. These are rhetorical questions, really. I can see that you are thinking about what I say, and that is all I ask." He smiled again. It reminded her of a lizard that had just swallowed a bug. But she listened, and as she listened, an old uneasiness returned.

"All right," Erin said.

"Surely Mr. Scott is aware of the economic problems the enzyme can cause if marketed improperly, especially to those small nations who presently supply much of the metals found in the manganese nodules." He paused, pleased with the interest he saw in her eyes. "Why, therefore, isn't Mr. Scott talking with the United Nations? I know that they are very anxious to speak with him," he added with a sad expression. "Your process can bring great benefit to the entire world. It can also bring great calamity and economic upset. Why is the Scott Corpora-

239

tion not taking steps to make sure the possible problems inherent in this kind of international situation do not outweigh those benefits?" He leaned closer and put his hand on Erin's. "In short, Erin, and if you will excuse my strong language, just what the hell does Logan Scott think he's doing?"

Erin had been so absorbed in his words that she barely felt the cold touch of his hand on her skin. "How do you know he's not taking such steps?" she asked suddenly, jerking her hand out from under his.

"Because I *have* initiated discussions with Third World countries already," he announced triumphantly, "and I can assure you that my company is the only one to do so. I already know the answers to the questions I asked you. Logan Scott is concerned only with Logan Scott and is willing to cause the downfall of entire nations to get what he wants."

With that he clapped his hands once, and Erin's old friends Armando and Carlos came out on deck. They looked at her and smiled. "He tells the truth. He is helping us, helping Chile and the world. Your Logan Scott will not even talk with the agencies we alerted to our plight. Seth is a fine man and a true humanitarian."

Erin sat there, dumbfounded, staring back at the three men who were watching her so expectantly. She didn't know what to say. She looked at the "fine man and true humanitarian" seated before her and sighed.

"I'm afraid, Mr. Reynolds, that I have to ask

you the same question I previously asked Armando and Carlos here. What's in it for you?"

"Well, naturally, my company will make a small profit—"

"Naturally," Erin interjected.

"But you must take the large view here, Erin. We—"

Erin cut him off. "Listen, buster. I told you before. I'm an employee of the Scott Corporation. The questions you've been asking me need answering, that's for sure. As a scientist and a member of the team," she continued with a feeling of pride that surprised her, "I'm duty-bound to get those answers. But if there's a profit to be made, I'm also duty-bound to make sure the Scott Corporation makes it!"

A hard, dangerous light had come into Seth Reynolds's eyes as she spoke. "I see," he said quietly.

"But, Dr. Barclay!" Armando protested.

Reynolds held up his hand to cut the man off. "Brian! Robert! Get out here!"

The two men who had pulled her from the water rushed to his side. They glared at Erin. The one with the tape on his nose spoke up. "Something we can do for you, Mr. Reynolds?"

Erin suddenly felt sick to her stomach. No wonder the other man hadn't let Robert speak before. Even with those few gruff words she recognized his voice, would never forget it, in fact. He was the man on the phone, the one who had made the threats that had started this whole mess. And he was leering at her as if he

241

were now ready to make all those threats come true.

She jumped to her feet, but Brian caught her with his good hand before she could jump overboard, and slammed her back into her chair. "Has she gotten tired of our hospitality already?" he said with vicious humor.

"Yes. I'm afraid she has." Reynolds looked at her thoughtfully. "What are we going to do with you, Dr. Barclay?"

"I've got *lots* of ideas," Robert announced in that voice that made Erin physically ill.

"You see, Erin, Brian and Robert here have many scores they feel they have to settle with you. They nearly got pneumonia while keeping an eye on you, Brian almost got his hand twisted off by Logan Scott, and poor Robert, here, may have had his ability to father children impaired permanently."

So he was the one she had gotten with her knee that night on her patio. She summoned up whatever defiance she could muster. "Good. I'm glad."

"Hey," Robert shot back, "don't you worry about it. The equipment still works." He gave her a nasty wink.

Reynolds seemed to be enjoying all this immensely. "Not to mention the broken nose he got while pursuing your cab after you left Armando and Carlos."

Brian squeezed her arm until she cried out. "Yeah. That was a real fun day. We got in a wreck trying to follow that crazy cabdriver of

242

yours off the freeway. Our car went up in flames."

"Oh, gee," Erin ground out through clenched teeth. "I hope you weren't hurt."

Erin saw the murderous gleam in the two henchmen's eyes. She had to think, and think fast. Through her terror she managed to make her mouth work. "Some businessman. What use would I be to you after these two got through with me?"

Reynolds grinned. "My point exactly. One way or another you *will* do what I say—sooner or later. Make it sooner and these two will never lay a hand on you."

"Hey!" Robert cried.

"Shut up, or you'll be shark bait," Reynolds said in a deadly quiet voice.

Erin saw that he had complete control over them. For now. She had no reason to believe that he would keep his word. She looked to the two Chileans for help. "This isn't your style, Armando. You see what kind of humanitarian this man really is?"

They were both looking at her blandly. "A necessary deception, it is a pity it failed. Mr. Reynolds was kind enough to offer his help, and we are behind him completely, whatever his methods," Carlos replied. "Our country has just come through a very bloody revolution, Dr. Barclay. We know there are some things that can be accomplished through only violence and bloodshed."

Armando nodded in agreement. "The *rotos*, the broken ones. That is what the upper class

243

calls the poor in my country. Chile is divided into those who have power and use it to maintain privilege and those who will always be underdogs until they build their own power. Your enzyme can supply that power."

"What about him?" Erin asked, jerking her head in Reynolds's direction. "Don't you think he might have something to say about what you do with the enzyme?"

Armando shrugged. "We understand this man, Dr. Barclay. He is greedy for money; we are greedy for power. With a small fraction of the money he can get through judicious use of your enzyme, he can help us wrest control of Chile's mining industry from our government." He turned his gaze to Reynolds and smiled. "Our cooperation with him will in turn assure him a virtual monopoly of the copper market, something he is already in a position to exploit to the fullest."

"When you described Logan as a man concerned only with himself, you were describing yourself! You're a megalomaniac," Erin bit out as she glared at Reynolds. "And a traitorous one at that. Don't you know who these *gentlemen* will align themselves with once you give them the power they seek?"

Reynolds waved his hand in dismissal of her accusation. "I couldn't care less about international politics. What I am, Dr. Barclay, is an investor, and Armando and Carlos are offering me a very attractive investment." He smiled as he spoke, that same reptilian smile. But it disappeared suddenly.

"I am also losing my patience. Out of necessity I have already started my plans in motion, proceeding as if I had the enzyme." He leaned over and took her chin in his hand, digging his fingers into her cheeks. "And I *will* have it soon, won't I?"

Erin shook free of his grasp. "You don't leave me a hell of a lot of choice," she said, shivering under the cold, expectant eyes of Brian and Robert.

Reynolds stood up then. "That was exactly my intention, Dr. Barclay." He looked at each of his lieutenants in turn. "Understand this. Erin is now off limits to you two. Got it?"

They mumbled and grumbled, but they nodded their compliance. Reynolds looked at them, then stepped over to the side of the yacht to which Erin's sailboat was tethered and untied it. From inside his coat he pulled a very large pistol and proceeded to empty it into the boat's thin hull. It started to sink immediately. "Dr. Barclay is off limits," he said again, then disappeared below decks.

Her ears ringing from the gunfire, Erin watched sadly as her little boat sank beneath the waves. Armando and Carlos followed Reynolds below, leaving her with Brian and Robert. They stole covetous glances at her but kept their distance.

But she wasn't fooled. Once she produced the enzyme for their boss, she would cease to be useful, and he would turn them loose on her. Right now she was valuable; right now they wouldn't hurt her.

Right now they wouldn't hurt her! What was stopping her from jumping overboard and swimming away? *Your poor swimming ability, for one*, she thought. Swimming in a pool or the protected bay of Logan's retreat was one thing, but the currents around the yacht were strong; she could tell that by the way the big vessel moved against its anchor.

Then she saw it, bobbing on the surface about twenty feet away. A life preserver from the sailboat! Without stopping to think she climbed up on the railing and dove overboard. She landed a bit harder than she had planned but came up swimming, anyway, spluttering and splashing, making her way to the life vest. Behind her she could hear the shouts.

"Get her!"

"Don't shoot her, you imbeciles! Go in after her!"

She made it to the vest and started toward the shore, using it as a kickboard. But she could already hear the powerful strokes of her pursuers to her left, and she knew she had failed. And then she felt something slimy brush her legs.

Except that it didn't just brush them, it *slithered* over them, moving up her back. She screamed and nearly went under, thrashing and flailing the water around her. Her hand struck the slithery, slimy thing, and she screamed again.

It was a rope! Treading water with her legs, she grasped it, and it moved through her fingers. She looked wildly in the direction in which it was moving and saw that the rope extended from her hands to the small finger of land before her and up the grassy knoll beyond. At the top of the knoll stood Stephanos, the rope in his hand, miming directions so as not to draw attention to his position. Erin was valuable, and they wouldn't shoot her. He enjoyed no such protection. She did as instructed and took a firm hold on the rope.

It stopped moving through her hands. She looked up, and Stephanos was gone. Then she felt a hard tug that nearly pulled the rope from her grasp, and she was suddenly planing through the water on her belly, picking up speed as it dragged her toward shore. She braced herself for the impact but simply slid up the sandy beach, then dropped the rope and stood quickly, chasing the still moving rope over the rise.

Fighting to keep up with her lifeline, she followed it to a sleek catamaran, sails unfurled and taut with wind, heading back toward the mouth of the bay. It was heeled over at a precarious angle because of its speed. At the helm Stephanos was dividing his time between steering and looking over his shoulder. There wasn't anyone following. He started hauling the line in with one hand as Erin ran to the water's edge, a few feet from the catamaran.

"I can't take you aboard yet, they might catch us," he yelled. "Are you okay?"

"Just dandy," she yelled back. Her jeans were full of gritty sand from being dragged briefly across the shore, and the salt water stung the cuts and scratches on her arms and belly. Still, as terrified as she was, Erin had a grin from ear to ear.

Stephanos took a quick look at her and started laughing. "We're being chased by bloodthirsty criminals, and you're smiling?"

"I'm just so happy," she yelled, "that I didn't wear my bikini today!"

CHAPTER TWELVE

Logan hated helicopters. Not because he thought them more dangerous than other types of aircraft but simply because he wasn't qualified in them and had to entrust himself to another pilot. He was only in this one now because it was the quickest way back to Erin.

The moment he had gotten Stephanos's message about the occurrences at the retreat, an icy fear had gripped his heart. And even though Erin was all right, he had quickly terminated his business and arranged this flight, startling his client by giving him the best contract he'd ever acquired with the Scott Corporation.

Logan didn't care. He just wanted to see Erin as soon as possible. All it had taken was a short absence from her and the sudden shock of almost losing her to make him come to a profound realization: The rambling heart of Logan Scott had finally come to rest. He loved Erin. But he also realized that he wasn't just worried about her safety; she had him worried in other ways as well.

He had had time to think and found some of his old doubts returning. Erin certainly picked

249

the most strategic times to go wandering on her own. Stephanos had reported it as a simple error in seamanship on her part, which had then allowed her to fall into the hands of one Seth Reynolds, a man Logan knew of but didn't really know. Evidently it had been Reynolds and his lieutenants who had started this whole thing off, and now the munchkins were allied with them as well. It certainly was complex, but he had expected nothing less.

The enzyme was a tricky matter in every way. Complex and intricate plans were required in addition to a secrecy that had so far been thwarted at every turn. As the key link in the highly sensitive chain of producing, marketing, and controlling Erin's process, Logan felt torn apart. He wanted to trust Erin, wanted to tell her all, especially now that they had become so involved with one another in every other way.

But how could he? Even if she was completely guiltless, Erin still had an annoying habit of falling into the hands of the opposition. If he filled her head with knowledge about his sensitive plans and she wandered off again, that knowledge could conceivably put her in more danger than she already was in and could also do irreparable damage to the Scott Corporation. It wasn't pleasant to think about, but he knew everyone had their breaking point—or their price.

He wanted to believe that she was loyal, but he couldn't be sure. Loyalty could be just as nebulous a quality as love, could change from moment to moment and mean what one wanted it to mean. Logan had allowed her into his heart, and yet he couldn't bring himself to allow her into his confidence. He loved Erin but he didn't trust her. It was as simple as that.

Stephanos had assured Erin that Reynolds and his crew would probably depart in case the authorities were summoned. And, indeed, once they had gotten back to the relative safety of the bay, they had seen a brief glimpse of the yacht as it headed out to sea at a good clip. But she noticed that he stayed where he could see her at all times, and though he certainly wasn't obvious about it, she was also aware that Stephanos was now armed. The gloss was gone from paradise.

She found it hard to concentrate on her work—not that she was at all inclined to work anymore, anyway. Once she cleaned up, tended her scratched stomach and arms, and calmed down, the questions Reynolds had put to her started burning in her mind.

He had been trying to gain her confidence, questioning Logan's secrecy as a ploy to turn her over to his side. He had failed because she had been through too much to trust *anyone* so easily. But Reynolds was an intuitive man and had chosen exactly the right way of reopening the file of doubts Erin had about Logan and his plans. When Logan got back—around sundown according to Stephanos—he would have to answer her questions. She was desperately in love with him, and the thought that his answers might make a mockery of her love terrified her. But she *had to know.*

Erin's tension grew when she heard the sound of a helicopter in the distance. The noise got louder, and she could see the landing lights against the dusky sky, feel the blast of air from the whirling blades. The aircraft was equipped with floats and landed in the bay, then glided closer to shore, kicking up sand and salt spray as it neared the small pier. Logan stepped out, waved to the pilot, and came ashore. The helicopter lifted delicately off again and was soon fading in the distance, leaving silence behind.

"Are you all right?" Logan asked, sweeping her into his arms and kissing her before she could answer.

Finally he let her up for air. "Yes, I'm fine." Erin smiled at him hesitantly, reveling in just being in his arms again. For a moment the questions in her mind didn't seem to matter at all. But only for a moment.

Logan pulled back and looked at her, taking in her beauty. Her hips still pressed against him, their bodies fitted as well as he remembered. But there was a certain resistance in her, a stiffness he couldn't define.

"Is anything wrong!"

"No. "It's just . . . we need to talk, Logan," Erin replied.

He grinned. "I had other things on my mind. But if you insist—"

"I do."

Logan linked his arm in hers and accompanied her up the beach to the house, surprised by her serious tone. In the living room he removed his coat and tie, loosened his collar, and rolled up his sleeves, then made them both a tall drink before sitting on the sofa and looking at her expectantly.

"So. Tell me all about your exploits while I was gone."

Erin shrugged and took a seat opposite him, disdaining his unspoken offer to join him on the sofa. She couldn't think when he was touching her. As it was, she didn't know how to broach the subject of his secrecy. "Not much to tell, really. I imagine you got the whole story from Stephanos, anyway."

"Yes." His expression turned thoughtful as he sipped at his drink. "You're sure it was Seth Reynolds?"

"That's what he said. Know him?" she asked casually, though she was very interested in his answer.

"I know *of* him," Logan replied. "He's a rather powerful man in investment-banking circles, but he has a shady past. The Securities and Exchange Commission fingered him as a participant in a scheme involving the World Bank a while back, but he came up clean—barely," he explained. "It doesn't really surprise me to hear that he's got his hands in this."

"He's not a nice guy," Erin said sardonically. "I'm sure he's quite angry with me—us—right now."

"I'm sure." Logan looked at her, trying to figure out why she was so distant this evening. "Don't worry about him and his crew. He is not, as you put it, a 'nice guy', but I don't think he's the type to mount an attack on this place or anything like that. You're safe here." Was it reassurance she was looking for, or something else? "Just stick close to home from now on," he cautioned.

In her present mood his patronizing tone grated on her frayed nerves. "What's that supposed to mean?"

"It means, you pick the damnedest times to go searching for thinking room." Logan had the feeling she was trying to pick a fight, and he was tired and exasperated enough to give her one.

"As long as we're on the subject of trust, Logan," Erin shot back, leaning forward in her chair, "don't you think it's about time you gave me the whole story?"

"Like what?"

"Like everything! I can understand keeping the competition in the dark, but why aren't you talking to me about your plans?" she asked heatedly. "Surely I have a right to know what's going to happen with my own discovery, don't you think?"

His expression darkened, and he gave her a long, hard stare. "I think it would be safer if I didn't tell you anything."

"Damn you!" Erin got up and went to the window, turning her back on his suspicious eyes. "You make it sound as if I *tried* to get abducted today. Do you think I enjoy being manhandled and threatened?"

Logan jumped up and went to her side, wanting to touch her but thinking better of it. "Manhandled?"

She spun to face him. "Oh, don't worry." She held her hands up for him to see. "A few scratches, but everything still works. I can still use a microscope and handle my equipment. We won't fall behind schedule."

Glaring at her, Logan almost grabbed her and tried to shake some sense into her. But he stepped away before he lost his temper completely. "I meant . . . oh, hell, I don't know what I meant! I was trying to say that it would be safer for *you* if you don't know everything." Her body still taunted him, but the thoughts of a pleasant evening together faded from his mind.

"If you're so worried about my safety, why don't we call in the police? I have enough grounds to charge Reynolds and his henchmen with attempted kidnapping at the very least."

Logan groaned. "We've been over this before! Stephanos and I can handle your security, if you'll only do as you're told." Running his hands over his face in exasperation, he added, "Besides, kidnapping is a federal offense. That would mean the FBI."

"Why does that worry you so much?" she asked suspiciously.

"I don't need a bunch of guys in dark suits running around poking their noses into my business," Logan replied.

"Why not? Are you hiding something you don't want them to know about?"

Logan looked heavenward in a silent plea, then looked back at Erin. "I just don't need the aggravation. *You* provide me with more than enough of that!" he shouted.

"Then tell me what I want to know and I'll stop!" Erin shouted back.

Throwing his hands into the air, Logan turned, grabbed his drink and drained it, then went for a refill. "It's a very complex situation," he said in a quiet voice.

"Do you think I'm too dumb to understand?"

Muttering curses under his breath, Logan returned to his seat before he did something he'd regret. He was trying to remain calm, but it wasn't working very well. "I think you're too damn smart for your own good. That's what I think!"

"I'm smart enough to know that mining done in international waters is of concern to the United Nations," Erin said at last. "And I know that the metals my process can separate from manganese nodules can affect the economy and livelihood of a lot of people, American and otherwise."

"Then you see how sensitive the whole thing is. Either nobody owns those nodules or everybody does. We're in the position of setting a precedent here, Erin," Logan said, "and I am not going to hand control of that position over to a bunch of diplomats—at least not until I have to."

"Who's asking you to?" Erin countered. She sighed and returned to her chair facing him. "I'm not begrudging the Scott Corporation its profits. All I want is to see the product of my hard work used to its fullest and best."

Logan nodded impatiently. "So do I. But

256

you're an optimist if you think the solution is to open the matter up to friendly discussion between nations. It's not that easy, and it sure isn't that simple." He met her penetrating gaze. "What do you want from me?"

How could she answer that? She wanted more of the happiness they had shared; she wanted trust and friendship and love. All that and more could be theirs if he would only tell her the truth. "I just want to be let in on the secret, Logan. Either I'm a member of the team and with you, or an outsider and against you. Which is it to be?" Erin asked, her throat tight with emotion.

She hadn't seen his eyes so cold in a long time, and that made them even colder. How could she have fooled herself into believing that there ever had been love for her in them? Before he even spoke, she knew he wasn't going to tell her anything, but she hadn't planned on what he did say.

Logan felt his temper snap. He should never have let it go this far, but it had, and there was no stopping the boil-over. Who was *she* to be giving *him* ultimatums? "For me or against me, it doesn't make the slightest difference. You can consider yourself whatever you want," Logan announced in a voice so cool, Erin could practically feel it on her skin. "As long as you produce that enzyme, I don't give a damn what your feelings are. You will know what I want you to know, when I want you to know it."

He was throwing it all away, as casually as taking out the garbage. How little she must really mean to him! To her their time here had been paradise, but to him it must have been no more than another part of his plan. To him, making love hadn't been a tender give-and-take but just another method of getting and keeping her under his control. How blind she had been!

And, still, a part of her heart refused to believe this was happening. "Logan, please . . ."

Logan didn't understand his anger, but he had never been angrier in his life. His temper was out of control now, and he was barely aware of the threatening tone his voice took on. "And while you are busy reproducing *my* enzyme, I'd keep something else in mind. If I were you, I'd be glad I'm being so secretive."

Fighting to keep tears from her eyes, Erin barely managed to ask, "And why is that?"

"Because, dear lady, some of the metals obtainable through your discovery have strategic importance. And now you've destroyed the enzyme. In some law-enforcement circles, that's bound to look like sabotage. Maybe even treason."

"That's blackmail!" Erin cried, jumping up.

Logan suddenly realized what he had done and grabbed her before she could make it to the door. "Erin, I'm—"

"Let go of me! You don't own me! I'll give you your damned enzyme if I have to work around the clock to do it. It's obviously the most important thing in the world to you, and far be it from me to stand in your way." She looked him in the eye, trying to force the shakiness from her voice. She wasn't going to give him the satisfaction of seeing her cry.

Logan let her go, as if her skin suddenly burned his hands. Damn this foul temper of his! And damn her for having wound her way so deeply into his heart! "I'm sorry, Erin. I got carried away."

She smiled bitterly in the face of his apology. "Don't look so worried, Logan. You haven't upset me so much that I can't work."

"You don't understand—"

"I understand as much as I want to," she interrupted quietly. "Keep your stupid secrets! But you keep your hands off me. You've had your fun, and now you hold all the cards. *But nobody owns me, Logan. Not even you!*" She left, slamming the door behind her. He didn't follow. Why should he? He's getting what he really wants. All he'd lost was his willing bed warmer. And with that thought she finally allowed the tears to come.

The next morning Erin watched the sunrise through the small window in her lab, her eyes red and bleary from lack of sleep. To her it was just a sunrise, flat and lifeless just like her feelings. She was numb, and she just didn't care anymore.

She didn't care about secrets, the enzyme, or any of the myriad people vying for her attention. She didn't care about Third World countries or strategic metals. She *did* care about Logan, but she refused to allow those feelings to see the light. He had hurt her enough, had stepped on her heart and her pride for as long as she could bear. All she wanted now was to leave this mess behind her, to disappear and run far away to be alone with her misery.

The door swung wide open behind her, but she didn't bother looking to see who it was. She knew, was still so aware of what his presence felt like that she decided it must be imprinted on her soul.

"Erin?" he said softly as he came up behind her.

"Yes?"

"Erin, you can't work all night like this again. I won't allow it." He took her by the arms and turned her to face him. He was smiling, expecting her to rant and rave about giving her orders. But she was limp in his hands.

She simply stood there and looked at him, pushing down the excitement her traitorous body always felt when he touched her. What did her body know? They were good together. Better than good. But that was over.

"I won't," she replied flatly.

"Good," he said, taking her answer for agreement.

"I don't need to."

"Excuse me?" Logan asked with a frown.

He released her, and she went to a counter in the middle of the room, opened a drawer, and took out a wooden box. From the box she took a stoppered glass flask the size of an orange, very aware of his suspicious eyes on her. He joined her at the counter, and she handed him the flask.

"There. I quit."

Logan's gaze went to the flask, which was

filled with a greenish-gray powder, then back to Erin's eyes. "What's this?"

"The enzyme. It's in a dried, stabilized form. It only becomes active when hydrated and in the presence of the substrate."

"What?"

Erin sighed. "It's all in here," she said, putting her hand on her notebook. "With this, the sample, and a decent biochemist, you're all set to begin testing."

"No, I mean, I thought you were weeks and weeks from this stage," Logan said with a confused expression.

Erin turned her face away. "The work in progress here *is* that far from completion. Get yourself a better-than-decent biochemist, give him—or her—my notebook and the sample, and soon you can be in production. Whatever suits your fancy." She looked back at him, her eyes stony. "I quit," she repeated.

This was all too much for Logan. He sat down in one of the chairs at the counter and gingerly put the flask back in its box. "Where did you get this?"

"Don't be so obtuse, Logan," Erin replied sarcastically. "I brought it with me from my lab. Just ask Stephanos; he's carted my stuff around often enough. This box was in my bag when he picked me up at the airport."

Logan's frown deepened, and the suspicion in his eyes grew more apparent. "Why wait till now to give it to me?"

"Does that really matter?" she asked impatiently. "You wanted it, and here it is."

261

"It *does* matter. How do I know this is real?" he asked, an edge of anger in his voice.

"What possible reason would I have to do that? You hold all the cards. You won't let me go until I give it to you, so here it is."

"That's precisely my point." He waved a dismissing hand at the flask. "Mix yourself up a little colored talcum powder and there you are, instant enzyme."

"Look, Logan, I'm going to lay this out for you. Okay?" she said through clenched teeth. Every moment here with him was sheer torture for her. "I couldn't bring myself to destroy my hard work. I wasn't about to give it to you until I knew what you were going to do with it, or until you forced me, one or the other."

"Nobody's holding a gun to your head," he countered.

"No, but that was next. Right?" she asked acidly.

Logan took her hand and squeezed it, as if touching her could explain all this to him. She only pulled it away. "I'm sorry about last night. I just got carried away. But you're being unfair, too, Erin."

She sat down in another chair and looked at him glumly. "Maybe so. But if it wasn't you, it might have been someone else. I do, as you observed, seem to have a talent for getting myself into trouble," Erin said wryly. "I just can't take the strain anymore. Once word gets out that you have the enzyme, maybe everybody will leave me alone." She sighed heavily. "At long last."

"And what has become of your high standards? Don't tell me you've lost your sense of scientific responsibility?"

Erin chuckled, but there was no humor in the sound. "Okay, I won't tell you. But it's true. I just don't care anymore. I am tired of being badgered and bullied, threatened and mauled. You hired me to work on this project. I worked on it. You wanted me to produce the enzyme, and here it is." She tapped the flask with her finger. "What you do with it is your affair. I guess I just came to the realization that it always has been your affair, high standards or not."

Logan shook his head. "This isn't like you, Erin. I can't believe it. You're not quitter."

"Believe it. I quit. Everyone has their breaking point, Logan, and I've finally reached mine. All I want is to get out of here and go back to leading a normal life." Was there life after Logan? Perhaps, but she imagined it would be very cold and empty indeed.

Logan saw something in her eyes, a touch of warmth he had been searching for. Why was she doing this? "I can't let you go," he said softly.

Erin stood up and leaned toward him, fists clenched at her sides, her voice sharp and bitter as she spoke. "Dammit, Logan! You have *no right* to keep me here against my will! You have no justification at all now. You have the enzyme, and you can test it, sell it, or pour it down the sink for all I care."

Logan reached out a hand to stroke her face, but she pulled away, something akin to fear in

263

her eyes. He refused to show her the pain that fear caused him. "Is there anything else?" he asked.

"All I want is to get the hell out of here," Erin replied vehemently. She turned on her heel and strode toward the door.

"Erin?"

She stopped but didn't turn. "What?"

"Tell Stephanos I want to see him. And you can pack your things. I'll have him take you to the train station in town."

"You're letting me go?" There was no surprise in her voice, because this was exactly what she expected. He had the enzyme, and it really was all he wanted. But she had allowed a lingering hope to stay alive in her heart, and he had just crushed it. A wave of pain hit her then, but she ordered her mind to push it away. There would be plenty of time for pain.

"You're right. You've completed our agreement. If there isn't anything else to hold you here, I have no right to stop you from leaving. I'm sorry for all I've put you through."

Erin suppressed a sob and walked out the door.

Logan sat and looked at the flask. He picked it up, held it tightly in his hand, and thought, *Here it is. I finally have it. So why do I want to throw it against the wall?* Lord! He wished he'd never even heard of the damn stuff! He was irretrievably in love with Erin, far past the point of caring about the process or anything except making her his own.

But he still had his pride. And his anger. He

wouldn't go chasing after a woman who didn't love him. No way. She had made it very clear that she didn't want to stay here, didn't want him to touch her anymore, didn't want anything from him except for him to let her go. So let her go! He had the enzyme, so why keep her around?

But who was he trying to fool? Having the enzyme in his possession was small compensation for a broken heart. Having her around may have been trying at times, but living without her was going to be sheer hell. The plain truth of the matter was that he loved her too much to hold her here if she wanted to leave. But he felt as if a large part of himself died right then and there.

CHAPTER THIRTEEN

The road from Logan Scott's retreat wasn't really much of a road, sand and gravel only, and it wandered along the coastline for ten miles or so before veering off and turning into a winding, tree-lined lane. Good road or not, it suited the purposes of the two men lurking in the shallow gully beside it.

They had been waiting patiently since before sunup, checking and rechecking their preparations, getting promising reports over their walkie-talkies. She was coming, just her and the big one, just like they had hoped and planned for. This time they would not fail, because they knew that if they did, there wouldn't be a hole deep enough to hide them.

The sound of a well-tuned truck engine interrupted the quiet morning air, and the two men pressed themselves even flatter against the ground, tense with anticipation. The truck crested the hill to their right, then immediately slowed down.

"What the . . ." Stephanos started to say. He had been having trouble concentrating, upset as he was by the state of affairs between his old friend and Erin. The man standing in the road ahead, therefore, took him completely by surprise.

Erin had been staring at her hands, paying little attention to her surroundings. Depression was too mild a word for what she was feeling right now. She looked up when Stephanos spoke, her sluggish mind trying to assimilate what she saw.

The truck slowed to a stop about twenty feet from the disheveled-looking man in the middle of the road. He looked drunk, or at least he was swaying in a breeze that wasn't there. All was quiet. His head turned slowly from the truck to the side of the road and then back, as if he were trying to decide in which direction he wanted to go.

Recognition dawned slowly in Erin's sluggish mind. She gripped Stephanos's thick arm. "That's David Turner!"

"What's he doing here?" Stephanos wondered aloud.

Erin started to get out of the truck, but Stephanos stopped her, every part of him now suddenly alert. "I'll go. You stay here and stay down." He pulled a wicked-looking revolver from beneath his shirt. "I don't like the feel of this."

Erin did as she was told, or almost. She peered over the dashboard and watched as Stephanos cautiously went up to Turner, turning around slowly as he walked. When he got to him, the man just seemed to topple over. Stephanos got his shoulder underneath him as he fell and draped him over his back, holding his legs with one hand and the gun in the other. He started back to the truck, but he was too late. The trap had been sprung.

An object that looked like an olive-drab soup can landed in the road before him and started emitting noxious white smoke. Another and still another tear gas canister fell around his feet, enveloping Stephanos in a thick, choking cloud. He couldn't see his hand in front of his face. The vapor biting at his eyes and nearly suffocating him, the big man unceremoniously dumped Turner to the ground and ran in the direction of the truck, somewhere in the haze before him.

"Erin!" he choked out. "Run!"

From up ahead he heard her scream, fought off the wave of nausea threatening to double him over, and staggered on, guided by the sound of her choking, gasping cries. The truck suddenly loomed in front of him, his vision so badly blurred from the tears flowing from them that for a moment he thought it was moving toward him. He reached out a hand and touched it, then moved to the passenger side. Erin wasn't there, and her cries for help had ceased.

Stephanos heard someone yell "Let's go!" just before the lights exploded in his head. Then the lights were gone and a soft, comforting blackness descended around him. Somewhere, a million miles away, it seemed, he heard the helicopter coming.

"Medic!" he hollered in his mind. Thank God for the choppers, he thought as he let the darkness claim him. They'd find him. They always had.

*   *   *

Texas hill country, Erin thought. That could be where I am. She rubbed her arm where a roughly administered hypodermic needle had pierced her skin. The tear gas had burned her eyes red, had made her physically ill. She hadn't had the strength to fight whoever had pulled her from the truck, jabbed her, and pushed her into the midnight-blue helicopter. All but unconscious from whatever sedative they had given her, she hadn't been able to discern direction, time, or distance on the way here.

Upon arrival at the Reynolds ranch, Brian and Robert had summarily thrown her into a small cubicle adorned with a cot and the barest minimum of plumbing, locked her in, and left her. She had been exhausted and sick and had blacked out while waiting for Seth Reynolds to come for her.

She had awakened to find that she'd slept the clock around. It was morning now, and Brian had escorted her to a fantastically equipped laboratory. It even had windows looking out on green fields and the rolling hills that tipped her off to where she must be. Knowing approximately where she was in the state didn't comfort her much. She knew where she really was. Prison.

Oh, this place was elegantly decorated, at least the parts she'd seen as Brian had walked her through the halls from her cell. But this was definitely not the velvet captivity of the *Tempete* or Logan's retreat. She was *really* a prisoner now. The windows were a nice touch to the sterile surroundings, but they were barred. Brian

269

had a gun, and he was right outside the only door. Robert was nowhere to be seen, but Erin didn't doubt that he and Reynolds would show up soon enough.

She knew she should be terrified. But she wasn't. She was just . . . resigned. Resigned to her fate. Bitterly false hopes of rescue only taunted her. Reynolds had gone to a lot of trouble this time to acquire her, and she hadn't a doubt that he would now make doubly sure that he didn't lose her again. Logan would probably decide to cut his losses by washing his hands of her and her talent for falling into the wrong hands. Even if he didn't, Reynolds would probably shuttle her around enough to confuse even the most outraged of rescuers.

Other thoughts taunted her as well. She was a prisoner of love, too, and the one thing she had managed to do well so far was to convince Logan that she didn't need or want him. From the cold, forbidding expression on his face as he had watched her leave, he obviously didn't need her, either.

But hadn't there been more than frost in those cold cobalt eyes? He had looked betrayed. Wounded. That was what really tore at her insides. She would never know now if he had simply been disappointed in her or if she had actually managed to touch his heart.

Seth Reynolds stepped into the room. "Beautiful, isn't it?" he asked, waving his hand at the view.

"Save the pleasantries, Reynolds. Let's just get on with this," Erin snapped.

270

He gave her a cool smile. "Despite our earlier hostilities, Dr. Barclay, this still doesn't have to be as unpleasant as you are trying to make it."

"They'll be looking for me soon," Erin said, only a small part of her heart believing her own threat. "I don't have enough time to produce the enzyme for you." She looked around at the equipment filling the room. "Even if I planned on doing so. Looks like all your preparations have been to no use."

That disgusting smile formed itself upon his features. "Oh, you'll produce the enzyme for me. You may be defiant now, but that will change." He glanced around the room, his eyes dismissing what he saw. "As for this, well, this was simply a bad investment. I'll write it off somewhere along the line. It won't be needed now."

"They'll catch you wherever you take me. It takes weeks to recreate my work. You can't—"

"But I *can*, Erin," he interrupted calmly. "I can. Your industrious Mr. Scott will find this place easily, but that is all he will find. By the time they carefully follow the trail I've taken such pains to lay down, you and I will be in Chile." He showed his brilliant white teeth as he grinned. "Along with Brian and Robert, of course. The government there will be more than happy to tie up any inquiries in red tape when they know the importance of your research."

Erin was confused but tried not to show it. "Armando and Carlos won't like that," she cautioned sarcastically. "They don't like their government. They'll—"

Reynolds started laughing, blocking out her words. "They are fools! Power buys power. I have no interest in their cause. By the time anyone questions me, I will have the enzyme and all the power I need to buy off anyone I need to buy off." He stepped over to her and stared into her eyes. To her it seemed his had the gleam of a madman's.

But he wasn't mad. Just very greedy, willing to subvert the needs of his own country or anyone else who stood in his way. "You are mine, Dr. Barclay. You are completely under my control."

Logan had relentlessly pushed the powerful engines of the *Tempete* from sundown to sunup. He could still feel the vibrations in every part of his body, even though they were now barely at idle as he maneuvered her into her sheltered birth at the marina anchorage. The all-out night-time journey had been a reckless thing to do, but it had kept him so completely occupied, he hadn't had time to think, and that was what he wanted.

His once-cherished retreat had become too painful for him, holding as it did such magnificent memories of the time he and Erin had shared. In his mind's eye he could still see his final glimpse of her as she had gotten sullenly into the truck with a protesting Stephanos and driven off. All he could think to do was to return here, immerse himself in his business, and try to forget. He knew it wouldn't work, but it was all he had left.

Shutting off the overworked engines, Logan went out on deck to make fast his lines. Only then did he notice the two men sitting on the dock waiting for him. One was Stephanos. That was his first surprise, for though they had planned to meet back here, Stephanos was supposed to take Erin wherever she wanted to go, to make sure she got there safely, and to protect her until word of the enzyme got out.

His second surprise was his old friend's appearance when he got close enough to get a good look at him. He looked very bedraggled and had a grim set to his big jaw. But the biggest surprise of all was the presence of another equally worse-for-wear companion. The numbness that had come over him on his trip back disappeared in the face of an overwhelming feeling of dread.

His first words when he joined them on the dock were filled with that same alarmed apprehension. "Where's Erin?"

Stephanos didn't bother apologizing. He knew that wasn't necessary. "Reynolds has her." He saw the dangerous gleam in Logan's eyes as he looked at Turner. "They had him too," he explained, jerking his thumb at the other man. "This is David Turner. They drugged him and used him as bait to set a trap for me."

"Your buddies turn on you?" Logan said sarcastically.

Turner shook his head. His eyes still looked a bit glazed. "Reynolds isn't anybody's friend. He'd managed to buy up a batch of gambling debts I had and used them to coerce me into feeding

273

him information on the enzyme project." He, too, saw the anger raging in Logan. "I didn't expect things to end up like this, honest."

Logan grabbed him by the lapels of his jacket, nearly lifting him off the ground. "Well, they did. I ought to—"

Stephanos put a hand on Logan's shoulder. "Easy. This guy probably saved my life." He showed him the back of his head, and when Logan saw the bandage, he put Turner down. "I don't know what they hit me with, but I came to in that little hospital near the retreat."

"You took him?" Logan asked.

Turner nodded. "Yeah. Least I could do." He looked at Logan, his jaw set in determination. "Listen. I know I'm going to have to pay for what I did. But I'm not going down alone. I've experienced Reynolds's hospitality firsthand, and we've got to get Erin away from him."

Logan shook off his anger. "You know where he's holding her?"

"I do, but I don't know if we can get to her in time."

An icy fear gripping him, Logan had to fight to keep from shaking answers out of Turner. "What's that supposed to mean?"

"He's planning on taking her out of the country. Chile, I think. I overheard him talking to these two guys named Armando and Carlos."

A dim hope flared in Logan's heart. "Do you know how to get in touch with him?" he demanded.

"A radio frequency, but—"

Logan took his arm and nearly dragged him

on board the *Tempete*. "Then let's do it! I only hope to God he hasn't left yet."

Stephanos followed along behind. "What are you going to do?"

"Make him an offer I pray he can't refuse. I'm betting he's in one hell of a hurry to get the enzyme and that he'd be willing to trade Erin for it." He pushed Turner ahead of him into the control room and sat him down in front of the radio.

A sly grin slowly spread over Stephanos's face. "You'd do that for her?" he asked softly.

Logan looked at him, gave him a wry smile, then shrugged helplessly. "I'd do *anything* for her. I love her."

Stephanos punched him on the arm. "If you hadn't been so stubborn and told her before, we wouldn't be in this fix." He gingerly touched his bandaged head. "And I wouldn't have this headache."

"I'll remember that next time." A worried frown furrowed his brow, and he prodded Turner with his finger. "If there is a next time," he muttered. "Hurry up!"

Erin looked up when Seth Reynolds entered her room. He evidently had decided to show her the opposite side of his rough treatment earlier. She had been fed, allowed to take a bath, and had been moved into a very nice room in the rambling Tudor house. So she now expected him to offer her some other morsel of decency to persuade her to do his bidding.

But the thought went right out of her head

275

when she saw his face. He was smiling, but it was that smile Erin had learned to despise. Robert entered the room behind him, smiling in his own evil way. Her heart thumped in her chest with fear.

"Robert," Reynolds said quietly, "if Dr. Barclay even hesitates in answering my questions, she's yours." With that threat hanging in the air, he approached her where she sat on the bed and fixed her with a hard stare.

"Does Logan Scott have the enzyme?" he queried in the same quiet tone.

Erin's eyes went wide. "I . . ."

Robert started to move forward, but Reynolds held up his hand. "Does he?"

"Yes," she replied, looking at her hands.

"That's better." He waved Robert back. "Would he trade it for your safety?"

She met his intense gaze, confusion plain on her face. "I—I don't . . ." She hesitated, saw Robert move again, then blurted, "I don't know. I don't think so."

"He says he will. He is awaiting my answer now as to where and when." He came closer to her and took her chin between his thumb and forefinger. "You *are* a pretty little bit of fluff, I suppose. But I can't imagine why he would trade such wealth and power for you."

Erin shrugged. "We—we became close. I don't know. He might—"

"Love you?" Reynolds completed derisively. "I don't know about that. He's got quite a reputation with the ladies." He released her and stepped back, looking at her thoughtfully. "Still,

I suppose that particular flight of fancy has turned even greater men's brains to mush. History is full of that kind of sorry circumstance."

Erin's mind reeled in confusion. She was almost afraid to let the hope she felt work its way into her heart. "I don't know," she repeated.

"Neither do I. But it is tempting. A very tempting offer indeed. If I set it up right . . ." He trailed off, pacing the room slowly. Suddenly he stabbed a finger at her. "Can you identify it when he gives it to me?"

"Yes." Afraid or not, hope sprang within her.

"Now, Robert," he said to the obviously disappointed man, "don't give up yet. There's still a chance for you." He looked at Erin and smiled that smile. "Do not doubt for a moment, Dr. Barclay, that if anything goes wrong, if I later find you have led me astray . . ."

"I won't!"

"Lovely. Such lovely terror in your eyes. I like that because it tells me we understand each other. There isn't a place on earth you can hide from me, Erin. Give me what I want and you will be fine. Double-cross me and you will live to regret it. But not for long." He turned crisply on his heel and went out the door. "Come along, Robert. We have plans to set in motion."

Once outside the room and down the hall, Robert asked, "Don't you know a trap when you see one?"

Reynolds chuckled mirthlessly. "I'm not at all sure this *is* a trap. Something in Scott's voice and something in that woman's eyes tell me they are willing to sacrifice the enzyme for love."

"Bull—"

"Oh, I know you don't understand," he interrupted. "But this is too good an opportunity to pass up. In the end I shall have Dr. Barclay, what is most likely the enzyme, and I'll be rid of Logan Scott's interference as well."

"I still think we should have let the authorities in on this," David Turner said. "I don't like it out here."

The *Tempete* was out on the Gulf of Mexico, far from land, with the sun just beginning to spread light upon the choppy gray ocean. There was a heaviness to the air that even the slight breeze couldn't discourage. Logan, Stephanos, and Turner were in the control room, peering into the hazy dawn together and drinking coffee.

"No way," Logan replied. "It's better with just the three of us. Even if Reynolds didn't catch wind of the law, one of them would probably get jumpy, and Erin might get hurt."

"I still don't like it."

Stephanos peered at the radar scope, smiled, and turned the wheel hard to port. "Got 'em. Only about five miles from where they were supposed to be. Not bad."

"Jerks," Logan said. "I don't like it, either, David, but we just have to play it by their rules."

Stephanos smirked and patted the sharpshooter's rifle carefully concealed near the helm. "Sort of."

Reynolds's yacht came into view, and all three stopped talking, tension apparent on their faces. Stephanos steered a course to it and pulled alongside with enough distance between to keep the swell from causing a collision. They waited.

Nobody hailed them or even showed their face. Logan bided his time, figuring that they were waiting to see if the Coast Guard showed up. Finally he grew restless and went out on deck, a bullhorn in his hand.

"Reynolds!" No answer. He tried again and got the same results. But listening to the quiet surrounding them, he did hear something.

Stephanos joined him on deck. "Helicopter," he announced, his tone ominous.

"Yeah," Logan agreed, just as grimly.

The sound of the helicopter grew louder, and then they saw it. It was a big machine, one similar to the craft the Coast Guard used for search and rescue. But this wasn't the Coast Guard. It circled the area once before coming to hover over the *Tempete*.

"Scott!" The voice was booming, amplified as it was by the public address system of the aircraft.

Logan lifted the bullhorn to his mouth. "Give us Erin!"

"Us?" Reynolds asked.

Logan motioned Turner out on deck. "Just us three."

"Why, hello, David. How's your head?"

"Buzz off," Turner muttered angrily.

"I will allow Dr. Barclay to climb halfway down the ladder." A rope ladder dropped from the open door of the helicopter, and Erin climbed down until she was dangling underneath.

"Are you all right?" Logan asked with the help of the bullhorn.

She waved and yelled back at him. "I'm okay."

"Now. Send the enzyme up in this." A rope with a bucket dropped from the door and was lowered to the deck of the *Tempete*. Logan caught it and stopped it from swinging.

"Let Erin go first."

"Do as you are told, Mr. Scott."

"I'll get it," Stephanos said with a wink. He stepped into the cabin, grabbed the rifle, and propped it near the door, then handed out the wooden box containing the enzyme.

"Please come back on deck, Stephanos, and keep your hands where I can see them," Reynolds said. The big man shrugged and came back out, his hands in plain sight.

Logan put the box into the bucket and watched tensely as it was gingerly hoisted up. But they didn't take it into the helicopter right away. They stopped it at Erin, and he could see her check the contents. Satisfied, she looked up and yelled something he didn't catch, but it must have been approval, for they yanked the bucket and its cargo up inside.

"Thank you, Scott," Reynolds's voice boomed. He sounded positively jolly.

"I hope you gag on it, Reynolds," Logan said bitterly. "Now hover closer so Erin can climb down."

The helicopter remained where it was, the sound of its motor a monotonous drone. "No. I don't think so, Mr. Scott. Have a nice voyage—to the bottom!" The whine of the engine increased, and the helicopter started to pull away, gathering speed, with Erin still dangling beneath.

"Stephanos!" Logan cried.

"Way ahead of you." He ducked quickly inside and threw Logan the rifle, then headed for the helm.

Logan snapped the rifle to his cheek and took aim through the powerful scope attached to it. He squeezed the trigger once, took aim again, and fired once more.

In the helicopter they couldn't hear the shots, but they did feel a sudden shift in weight. Robert pulled up the ladder and sat looking dumbly at the two severed ends of the rope. "She's gone!" he exclaimed.

"What?" Reynolds cried, grabbing the rope from his hands and staring at the frayed ends. "Dammit!"

"You want me to go back?" the pilot asked.

"Yes!" He ran a hand over his face and looked at the wooden box containing the enzyme. "No, no. Keep going. I heard the defeat in Scott's voice. I have what I wanted." He lovingly caressed the remote control device he held in his hand. "And a little bit more."

Erin was treading water. She wasn't really sure how she got here. She only knew that one moment she had been dangling in midair and falling the next, still clinging to the rope ladder. The helicopter was behind her, and the *Tempete* was bearing down on her. It didn't look like it was going to stop!

A round life preserver landed beside her, but she couldn't take her eyes off the looming prow of the boat as it barreled toward her. "Don't hit me!" she screamed.

Logan and David Turner were on the bow, jumping up and down and yelling. "Grab it! Grab it!"

She grabbed it and closed her eyes. The wake kicked up by the approaching yacht lifted and buffeted her around. She risked a look, expecting to see it right on top of her.

But Stephanos had veered off abruptly without any change in speed. The only thing she couldn't figure out was why they weren't following the helicopter disappearing in the distance. It ceased to be of concern to her as the slack went out of the rope with a jerk that nearly took her arms off.

"Oh, God! Not again!" But she held on, and Logan started pulling her in, hand over hand as fast as he could go.

"Hold on!" he hollered at the top of his lungs.

"No kidding!" she yelled back, practically drowning from the force of the water flowing past her.

Her hand locked on to his, she took one more violent bump against the *Tempete*'s hull, and she was aboard, coughing and choking. "Why didn't you just stop and pick me up?"

"Because—"

He didn't have time to explain. A violent explosion split the quiet morning air, deafening them temporarily, and they watched as the sky lit up behind them. A moment later a wave hit, which knocked them off their feet, and they slipped and rolled across the deck along with a great rush of sea water washing over the railing. It almost swamped the resilient *Tempete*, but

282

Stephanos kept pouring on the speed and they outran the wave's crest. Then the debris started falling, bits and pieces of Reynolds's yacht and other flotsam thrown skyward by the blast.

"Because," Logan continued as he helped Erin to her feet, "Reynolds is just the kind of scoundrel to destroy his own ship in an effort to sink ours. It's been done before you know."

"Go tell Stephanos to head for home," Logan told Turner. "And then you'd better alert the Coast Guard. It's time some form of law was brought into this mess."

"Right," he replied. He started for the wheelhouse, then hesitated. "I suppose this will open the whole can of worms?"

Logan grinned wryly. "I imagine. There will probably be more people in three-piece suits waiting for us at the marina than we'll be able to count." He squeezed Erin's hand. "And thanks, David," he added. "We couldn't have done this without your help. I'll put in a good word for you."

Turner smiled and continued on, leaving Logan and Erin alone on deck.

"Do you think they'll catch him?" Erin asked.

"Probably not in time. Reynolds will be a very powerful individual soon," Logan replied in disgust.

Erin smiled a secret smile. She looked at Logan, at the man she loved. He loved her, too; she knew that now, even though he hadn't put it into words. He loved her more than the money and power the enzyme could have brought him, had proved that and finally brought an end to all her doubts.

Seeing the warmth in her eyes, Logan released all the worries and concerns pressing in on him. Let Reynolds have the enzyme. He had what he wanted, standing here next to him. He pulled her into his arms, thrilling to the willing warmth of her body.

"You are positively the best-looking drowned rat I've ever seen," he said playfully. He brushed waterlogged tendrils of hair away from her face and planted a tender kiss on her parted lips. "I love you, Erin."

"Logan—"

He silenced her with another kiss. "I know it will take time for you to trust me," he murmured. "And we'll take it slow and easy."

"I don't want to take it slow and easy anymore," she objected. She sensuously pressed her body against his, her hand wandering to the back of his neck to pull him into a much more demanding kiss. Thier lips met, hungry for each other, searching deeply for the fire within each other. "I love you too. I don't know how I'll ever show it as strongly as you just did, but I'll try."

Their bodies tried to melt together as one, desperate hands delighting in the feel of their warm bodies through their wet clothing. Erin drew away slightly, breathless, not wanting the moment to end but knowing that she couldn't keep him in darkness any longer.

"Logan," she said, her mind reeling from the

love and passion she saw in his eyes. "The enzyme—"

"I don't care about that, my love. All I care about is you," he returned softly.

"It doesn't matter to me, either. But I have to tell you . . ." She trailed off, suddenly unsure. Would he be mad? Would this put a sudden end to the love they shared? No, that wasn't possible. It was too strong. She could feel it flowing through her, through him, wrapping around them like an all-encompassing web. "I have to tell you that I lied."

"About what?" He looked confused.

"The enzyme. The one I gave you and which you just gave to Reynolds. It—it isn't real. I mixed it up just like you said. I thought it was all you cared about, and that hurt me so much, all I wanted to do was run away and hide." She reached out a hand and touched his lips. "When you let me go, that only seemed to prove that you had what you wanted. I never thought I'd see you again."

Logan's eyebrows were arched in surprise. "That wasn't the enzyme?" he asked in a bewildered voice.

Erin shook her head. "No. Colored talcum powder, just like you thought. Are you angry with me for deceiving you?"

"Angry?" A smile tugged at the corners of his mouth, then slowly spread across his rugged face. He pulled her against him again. "I *do* have what I wanted," he said gruffly. "But I just made a grand gesture with talcum powder?"

"It *was* a grand gesture. Now I know what

was really important to you," she said, coyly averting her eyes.

He turned her face back to his with a finger on her chin, then kissed the tip of her nose. "You missed your calling. You should have been an actress." He started laughing as if he couldn't stop. The sound sent shivers of happiness through Erin as she felt the vibrations of his chest against her breasts.

"What's so funny?"

"Nothing, at least not for Reynolds," Logan finally managed to say. "Can you imagine what will happen to him when he starts kicking up a fuss in Chile, making demands they'll probably gladly meet, only finally to discover all he has is talcum powder?" Logan shook his head sadly, but he was grinning from ear to ear. "They'll toast him alive—if he's lucky. That can be a very rough part of the world down there. They're very proud, and to be made a laughingstock like that will just . . ." He trailed off and started laughing all over again.

"But once we announce that *we* are the only ones with the real process, won't that let him off the hook?" Erin asked.

Logan grinned wickedly. "Let's take a good long time in announcing it then, shall we?"

"Logan!" she objected, then thought back to just how despicable Reynolds and his crew really were. Whether it was prison here for the crimes he had committed in his bid for the enzyme or heaven only knew what kind of end at the hands of his embarrassed Chilean cohorts, Reynolds deserved whatever he got. "I hope they toast him slowly. Snake can be very tough if it isn't cooked right!"

"Come on," Logan said, "we'd better get dried off."

They started aft, but Stephanos stuck his head out of the control room. "Some lady named Megan something or other on the radio wants to talk to you." He raised his black brows theatrically. "CIA," he whispered in a dramatic tone.

Logan looked into Erin's eyes, felt the heat of her hip against his. "Tell her I fell overboard."

Stephanos grinned. "Oh, good. I was hoping you'd let me do the talking. She's got the most fantastic voice." He put his massive hand over his heart. "I think I'm in love!"

Erin wrapped her arm around Logan's waist and let him lead her below to his cabin. "I have a very good idea of how we can warm up," she said, stripping off her wet things and throwing them in a corner.

Logan looked at her in all her damp, feminine glory and felt himself come alive. He definitely had what he wanted, had wanted, all along. He intended to keep and cherish the love he felt and the beautiful woman he would love forever and beyond. "So do I, my love. So do I."

Now you can reserve June's Candlelights *before* they're published!

♥ You'll have copies set aside for *you* the instant they come off press.

♥ You'll save yourself precious shopping time by arranging for *home delivery.*

♥ You'll feel proud and efficient about organizing a system that *guarantees* delivery.

♥ You'll avoid the disappointment of not finding *every* title you want and need.

ECSTASY SUPREMES $2.75 *each*

At your local bookstore or use this handy coupon for ordering:

DELL READERS SERVICE - Dept. B653A
P.O. BOX 1000, PINE BROOK, N.J. 07058

Please send me the above title(s). I am enclosing $_____$ (please add 75¢ per copy to cover postage and handling). Send check or money order — no cash or COBs. Please allow 3-4 weeks for shipment.
CANADIAN ORDERS: please submit in U.S. dollars.

Ms Mrs Mr _____

Address_____

City State_____ Zip _____